JINXIE'S WISH

JINXIE'S WISH

Geoff Dickinson

authorHOUSE®

AuthorHouse™ UK Ltd.
1663 Liberty Drive
Bloomington, IN 47403 USA
www.authorhouse.co.uk
Phone: 0800.197.4150

Published by AuthorHouse   03/21/2014

ISBN: 978-1-4918-9795-9 (sc)
ISBN: 978-1-4918-9796-6 (hc)
ISBN: 978-1-4918-9797-3 (e)

Library of Congress Control Number: 2014904744

CONTENTS

CHAPTER 1

CHRISTIAN WAS NEVER going to forget the day Brimhall Press delivered a truly bizarre gift box to Mike Tyler for his birthday. Its contents included an old beer can, a dead rat, a dog turd, and some gravel-speckled vomit.

Christian sat behind his desk and shook with laughter for the tenth time that day. He had spent the morning with Malcolm, the owner of Brimhall, trying to negotiate a price to print his new magazine. Brimhall were quality printers and offered competitive print prices. Located in Farringdon, London, they were close to many of the leading magazine publishers.

Malcolm worked from a small office next to the goods entrance of the print works. He was short staffed as always, and he kept popping out of his office to check on the numerous print jobs.

When Malcolm apologised and popped out for the fourth time, Christian was left alone yet again in the small grubby office. He found himself staring at a wooden presentation box sitting on the desk. A card stuck to the box read, 'To Mike Tyler. A very happy birthday from Malcolm and the team at Brimhall Press.'

He flipped open the clasp on the box and looked inside. It was a nice gift set containing a bottle of vintage port, a mature Stilton cheese, oatmeal biscuits, and some fine Cuban cigars. The printers were always good at remembering clients' birthdays, and they sent nice gifts.

Christian immediately saw his chance for some fun. He emptied the contents of the box into his own briefcase and carefully crept out of Malcolm's office. He slipped out of the goods door and on to the street with the box tucked under his arm. The street was filthy and strewn with rubbish. It was the perfect place for Christian to construct a more appropriate gift box for the loathsome Mike Tyler.

His first selection was a chipped bowl languishing next to the rubbish bins. His next task was to find the perfect contents to go inside this vile little bowl. Then in an instant he spotted a nice puddle of vomit that one of the local drunks had probably deposited. He found a piece of cardboard and scooped up some of the congealed, gravel-speckled vomit to deposit it into the bowl. He then carefully placed the bowl in to the presentation box where the Stilton had formerly sat. To his delight he saw a dog turd. Using his cardboard shovel, he scooped it up and placed it in the presentation box in the slot that previously housed the cigars. His next discovery was an old, battered beer can, and this seemed to be the perfect item to fill the slot that formerly housed the bottle of vintage port. Finally to his delight he spied a dead rat sitting next to one of the bins. This proved to be the ideal item to fill the slot that had previously housed the oatmeal biscuits.

The box was now full, and Christian was proud of his superb gift selections. He closed the box lid, slipped the metal clasp shut, and retreated back through goods doors and back in to Malcolm's office.

Malcolm eventually returned, and Christian concluded his discussions, desperately trying not to burst out laughing as he thought about the new and improved gift box.

The meeting did not conclude well. Lancaster Publishing was a huge client for Brimhall, and Malcolm explained that he would have to ask their opinion. Most likely they were not going to be okay with him printing for Christian. The chances of them agreeing were frankly less than zero—particularly if Mike Tyler had anything to do with it.

Christian headed back to his office. He nestled behind his desk and returned to writing articles for his new publication. The day passed slowly, and as he pondered going home, Tom burst into Christian's office desperate to impart some hot gossip.

'Christian you are not going to believe this! I was speaking to Brian, one of my mates at Lancaster Publishing. He told me that Mike Tyler went fucking berserk with Malcolm on the phone today and fired Brimhall Press.'

'Why on earth would they want to fire Brimhall?' Christian asked.

'It was Mike's birthday today, and Malcolm sent a gift to him. When the gift arrived, Mike had a client in his office—Jill Johnson, a big media buyer from Wright, Biggs, and Stimpson. Jill was curious to know what was in the box, so she told him to go ahead and open it. Mike said that because she was his favourite client, she should do the honours and open it for him. So she opened the box, and to her horror she saw this piece of shit crawling with flies, a bowl of what looked like puke, and a fucking enormous dead rat. She ran out of Mike's office screaming.

'No one particularly likes Tyler, but Malcolm must be off his head to send such a weird gift. He must have known Mike would not see the funny side. It took Mike nearly an hour before he persuaded the directors of Lancaster Publishing to fire Brimhall.'

Christian suddenly felt guilty. He hadn't wanted to cause Malcolm any trouble, but he couldn't pass up the opportunity to have some fun with Mike. Hopefully Malcolm could persuade Lancaster Publishing that someone had interfered with the box. He was sure they would relent and restore the printing contract with Brimhall Press. In any case, Malcolm's print work was the best and the cheapest; Lancaster Publishing would find it hard to replace them. Christian relaxed and laughed his way though most of the afternoon, despite his guilty conscience about Malcolm. He would dearly have loved to have seen the look on Tyler's face when Jill opened the box.

He did his best to regain his concentration because he still had a lot of articles to write for his mag. He was going to have to work late again tonight. He suddenly felt bad. He had been neglecting Lizzie a lot over the recent weeks.

He sat for hours hunched over his computer trying to write some good stories. Christian saw the office workers empty out onto the streets, chattering and laughing as they either headed home or went to the nearest pub.

The time passed quickly, and before he knew it, even the pubs were emptying out. The noise outside had robbed him of his concentration; he could hear the high-pitched screeches and laughter of London's finest pouring out of the Pig and Whistle.

It was a little after 11.00 p.m., and the year was 1987. He was only twenty-six, but most people guessed his age as early thirties. He was only five years out of university, yet those easy days seemed so very far away. On numerous occasions he had been described as an old head on young shoulders, but tonight even his shoulders felt old.

Sometimes he wished he was still back at university. Tonight he would have paid dearly to recapture the days when the Human League topped the charts, and Floyd had come back with *The Wall*. Roxy Music was cool and enigmatic then, and he and Lizzie had enjoyed the nervous excitement of their first serious relationship. New and Old Romantics dominated the music scene as the seventies passed away and the eighties were born. Those were good years . . . but tonight they seemed so very far away.

Christian Davidson had taken the plunge and launched his own publishing company with Tom Stevens. Tom was a brilliant, young advertising salesman who could do ten deals a day, drink ten pints of a lager a night, and still remember one hundred great jokes. Christian was a magazine editor who could write a thousand words of good copy in an afternoon and drink nearly a litre of scotch without vomiting, but recent weeks had seen him skip the after-work boozing as he fought to run a business and try to bring out the first issue of *Style Inc*.

Style Inc was Christian's brainchild: a magazine for men that looked at fashion, food, and fast cars. The publication covered suits, sounds, and super achievers. Women's magazines had grown up in the eighties and no longer covered knitting patterns and nappies, but men's magazines still only catered for pot-bellied porn addicts, and it was time for a change. His last company, Lancaster Publishing, had rejected his concept, but since leaving they had decided to launch against him. The race was now on to be the first publication on the bookstalls.

Christian felt the burden tonight. Tom had done well, the advertising revenue was on budget, and they would have enough cash to cover the costs for artwork, typesetting, and printing. Despite this good news, their company, ChrisTom Media, still had limited funds, and consequently the staff list still consisted of the two partners and one other employee. They had limited resources to buy articles, features, and photos. The vast amounts of research and writing for the first issue was making him very stressed and incredibly tired. His back ached from hunching over his computer, and his head ached from staring at the screen for too many hours.

It was now 11.33 p.m., and his article was finished. He should be getting back; Lizzie was going to be pissed off because he had promised he would not be late again. She still worked for Lancaster Publishing—and worse still, she worked for his old boss, Mike Tyler.

Mike was two years older than Christian. Mike's smooth and sneaky style had endeared him to the Lancaster directors, who had rewarded him with the position of publisher a year back. Mike had never liked Christian and saw him as a threat.

When Christian had come up with the idea for *Style Inc*, Mike had encouraged him to present it at a board meeting. The presentation was an unmitigated disaster. The board hated it, and Christian resigned in a fit of anger. But now, bizarrely Lancaster Publishing was launching *Alpha Male* with the same editorial concept as *Style Inc*, and Christian simply could not understand it.

He loathed the idea that Lizzie still worked for Mike. The only compensation was that she worked on a business publication, so at least Christian would not be in competition with his own girlfriend. Lizzie was good at her job, she was a great adverting sales manager, and her team would do anything to help her hit the revenue targets. Despite the fact that she was his girlfriend, Lancaster Publishing would never fire her because they could not afford to lose her.

He had met Lizzie at university; they had studied economics together. Christian loved university, but he had chosen the wrong degree course. He should have taken English. He loved English literature, and most of all he loved poetry. In most of the lectures he attended at Midlands University, he would sit at the back of the lecture room day dreaming and writing poetry. His poems always started reasonably but then collapsed into stupid endings. He never could take anything seriously, not even himself.

As he sat in his office, a poem came flooding back to him. His eyelids began to close, and gravity sucked his head towards the desk. He drifted back in time to 1979 and a particularly tedious lecture. He was there as always, a committed backbencher scribbling nonsense on an A4 pad. The words on the pad were as clear as if he had just written them.

> I looked through the blinds of my shuttered mind,
> A mental jumble there defined.
> I sat and wrestled with tortured thoughts,
> 'Coz what kind of a wanker
> Writes financial reports.

Always the same, a few half-decent lines and then a badly constructed nonsense ending. He had always wanted to write from an early age, but something anarchic always got the better of his deeper feelings and turned his jottings into drivel.

He was now in deep sleep, his head resting on the desk. He was seventeen again. It was the summer before he went to university, and he was very drunk and was laughing so hard that tears rolled down his face. His best friend William took another swig from his dad's scotch bottle and passed it to Christian.

Christian and Will had just worked a half day in the warehouse of a local supermarket. After completing the morning shift, they decided to go for a sandwich and a few pints in the Dog and Duck. Will suggested that they go back to his dad's house to have a few more drinks. On the way back to the house, they stopped in at the local bookstore and bought an *Asterix the Gaul* book. Will's dad was a local artist, and Christian envied Will for having such a cool and bohemian father.

The two young men sat in Will's father's studio, and with a bottle of scotch and some artist's tools, they turned the dialogue of Asterix and Obelix into pure obscenity. It was Christian's idea; his perverse sense of humour and anarchic temperament were well developed at a young age.

Christian started: he pulled a hard swig of scotch and then set to work on the first words of Asterix. 'Hey, Obelix, you cocksucker, how did you get to become such a fat bastard?'

Will glugged back a good mouth full and wrote, 'Knob off, Asterix, you stunted, garlic-munching gimp.'

And so it went on for hours as the pair whitened out the original words and replaced them with expletives and insults. Some hours later they staggered giggling and very inebriated back to the bookshop, where they carefully placed the book back on the shelf. Then they went back to the Dog and Duck and had a few more pints, laughing like fools as they imagined an irate mother screaming at the bookstore manager. They could imagine her telling him how her little Jimmy's vocabulary had been damaged forever by the filth that the store had sold her. She had been devastated that morning when Jimmy had called his father a fat bastard and his little brother a cocksucker.

Christian and Will howled with laughter and coughed beer through clenched teeth as they imagined the fallout from their afternoon's work. They vowed that next time they would buy a cookery book and change the contents of a few of the recipes. They drank on and imagined the text.

> 3 chicken breasts, lightly fondled
> 2 teaspoons of soy sauce, or improvise with engine oil as both look similar
> 6 Brussels sprouts, or substitute with large bogies as both are green and foul
> A pinch of salt—preferably sea salt as road gritting salt tends to be too coarse
> 1 diced green pepper, or green chilli if incinerating guests' colons amuses you
> Large side dish of couscous, or donkey's vomit as consistency/texture are similar
> 8 pieces of fresh asparagus, or some flower stems as both are quite similar
> 8 wild mushrooms, or magic mushrooms if your guests need livening up
> Cook for 20 minutes in a preheated wok, or use a blowtorch if you are rushed

At closing time they fell out of the bar and into a Chinese takeaway, where they bought some sweet and sour pork balls, spring rolls, and chips. On the way back to Will's father's house, they demolished the lot but failed to sober up, so they reached the house and headed for the kitchen for some coffee. They got back just in time: the heavens opened, and rain started to pour. But Christian and Will could not stop their day of madness just yet. It was time for coffee catastrophe. This was a game that required a cast-iron stomach. Tonight's coffee was to be a mixture of coffee, curry powder, a dash of washing liquid, mint sauce, peanut butter, and hot water. The game was simple: you either drank it or performed the dare.

The dare was to take off all their clothes except for their underpants, put another pair of underpants on their heads, and then run round the block singing the Alvin Stardust song 'My Coo Ca Choo'. As always Christian drank the coffee catastrophe, and Will ran round the block in the pouring rain as fast as possible in the hopes he would get back in time before his father arrived home with his latest girlfriend.

Will nearly made it. He arrived at the front door singing at the top of his voice with Christian standing in the doorway howling with laughter. At that moment Will's father's car pulled up.

'William, were you born to embarrass?' his father said as he climbed out of the driver's seat.

Then Will's father's girlfriend got out of the car. Amazing—she was in her early twenties, looked like a model, and spoke with a nice, clipped, upper-middle-class accent. 'You must be William. Nice outfit, but I think you need an umbrella,' she said.

Will's father liked everyone to call him Ray, even Will's friends. Christian flushed red and said, 'Good evening, Mr Hughes.'

Will's father responded with tremendous composure and charm. 'Christian my name is Ray. Get yourselves tidied up, and you can join Julia and me for one last drink.'

Will dressed, Christian cleaned up the kitchen, and the boys went into the sitting room.

'A Remy suit, you both,' Ray stated as he poured four generous measures in to four large brandy balloons. Bob Dylan was playing on the stereo: 'How many roads must a man walk down, before you can call him a man?' Christian guessed he would have to walk down about three and half thousand roads before he could be cool like Ray.

Christian could hear a phone ringing, but it was not part of the dream. He made a grab for the phone and knew it was going to be an irate Lizzie on the other end.

'Nice of you not to show up,' she said.

Then Christian remembered it was Simon's birthday—he had forgotten. Simon was Lizzie's younger brother, and Christian liked him a lot. He had let them both down, and Lizzie was not going to let him forget it. 'Sorry, Lizzie. I had an article that I needed to finish, and I forgot the time. Where are you now?'

'Well, if you can bear to drag yourself away from the office, a small bunch of us have gone back to Simon's flat. If you hurry, you might still have time to make it up to my brother.'

Christian locked up the office and went down to his car at the back of the building. But things were about to get worse for him. He could not believe it—all his tyres were flat, and someone had snapped off the valves. 'Bastards!' he howled. He guessed some kids had vandalised his car for a bit of fun. He walked for ten minutes and then successfully flagged down a black cab. This was going to be an expensive ride.

Forty-five minutes later and with an empty wallet, he was standing by the front door of Simon's flat in South Ealing. He rang the bell, and to his horror Mike Tyler opened the door. 'Lizzie is really pissed at you, Chris,' he said in greeting. Mike tried his very best to exploit Christian's discomfort by commenting, 'Can I recommend a tin hat, a convincing excuse, and an expensive present?' It was clear that Mike was going to enjoy Christian's embarrassment. 'You are going to have to eat a large helping of humble pie tonight, Chris. Still, it's better than being in the SAS—I hear they have to learn to drink their own piss in training. Speaking of which, I need to visit the little boys' room.' With that Mike headed off in search of the toilet, clearly feeling satisfied at having irritated Christian.

After seeing Mike's drink unattended, Christian's mind once more returned to coffee catastrophe. Tonight he was going to serve up pissed-in pint. He nipped out of the back door and into the garden, where he urinated just a little into Mike's pint glass. He then relaxed and emptied the remainder of his bladder up against the fence. He dashed back inside just in time to see Mike coming out of the toilet. Mike strolled back up to Christian hoping to irritate him a little more.

'So what did you get for the birthday boy? No, don't tell me—let me guess. Bugger all.' And with that he picked up his drink and took a large gulp.

Christian held back his joy and amusement at seeing Mike drink the foul cocktail. He coolly said, 'Can't stop and talk, Mike, but good luck with your SAS training. I must say I am impressed—you drank that without flinching. You certainly are a true professional at taking the piss.' Mike seemed totally confused by Christian's comments.

Christian saw Simon pouring drinks in the kitchen and hurried through the doors to reach him. 'Sorry, Simon, I really am. Hope you had a good birthday. I meant to get here sooner—just got tied up.'

'Grab a beer, you dickhead, and don't worry about it. There's plenty of drinking time left.'

Christian was very fond of Simon, and at that moment he loved him. Simon was always quick to forgive. He was a warm and fun personality who never made anyone feel bad. 'What's that git Tyler doing here?' Christian asked.

'Lizzie asked him to the pub, and the he sort of invited himself back here afterwards,' Simon replied.

'He is always following Lizzie around. Why does she encourage him?' asked Christian.

'Well, he *is* her boss, even if he is a prat. Don't be so jealous—Lizzie loves you despite the fact that she sees sod all of you these days. Come on, let's go in to the sitting room, and you can try to placate my scary sister.'

Christian found Lizzie and suffered her wrath. All his excuses failed to work, as he had expected. Then Mike, the master of insensitivity, staggered over wearing a hideous grin.

'Hear you had a spot of car trouble.'

'How did you hear that?' Christian asked, surprised to find that Mike knew about this.

'Oh. Um, Simon told me.'

'That's very strange, Mike, because I didn't tell Simon about my car.'

'Well, I must be psychic.'

'Psycho, more like. You bastard—you must have done it!'

'How could I? I was at the pub all night with Lizzie and Simon.'

Mike and Christian traded insults and would have traded blows if Lizzie had not insisted that Christian take her home.

Back at the flat, Christian broke the frosty silence 'Lizzie, he must have vandalised my car.'

'Christian, he was at the pub all night, stop being so paranoid.'

'Why do you encourage him? He is a total arsehole. You know he fancies you.'

'Let me remind you that Mike is not an arsehole—he is the man who gave me my first job. You also know that as a boss, he has been good to me. And you know damned well that he has never once made a pass at me.'

Christian snorted. 'Well, just give the creep a bit more time, and he will.'

'Christian, you seem to forget that it was Mike who also helped you to get a decent job at Lancaster Publishing. If it wasn't for him, you would still be working for that bloody awful local rag.'

'He only helped me to get the job so that he could play the big man. Then when he saw me doing well, he took the first chance he could to get me sacked. And now to make matters worse, he has even persuaded Lancaster to launch a magazine *against* me.'

'Christian, when the Lancaster directors rejected your magazine idea, you just as good as said they were a bunch of wankers. It was *you* who resigned—no one pushed you.'

'I *had* to resign! I was made to look like a total idiot in the meeting. If my magazine was such a bad idea, then why are they now launching against me?'

'Christian, you made them angry, and that was stupid. You could have just left quietly and done your own thing. But you had to thrust your ego in their faces, writing letters to the directors telling them what a big mistake they had made and how you would succeed and make them regret it. It's your own bloody fault, and if they beat you, you will lose your precious little magazine. You'll also find it fucking hard to find another job.'

She was mad now, and he wished he had just said sorry about tonight and left it there. Now she was going to let him have it. They argued well into the night, and when they both ran out of energy, she went to bed and he slept on the sofa.

He lay awake for an hour, frightened of the present and the future. He pined for his uncomplicated, carefree past. Before he went to university, he saw himself as a rebel, shy of responsibility and open to new experiences. What had happened? He was still young but was already suffering the stresses and strains of his own business, and he had a relationship that was falling apart. Eventually he drifted off to sleep, and his mind slipped back once more to when he was seventeen.

It was Friday night in the Dog and Duck, and they were all there— Christian, Will, Steve, and John. The Boomtown Rats song 'I Don't Like Mondays' was playing on the jukebox. Even if the words of the song spoke of depression, there was none of that in the air that night.

Steve was getting them all excited about their great summer adventure plans. 'So the plan is that we all go on one last holiday before university,' he said.

'It's a great idea,' said John.

Steve's mother worked in a travel agent. She had told him that she could get the lads a great two-week deal on a camping holiday in the south of France. It was going to be a long trip with a coach from London to Port Grimaud, but on the plus side it was very cheap: the holiday would cost them just sixty pounds a head for their travel. It included accommodations: a pre-erected tent on a quality campsite next to the sea. Christian thought that it was a great idea and a good way to celebrate his eighteenth birthday. It would be a last opportunity for four good friends to have some fun together before departing for their degree courses.

As they raised their glasses and toasting their future fun in the sun, Mike Tyler walked in. Mike was two years older than the lads and was back home on holidays from his degree studies at Midlands University. 'Good God, things have gone downhill in this pub since I've been away. They really are letting in the dregs now,' Mike sneered as he walked up to the guys.

Christian's heart sank, because he hated Mike. They had attended the same school, and most of the pupils regarded Mike as a loudmouth bore with few, if any, friends. He had no feeling for when his company was not required, and he was harder to get rid of than the fleas on a hedgehog. The bar was packed, with standing room only. They were now faced with the awful prospect of having Mike joining their group and talking at them about all his conquests at university.

'Hey, Christian, got a love life yet, or are you still practicing on your own?' Mike asked with a sneer.

No one offered to buy Mike a beer, so he went off to the bar and bought himself one without buying any drinks for the others.

'Tight, obnoxious git,' said Will.'

'How the hell are we going to get rid of him?' asked John.

'Let's poison his pint,' Steve replied.

'Leave it to me,' said Christian. 'I have a plan. When he gets back from the bar, I want Will to go and get me two wine glasses filled to the brim with blackcurrant juice.'

'Why?' questioned Will.

'You'll find out very soon. When I head for the exit door of this pub, I want you all to follow me as quickly as you can,' said Christian.

Mike returned from the bar. 'Well, that was a cheap round, must be yours next, Christian.'

Christian ignored him and said, 'Mike can you balance two full glasses of red wine on the back of your hands for thirty seconds without spilling any? Bet you a fiver, plus the two glasses of wine, that you can't do it.'

'Piece of piss. My hands are steady as a rock. Consider your money forfeited, loser.' Mike looked supremely confident and beamed his usual obnoxious, superior smile.

At that point Will returned from the bar holding the two full glasses of blackcurrant juice.

'Okay, Will, we are going to let Mike take this challenge first,' Christian said.

Mike stretched out his hands, his palms facing the ground as instructed, and Christian carefully placed the glasses on the backs of his hands. It was a delicate operation because the pub was packed, and it was difficult for Mike to stretch out his arms.

'Time to go,' Christian said to his mates. They all followed him swiftly as he made a hasty move to the pub exit. Mike was unable to move an inch for risk of sending the glasses flying from his hands. He stood frozen to the spot, his face turning crimson with fury.

They pushed their way through the crowd and burst out into the summers' night. Christian broke into a sprint and fits of laughter at the same time. He could hardly draw breath for laughing, but he kept going until he reached the Swan. He dashed into the pub lounge and made his way to the bar with his friends in hot pursuit.

'Four large scotches please,' he ordered. When they were poured and they all stood holding their glasses, he proposed the toast. 'Gentlemen, raise your glasses to moronic Mike. He is a git and a shit, and we thank God that he fell for it.'

*   *   *

Meanwhile, Mike was heading home, furious and vowing vengeance. As the boys disappeared through the door, a man accidentally bumped into Mike, sending the glasses flying. One glass fell onto Mike's leg, depositing the sticky liquid down his trousers. The other fell forward and poured over a man in front of him. The next thing Mike felt was the man's hands around his throat. If Mike had not squeaked out an apology and quickly proffered a ten-pound note for dry cleaning, the man probably would have beat the crap out of him.

That was the end of Mike's Friday night. He had stained and sticky trousers, was broke, and had a long and uncomfortable walk home. He vowed he would get Christian for this, even if he had to wait years to do it.

* * *

Back in the Swan, the guys replayed Christian's victory and laughed at the look on Mike's face as they ran for the door: horror and anger combined.

'Great trick, Christian, but when he catches up with you, he is going to go bloody mental,' said Will.

'He'll never catch me—I'm far too quick for him,' said Christian.

Christian smiled with joy at his success, and he smiled again now as he turned over in his sleep. The satisfaction of that night flooded through his dreams, and it felt good.

CHAPTER 2

CHRISTIAN WOKE WITH the sunrise, not out of choice but because he had forgotten to pull the curtains in the sitting room. He went into the kitchen and made himself a cup of instant coffee. He sipped the hot brown liquid and began to regret his argument with Lizzie. He knew it was his own fault. How could he have forgotten her brother's birthday? And why had he let Mike Tyler make him angry?

There was a time when he could deal with Mike without getting upset. He had always prided himself on the fact that no matter how much Mike tried to irritate him, he could always brush it off and irritate Mike even more. But Christian was feeling the pressure now. He had ten days to complete the first issue of his magazine, and he was still running thin on good content. Most of the bread and butter stuff was written. He had good test-drive pieces on new sports cars, some hot style tips from leading fashion designers, a few interesting reviews of some new pop albums, a round-up of happening clubs, and some celebrity interview pieces.

But, he still did not have anything in sight for an attention-grabbing cover story. He needed something sensational. He knew that if he could find a great story, he could run a picture and a banner on the front cover that would make people want to buy the magazine. He had phoned round some of the best freelancers from the tabloids and had asked all of them if they had a sniff of something hot that he could pay them to investigate. But every call ended without a result. If only he could find a retired MP who was prepared to spill the beans about his former colleagues. Now *that* would make great copy. Or an ex-girlfriend of a pop star who was willing to tell all about her ex-lover's strange tastes and habits. Something with secrets, something with sex, something with scandal. He badly needed something that would really sell the first issue.

If issue one sold well in the early weeks, then he would never have a problem fighting for shelf space in the newsagents. Good sales would help Tom sell lots of future advertising space. Time was running short now. He needed to decide today on where to look for a good lead. He slugged back the last dregs of his coffee and set off for the office.

Once more behind his desk, he took six sticky notes and wrote down a category on each of them: politicians, pop stars, tycoons, criminals, actors, and sports stars. He then carefully folded up the notes and put them in a tin.

When Tom arrived for work, Christian told him to close his eyes and pick a note from the tin.

'What's this in aid of, Christian? Are we betting on something?' asked Tom.

'You could say that. We are betting on our future,' replied Christian.

Tom made his selection and handed it to Christian. 'Politicians,' said Christian.

'What about politicians?' asked Tom.

'That is where we are going to begin our search for a cover story. You are going to take a day off from flogging ads to come and help me in our quest.'

Christian explained that they were going to spend the day visiting haunts that might be frequented by retired government ministers who liked to drink. Once merry, the men would often recount old stories to anyone who would listen.

Their first stop was the Wig and Pen Club on the Strand. Christian knew some old hacks in there. These journalistic legends were great fun to drink with, and they were often good sources of hot leads. Tom was smartly dressed in a suit and tie, as usual. Christian wore smart trousers and an expensive shirt, but no jacket or tie.

'You know the rules, Christian,' said the man at the door.

'I know. Can you find me a jacket and tie? And ideally a jacket that fits?' Christian replied.

He was presented with a creased jacket a couple of sizes too big and a tie with more gravy on it than the house steak and kidney pud. Christian now only needed to clasp a bottle in a brown paper bag, and he would have blended in well with the tramps down at the Embankment. He found it ironic that in order to obey the house rules, he had to end up looking like a down and out. Still, for all its idiosyncrasies he felt at ease in the Wig and Pen. The usual crowd was in: a mix of old newspaper hacks talking about old times, some hard-drinking PR and ad agency types, and some old lawyers living out their greatest cases. The club had a great buzz of excited chatter, a strong waft of solid British grub, and a warm feeling of being part of London's history.

'Dior, old boy, what a pleasure to see you,' came a gravelly voice from the bar. It was James Jinks, known to everyone as Jinxie.

Jinxie's pet name for Christian was Dior. Christian thanked God that his name was not Channel, or perhaps he would have been given the name Coco.

Jinxie was a soon to be retired journalist working for the *Daily Mirror*. In his youth he had been a well-respected war and troubled hot spots reporter. As a young man he was highly regarded for his courage, honesty, and impartiality, but most of all for his gift at writing brilliant editorials. His articles had often truly portrayed the real horrors of war.

'Tom, meet Jinxie, a good friend of mine and a joy to converse with,' Christian said. 'Jinxie, can you give us the low down on latest juicy gossip?'

Jinxie mostly wrote gossip and scandal these days, and he could be relied upon to provide some very useful tips at times. 'Well, if the drinks and steak and kidney pud are on you, then I am happy to give you my views on the dirt that will soon be making the headlines.'

Christian happily agreed; it was never going to be a big bill in the Wig and Pen. Even if Jinxie's information proved to be useless, it was always fun to spend time in his company.

'Normal rules apply, Dior. If I say a story is for your ears only, it never leaves this room. If I say general release, you can use it. If I give you a useful story, you pay the bill with good grace; if not, then we will spoof for the bill.'

'Okay, Jinxie, normal rules.'

They ordered a bottle of stiff red plonk and the obligatory steak and kidney puds, and then they made their way to a table. Jinxie began with a 'for your ears only' story of the continuing joys of working for the *Daily Mirror* and its well-known proprietor, Robert Maxwell. Jinxie confided that for some time, Maxwell had harboured great ambitions to get to meet Gorbachev. In doing so, he hoped to gain opportunities to publish newspapers and magazines inside Russia. As luck would have it, Gorbachev had announced that he was going to visit the UK and wished to meet some leading industrialists. Maxwell was desperate to have a meeting with Gorbachev and hatched a plan.

Gorbachev was currently promoting a programme of liberalisation and openness in Russia that had come to be known as Perestroika. Maxwell announced that he was going to hold an exhibition of great Russian achievements, to be called Perestroika. The exhibition was to be held on the ground floor of the Mirror Building, and a number of leading journalists were to be forced to camp out on temporary desks in other parts of the building. Naturally, many of them were not happy, and some were even prepared to risk their jobs to get revenge on Bob Maxwell.

One night in one of the numerous watering holes off Fleet Street, a small group of disaffected hacks got roaringly drunk and forged a plan.

Upon hearing about the exhibition, Gorbachev had indeed agreed to meet Maxwell. The time had passed, and Maxwell was going to meet him the next day. Maxwell stage-managed a photograph of himself inside his Perestroika exhibition. The headline for the next morning's front page was to read, 'Maxwell Hosts Perestroika Exhibition to Welcome Gorbachev'.

The hacks conspired together to sneak back in to the building and create a new front page. Of course they knew they would be fired, but after being fortified with copious quantities of booze. they decided it was worth it. In any case. they were all close to retirement.

One of them telephoned a page-three topless model who often appeared in a rival paper and asked her to meet him in the bar, promising her a fat fee for an urgent photo shoot. One of the other hacks rang the number of a man whom he had used for a recent photo shoot because he looked exactly like Gorbachev.

The model arrived some thirty-five minutes later, and shortly after that the Gorbachev lookalike showed up. They all then left the bar and sneaked back to the Mirror Building. They told security that they had to run an urgent story for Maxwell and had no trouble getting in.

Once inside, they entered the Perestroika exhibition on the ground floor. They asked the model to strip down to her underpants and sit legs astride the huge gun barrel of a Russian military tank that sat in the centre of the exhibition. They then asked the Gorbachev lookalike to stand in front of the tank, pointing at her with his mouth wide open in a look of surprise. They photographed the scene and hurriedly developed the pictures in the building's photo studio.

The team then set about creating a new front page for the morning's paper, with the new photograph and with a new headline that read, 'What a Pair of Stroikas!'

It was brilliant—this newspaper was going to be a thing of legend. Career-ending, of course, but totally worth it.

Sadly, the new front page never ran. Maxwell returned late at night to check on the paper. He went berserk, pulled the new front page, reinstated the old one, and fired all the hacks.

'Great shame, Dior. It would have made a great front page. It would have been the spoof of the decade.'

'Is that story really true?' asked Tom in disbelief.

'Of course, dear boy,' replied Jinxie, seemingly a little hurt by the question.

'Great story, Jinxie, but I need something that I can run. What have you got that is printable and sensational that will send people rushing to buy my mag?' asked Christian.

'Oh yes, I forgot. Soon you shall be making history and publishing your new, glossy, first non-masturbatory men's mag. Well, let me rack my brains and see what I can come up with.'

Jinxie asked Christian if he had any particular type of story in mind, and Christian said he would like some scandal on a politician. The lunch moved on and the red wine flowed. Jinxie told more amusing stories but failed to think of any leads for scandal concerning a politician. Nevertheless the lunch was fun, and Tom clearly enjoyed Jinxie's stories—particularly the funny ones about working for the *Daily Mirror*.

'Jinxie, for a man who has clearly done and seen so much in his life, how can you possibly go on working in an environment that you so clearly hate?' Tom asked.

Jinxie replied with part of a poem.

> It matters not how strait the gate
> How charged with punishments the scroll,
> I am the master of my fate:
> I am the captain of my soul.[*]

---

[*] Taken from the poem *Invictus* by W. E. Henley.

'Good answer Jinxie,' said Christian. 'W. E. Henley, if I'm not mistaken. A great poet who suffered a lot in his life but stayed positive. Just like you, eh, Jinxie?'

'Yes, Dior. I should have known you would recognise the reference. So what pieces of poetic perfection have you committed to paper recently?'

'Oh, you know me, Jinxie: I can never finish anything. I just compose things in my head and dream that one day that I will put them down on paper.'

'Come on, dear boy, give us a few lines.'

'Okay, here's one I can never finish:

> What if my soul does not exist?
> What if my life shall not be missed?
> What if I leave no lasting mark?
> What if the end is only dark?
> What if this life is really it?
> Wouldn't that be bloody shit?

'Oh dear boy, why do you always do it? You have a poet's heart and a clown's head. Promise an old fart that one day you will write something with a proper ending, so that I can quote you before I die.'

'One day, Jinxie, I promise. Now, a deal is a deal—you did not give me anything I can use, so we spoof for the bill.'

The three of them took out three coins apiece and put their hands behind their backs. On the count of three, they all put out their clenched right fists. They were all clasping somewhere between zero and three coins in their right fists. The object of the game was to guess how many coins there were in all the clenched fists. Jinxie guessed first by saying seven coins, Tom said six, and finally Christian guessed four. They all opened their fists, and Jinxie was right, so he was eliminated. Tom and Christian put their hands behind their backs again and repeated the exercise. Christian guessed first at three coins, and Tom said two. They opened their fists, and Christian was correct.

'You bastard, Christian. You persuaded me to join you this lunch. Then we play some game at which you are well practiced, so I lose and cop the bill.'

Jinxie interjected to stop Tom from getting too upset. 'Calm down, dear boy, it's just a ritual. You asked me why I stick to the job. Well, my best excuse is that the expenses are generous, and no one else is going to allow an old fart like me to spend 50 per cent of his working week at lunch.' Jinxie paid the bill and said, 'Okay, boys, let's prop up the bar for a few liveners, and this time Christian is paying. You see, Tom, this is how it is with me and Dior here—the same performance every time. And so shall it be until he gets to write a decent poem as a eulogy for my funeral.'

They moved over to the bar and drank till 6.00 p.m., and then Jinxie announced that he was clocking off, proclaiming that another stressful work day was at an end. He was now going to cab it back to his dreary flat in Gloucester Road to drink himself to sleep with Gershwin playing in the background. He recited,

> It was fun, dear boys, I do profess.
> But I am tired, I must confess.
> So alas, farewell to the bar and you.
> Home for me and *Rhapsody in Blue*.

'Not bad, Jinxie. There is a poet inside you, too,' said Tom.

'Oh no, dear Thomas, I could never claim that honour. However, if young Dior here could ever dredge the depths of his finer soul, he just might write a few worthwhile lines.'

Jinxie departed, and Christian persuaded Tom to stay for a few more drinks. 'You really like Jinxie, don't you, Christian?' Tom asked.

'Yes, I do. He has lived a really full life. He was born in 1916 during the First World War. Sadly, his father died in the conflict a few weeks after Jinxie's birth. It has always saddened him that his father never even got to see him, and that he never got to know his father.

'Jinxie did well at school, and his writing talents led him to bag a good job as a newspaper journalist by 1938. One and a half years later, Jinxie decided that with the outbreak of World War Two, he should do the right thing and serve his country. He joined the army and, following a short period of training, was dispatched to France. By 1941 he was discharged with medals after being unlucky enough to have been shot and wounded a few times. By 1942 he was travelling alongside the action as a war correspondent, and he managed to get himself shot a few more times. He claims he is so full of holes that he sometimes leaks when he drinks too much.

'Jinxie is now seventy-one, and he should by rights be retired, but he cannot retire. He says death will be his retirement. The paper keeps him on through a mixture of his experience and sentimentality. They do not pay him much anymore because he only works part time, but they always pay his expenses.

'His wife died over twenty years ago from cancer, and his heart has never mended. He drinks to get himself through the days, and it seems to work. At night he hopes to be so drunk that he can sleep his way through without feeling the pain of his loss. He is a good man, Tom, but I do not think he will be around for much longer. He drinks too much, smokes like a maniac, and exists on a diet of steak and kidney pud.'

'Well, Christian, what about our lead story? There is not a lot of time left, we desperately need something big for our first issue.'

'Yes, Tom, you're right of course. I propose we hang around here until eight to see if any of the other Fleet Street hacks come in. If that fails, I have the perfect suggestion for dinner.'

Tom and Christian carried on drinking in the bar. Christian introduced Tom to a variety of journalists, PR agency owners, lawyers, and businessmen who were frequent patrons of the Wig and Pen. They talked a lot, but no one had anything that came close to providing a good story.

At eight o'clock they hailed a taxi and headed for the Gay Hussar Restaurant. 'Christian, you must be mad! We have drunk enough to floor a Rhino, eaten enough stodge to spoil the digestive system of a warthog, and smoked more than your average kipper. A session at the Gay Hussar will surely kill us.'

'Tom, we need some leads, and the Gay Hussar is the perfect place to earwig the conversations of some politicians.'

The taxi deposited them at the Gay Hussar, one of London's oldest and best restaurants. As always the menu offered a marvellous range of Hungarian food literally to die for in every sense of the word. The boys scanned the superb, high-cholesterol offerings and opted for goose and dumplings accompanied by a full-bodied Hungarian red wine.

'Not intending to live long, then, Christian?' remarked Tom as they tucked in.

'Why live a long, perfect life of boredom when you can live a short, rewarding life of fun?' responded Christian.

Christian had chosen a central table in order to earwig the conversations of his neighbours. The table behind was talking constantly about the health service, and the table in front was talking about the terrible dress sense of some of their colleagues.

'He dresses like Man at Oxfam. How will people take him seriously? He looks more like a geriatric student than a leading political figure.'

'I know, what a disaster. Not only are his views outdated, but so are his suits.'

'Have you seen his shoes? Looks like he has been working on a building site. Claims they are handmade, but by who, I ask? Cloddhoppers Industrial Outfitters?'

'Everyone thinks he wears patterned ties, but we all know they are plain and covered with such a wide variety of stains that they could keep a forensic scientist busy for a year identifying them.'

'His views went out with the Ark. The kids today think CND are a Hip Hop band and that Trotsky is a dose of the runny plops you get on a package holiday in Russia.'

'With a man like this, how will we appeal to the kids, the new voters? We don't stand a chance.'

From another table, Christian could hear some pretty disastrous ideas for the Health Service. 'Well, I know we cannot privatise it, but it's too bloody expensive to run as it is.'

'What if we turn hospitals into mini companies and local hospital authorities into corporations? They then have to operate like businesses and compete for funds, like businesses do for orders.'

'Brilliant—they will never get the hang of this. Most will fail to correctly complete the complex documents we create, and those that do will have to wait until the next millennium to get the cash.'

'Yes, great idea. We can talk about the Health Service operating like a business, offering patient choice. People can currently choose from which supermarkets to buy liver, and soon they can choose from which hospitals to get their kidneys. Ha ha!'

'No, no, no! Much better still, I can imagine the speech now: This government does not tell you which supermarket you should go to in order to buy your eggs. Nor will this government dictate from which hospital you can get your fertility treatment. Ha ha ha!'

'I love it! Let's talk to the PM. I can hear his opening remarks now: From the National Health Service to the National Health Supermarket—more choice at low, low prices.'

Christian began to feel unwell—not from the physical assault on his senses caused by too much booze, rich food, and cigarettes but from the assault on his ears from ear-wigging too many unpalatable ideas. He said, 'I vote we get the bill and move on to a nice, sleazy club to finish off an imperfect day.'

Tom replied, 'Okay, Christian, whatever you say. I'm too pissed to disagree.'

They paid the cheque and staggered off into the night.

CHAPTER 3

EARLIER THAT SAME day, Lizzie arrived at work in a very bad mood. As she walked through the reception area of Lancaster Publishing, the sour look on her face nearly caused the rubber plant to keel over and die. She had loved Christian once, but now she was not sure. At university he seemed so cool, witty, and full of drive. Now he was anxious, shitty, and driving her berserk.

She remembered when he stood for the University Students Union Guild Council, a kind of students parliament. The university was broken up into a series of constituencies such as Economics, English, Biology, and more. The size of the faculty dictated how many candidates they could elect. The Economics department had about six hundred students across the three years and could elect four candidates. Anyone could stand as a candidate, and the four who got the most votes would be elected. The normal political parties put forward their appropriate candidates: four from Labour, four from the Liberals, and four from the Conservatives. Then there were a few Monster Raving Loony candidates, a couple of Ecologists, and a variety of different Communist candidates.

Christian stood as a Nihilist. He thought this was highly amusing because everyone kept asking him for his policies, to which he proudly replied that Nihilists didn't have any policies. Naturally, he was elected—he was the only candidate with a 100 per cent honest campaign document that contained the following information.

Vote Christian Davidson
Your Nihilist Candidate

I do not have any policies.
I do not have any political views.

I probably will not do anything if elected.

But, at least I am honest.

He became a guild councillor and was promptly voted in to a number of positions from which he could abuse his newfound powers to the benefit of himself and his friends.

She remembered Christian's first journalistic job, writing columns for *Breezeblock*, the University student newspaper. He wrote articles on university news, local bands, and previews of upcoming events.

Lizzie was attracted to Christian. He was funny and carefree, and she wanted to be like him. She remembered how they first met. Christian was into sports, and he liked to run. Some afternoons if he got home early, he would run back to the university. Once at the sports complex, he would leave his clothes in the changing room, take a sauna, dress again, and run back home.

One day upon coming out of the sauna, he found some joker had stolen all of his clothes; naturally, he blamed Mike Tyler. Mike was now in his final year, and he and Christian despised each other. Christian had not intended to go to the same university as Mike, but he failed to get into the LSE in London, and he was offered a last-minute place at Midlands University.

Mike was doing History, so their paths rarely crossed, but they both enjoyed sports and did occasionally bump into each other in the sports complex. Christian had passed Mike on the way in to the sports centre that afternoon, so he figured that Mike must have stolen his clothes.

It was early evening when Christian had wandered over to the Physical Education department dressed only in a towel, to see if he could borrow any clothes. The only available clothing was a pair of old tracksuit bottoms left in lost property. The Physical Education instructor agreed to lend them to Christian along with twenty pence for a bus ride home.

Christian ran out barefoot and bare-chested into the cold night to the bus stop. He looked ridiculous. He tried to keep his cool through clenched teeth despite the fact that the cold, hard pavement hurt his feet and the wind chill on his nipples brought tears to his eyes.

He arrived at the bus stop, and as fate would have it, he joined the queue behind Lizzie. The queue gazed at him in amazement—who was this madman with bleeding feet and frosted nipples about to catch their bus? Lizzie grinned at Christian and tried to stifle a laugh.

'I expect, you are wondering why I am dressed like this,' Christian said to Lizzie. 'Well, my spiritual advisor, the Grand Yogi Oftenbare, has advised me that to find inner strength, you must feel the earth beneath your feet and the chill wind on your breast. He has given me a mantra to recite as I run:

> If you run without shoes or socks,
> You will never catch the pox.
> If you expose your nipples to the air,
> You will find good karma everywhere.'

Lizzie laughed and beamed at Christian, and he knew that he wanted to see her again, but next time he planned to be better dressed. They sat together on the bus, and Lizzie offered Christian her jacket, which he gladly accepted. She was going to have a party in a week, and she invited him to come.

The week passed quickly, and Christian arrived at her party with a couple of his mates, who proceeded to mix anything they could find in pint glasses and knock it straight back. Christian got very drunk, and Lizzie's friends told her they could not understand why she liked him.

By 2.00 a.m. all that remained in the kitchen were seven giant, party-size cans of beer. Lizzie found herself in the kitchen trying to open a tin by attempting to puncture it with a knife, but to no avail.

At that point Christian walked in. 'Any booze left?' he asked.

'Only these jumbo tins, but I can't open them,' responded Lizzie.

Christian took the knife, raised it above his head, and then brought it down hard on top of one of the tins. Beer exploded out of the tin and soaked the two of them.

'Oh shit! Sorry, Lizzie. You must think of me as a real yob. First you meet me half-naked at a bus stop, and then I come to your party and drink everything in sight. And now as my grand finale, I drench you in beer. I'm really sorry.'

'Don't worry, Christian. At least we can get a drink now. Oh, and in case you are wondering, I don't think of you as a yob—in fact I think you're rather sweet.'

'Oh god, girls normally call guys sweet when they feel sorry for them. Do I seem pathetic to you?'

'Christian, stop being so sensitive. I like you. Look, we are both soaked. I need to put on some dry clothes, and so do you. I can lend you a sweatshirt, if that helps.'

'Yes, great, thank you. This is getting to be a habit—me borrowing your clothes. I promise not to ask to borrow any of your underwear.'

They went up to Lizzie's bedroom discreetly, unseen by the few remaining drunken partygoers. Lizzie went to a drawer to find Christian a sweatshirt. As she walked back towards Christian, she tripped over a pair of her shoes and fell forward. Christian put out his arms and caught her, and within seconds they were kissing.

'Lizzie, penny for your thoughts,' said Mike Tyler, instantly bringing her crashing back from her memories.

There she was, behind her desk again—back in the present. 'Sorry, Mike, I was miles away.'

'You look sad, Lizzie. What's up? Want to come to my office for a coffee, to confide in a friend?'

'No thanks, Mike. I'm fine, just a bit tired this morning.'

'What did you get up to last night? Perhaps another fight with that loser boyfriend of yours? I really don't know what such a charming, talented girl like you sees in such a toss pot like Christian.'

Lizzie liked Mike, but she did not appreciate him offering up his negative views on Christian. But right now she was starting to wonder why she'd stayed with Christian. He never wanted to discuss marriage, although they had been an item for nearly seven years. These days he was hardly ever around, and when he was, they always seemed to fight.

She knew Christian and Mike hated each other, but Mike had always been kind and considerate to her. Lizzie sensed Mike liked her, and despite what she had told Christian, she knew that Mike would love to ask her out.

'Christian is just a bit stressed at the moment with his new magazine. I guess it's making him a little grumpy,' she said.

'Well, I guess the prospect of imminent failure must be what is getting to him. However, there is really no need for him to take it out on you.'

'Mike, that's not fair—I would really have expected better of you.'

'Sorry, Lizzie, it was a bit unfair of me. I admire your loyalty. If only I had a woman like you to care for me as much as you care for him.'

'One day you will find someone nice, and she will be a very lucky girl.'

'Thank you, Lizzie. That is very sweet of you. And my offer is always there: if you need someone to talk to, you know where I am.'

Mike returned to his office, and Lizzie got on with her day's work. In the afternoon she rang Christian's office but was told that Christian and Tom had gone to lunch. She phoned repeatedly during the afternoon and left messages. At 5.50 p.m. she phoned again and found out that Christian had not returned to the office.

She had hoped that perhaps Christian would feel guilty about last night and offer to take her somewhere nice for dinner, to make it up to her. But no, he had gone for one of his famous long lunches and would probably go on boozing until the early hours of the morning. She was upset and angry. She could not believe that Christian had turned in to such a selfish bastard.

There was a time when he could not bear to be parted from her. At university, when they went home to their parents during the holidays, he used to send her cards all the time saying how much he loved and missed her. Sometimes he would include silly little verses. She could still remember some of them.

> When shall we join again,
> Our bodies welded tight?
> I am alone, an empty soul,
> Tortured through the night.
> I wake often in lonely pain,
> Anxious, longing to join again.
>
> The pain from being parted
> Is too hard for me to bear,
> So catch a train and bring your bag,
> And we can have a damn good shag.

She would start reading his poems in the hope of finding some future classic piece of romantic poetry written in her honour. But no, always the same: a promising start and then a totally crap ending. All his poems were garbage, but years ago they had made her laugh. She had really loved him back then.

But tonight, as she sat alone in the office, she was sure she had fallen out of love with him. She wanted excitement back in her life, somewhere to go and to have a good time. She wanted someone to care about her and tell her she looked great, someone to be interested in what she said and not be self-absorbed with his new magazine. She wanted to look forward to something, and she wanted her ego stroked. But Christian was not going to do it—not now, not tonight, and now she was sure not ever.

Lizzie wanted to spite Christian. She wanted to grab his attention away from his own world, but she did not know how.

A voice from her doorway startled her. 'Start as you mean to finish, Lizzie. You started the day staring into space, and it looks like you are finishing the day in the same fashion.'

'Sorry, Mike, I didn't see you there. Lost in my own thoughts again.'

'Lizzie, let me cheer you up and buy you a G&T. You can either enjoy the drink and my scintillating company, or you can cry on my shoulder, whatever the mood takes you. Good offer?'

'Good offer, Mike. I need that drink—let's go.'

Mike and Lizzie went to a small pub around the corner from the office.

'Want to talk about it, Lizzie? Or just talk trivia and enjoy the drink?'

'Trivia sounds good to me Mike.'

They talked for a few hours. Mike cracked some jokes and flattered Lizzie a bit, and she began to feel happier. Mike suggested they go to an Italian restaurant nearby, and to her own surprise she readily agreed.

In the restaurant she felt warm, cosy, flattered, and a little tipsy. It was a good feeling. She knew she should not feel that way with Mike, but it felt pretty good—in fact it felt *really* good. They talked for hours, and Mike told stories of his early years in publishing and made her laugh.

He recounted a story of how he had once attended a client party and had mistakenly eaten a polystyrene table decoration that formed the centrepiece of a tray of canapés. He was talking to a client at the time and, with superhuman effort, restrained his desire to hit the floor choking. However, when he replied to a question posed by the client, small pieces of polystyrene flew out of his mouth and shot down the front of her dress. The woman rushed off to the toilet in disgust, and he got a huge bollocking from his managing director.

Lizzie was enjoying Mike's charming and amusing attention. When the waiters started fidgeting by the side of the table with the bill, she felt disappointed that the evening was drawing to a close. Then Mike asked her if she would like a nightcap back at his apartment. Mike lived nearby, so it was only a short walk away.

Lizzie was amazed at the words that came out of her mouth as she said yes to his invitation. Part of her said she should say no in order to be loyal to Christian, but a greater part of her said it was an innocent drink. Why shouldn't she enjoy herself when Christian was undoubtedly out on the piss somewhere?

Back at Mike's apartment, he opened a very good bottle of red wine. Lizzie became more tipsy, more flattered by Mike's charm, and more amused by his stories. He told another story about how he had once taken a client to a very nice, Far Eastern restaurant in Soho. To start, they had satay sticks. Mike struggled to get the chicken off the stick with his mouth. He tried to grip the chicken with his teeth and pull the stick away. As he pulled the stick away, he flicked a huge piece of chicken straight at a tray of food being held by a waiter. The tray tipped and deposited two bowls of hot, spicy soup and a tray of mixed appetisers on his client's head.

Lizzie laughed and rocked back in her chair, spilling red wine down her blouse as she did so.

'Oh Lizzie, I am so sorry! I made you spill wine on your lovely blouse. Best thing to do is for me to find you one of my shirts and pop that blouse of yours in soak before it stains.'

Lizzie agreed, and they went to Mike's bedroom to choose a shirt. Mike selected a shirt, and Lizzie walked towards Mike to collect it. She suddenly tripped on a pair of Mike's shoes and fell forward. Mike put out his arms and caught her, and within seconds they were kissing.

Lizzie felt that this had happened to her before, but she was too drunk to remember when. Before she knew it, she and Mike were in bed and making love.

CHAPTER 4

CHRISTIAN AND TOM staggered into Diamonds, one of London's sleazy, backstreet clubs. It was much like any other night in Diamonds, with the usual selection of MPs, judges, and businessmen wanting to feel that they were still young and handsome. They loved being flattered by young girls who would happily sit and drink with them for hours—for a decent hostess fee.

Christian knew the form: if you saw a girl you liked, you let the waiters know and went to a table with her. You paid a fee to sit with her, as well as a hell of a lot of money to drink champagne with her. If you did not want to select a girl, you went to the bar, ordered a drink, and stood there talking with other guests. Christian never selected a girl—he loved Lizzie too much, and he only came to the place for either late drinking or to try to get some leads for a story.

Christian led Tom to the bar, saying, 'Let's get talking to some of the punters. We buy them a few drinks and see if there are any MPs amongst them that are pissed enough to spill the beans on any of their colleagues.'

Christian ordered two large Lagavulins, and he and Tom propped up the bar. He instantly recognised a former Tory minister leaning against the bar. Christian opened the conversation. 'Never been in here before. What's the form?'

Christian knew how it worked but guessed that the old boy in that state of amiable inebriation would be kind enough to explain how things worked in the club. He guessed right. The former minister, now Lord Whitstop, took delight in explaining it all, and Christian and Tom offered to buy him more drinks.

Although Christian had recognised the former minister, he feigned ignorance and asked Lord Whitstop about his line of business. Whitstop proudly recounted his parliamentary career and bemoaned the fact that he had now been put out to grass in the Lords. He told them that he could offer so much experience and advice to his younger House of Commons colleagues, and they were foolish to have banished him to the Lords. 'Bloody stupid, making way for young blood. What the bloody hell do they know? Experience, that's what counts! How can you make judgements without experience? Bloody bollocks, that's what I say.'

He was a nice old boy and insisted on buying a round of drinks. And then he said it—he just came out and said it. 'Poor boys, poor young boys. Fought for their country in the Falklands, came back sick, and no one will ever own up or compensate them.'

'What do you mean?' asked Tom.

'Chemical and biological weapons, of course. The Junta used them, you know. We knew they were using them, but we couldn't tell the troops—it would have spoilt their fighting spirit. Of course we gave them injections before they were sent there, and we gave them gas masks. The ministry men said the injections would cover the biological stuff, and the gas masks would protect them from the chemicals released into the air. But it didn't, you know. Many of the boys are developing illnesses now, and we do not know how to treat them. The government will never admit what they knew because the compensation would go through the roof. And everyone is intent on keeping quiet because all their reputations will go up in flames, and no one will elect them again. Bloody shame. I took part in World War Two, fought for my country, even got decorated. I know what those boys went through in the Falklands, and now many of them are sick, and there is nothing to be done. Damn bloody shame.'

Christian could not believe his luck. A huge cover-up! If he could expose it, then this would bring down the government and shame a number of very influential political figures to boot. It could help some heroes and right a wrong. A great story: war heroes dying because of an uncaring government. This was the story he needed, it would make the first issue of *Style Inc* a total sell-out. Newsagents would be banging at his door for reprints, and the magazine would gain fame and popularity overnight.

But Lord Whitstop was fading fast. His day's alcohol consumption was so high that his liver was already looking to pack up and leave him. 'Sorry, boys, I have had enough for one day. Spoken too much and need to head for home.'

'Lord Whitstop, I have my own magazine and would love to run a story on your life because it sounds truly fascinating. Can we have lunch later this week?' Christian could not lose the chance to meet again to get the whole story. He prayed Whitstop would agree to his lunch offer.

'Sounds a super idea, young man. Here is my card. This number here will be answered by Beryl, my personal assistant. Just tell her we had a lovely drink together and that you want to get a slot in my diary for lunch. Only she knows when I am available—I would be truly lost without her.'

They all shook hands, and with that a waiter assisted Lord Whitstop out of the club and into a waiting limousine taxi.

Tom exclaimed, 'Christian, you are a fucking genius! I knew you would come up trumps in the end. What a great story! You'd better book that lunch and write the story fast—we are going to be publishers of the most famous magazine in Britain.'

Christian was very excited and couldn't wait to tell Lizzie. He phoned the flat from the club, but there was no reply. He suggested to Tom that they go back to Christian's flat, wake up Lizzie, and crack open a bottle of champagne to celebrate. Tom was sceptical and said he felt Lizzie might not wish to be woken in the early hours of the morning, but Christian persuaded him. So they headed off to Christian's flat.

They burst through the front door like two school kids. Christian called out, 'Lizzie, Lizzie wake up! Great news—we're going to be rich.' But Lizzie did not reply, because Lizzie was not there. Christian burst in to the bedroom to find no sign of Lizzie, so he searched the rest of the flat to see if she was still up. There was no sign of her. 'Where can she be, Tom?'

'Well, Christian, you are so often working late these days, maybe she got pissed off and went out with some friends.'

'Yes, you're probably right. I have been a git to live with recently, and Lizzie needs a life. Let's save the champagne for when she gets back. But as luck would have it I have a full bottle of Lagavulin that we can try to make a dent in.'

Christian found the bottle and repeatedly poured generous measures as they talked excitedly into the early hours. They constantly toasted their future good fortune until the sun came up. By 6.00 a.m. they had drunk themselves to sleep, and they both sat slouched in armchairs with their mouths open, dreaming of publishing glory.

Just after 10.00 a.m. the two men both woke from the sounds of road work outside.

'Oh shit, we should be at the office getting things done, and I feel like crap,' said Tom.

Christian searched the flat to see if Lizzie had returned home. 'Lizzie, didn't come home, Tom. I'm worried.'

'I expect she stayed with a girlfriend from the office. Don't worry—I'm sure Lizzie is fine.'

*   *   *

Lizzie was back behind her desk and fine, except for the hangover and the guilty conscience. Part of her could not believe what she had done last night, and she felt guilty. But part of her did not feel guilty at all, and she felt good about herself and the great night she had enjoyed.

Then the phone rang. 'Lizzie where were you last night, I was worried sick,' Christian said on the other end of the line.

'Christian, I find that hard to believe. I phoned your office all yesterday afternoon only to discover that you never returned from one of your famous drunken lunches. You don't give a shit about me. You are too wrapped up in your own little publishing empire to give a moment's thought to anyone else.'

'That's not true, Lizzie. I *was* worried about you. Where were you?'

'I went for a drink with a friend, and then we went on for dinner. We had quite a lot to drink. It was late, and she kindly suggested that I stay at her place because it was nearby.'

'Which friend?'

'Er, Jackie, from the subscriptions department,' Lizzie stated, hoping that Christian would believe her.

'I had no idea you and Jackie were such great mates. I thought you said she was an airhead with the dress sense of a pantomime cow.'

'Well, I seem to spend so much time on my own these days that *any* company is welcome,' she retorted. 'So why don't you just leave me alone and piss off back to your shitty little magazine.' And with that she slammed the phone down.

CHAPTER 5

CHRISTIAN AND TOM made their way to the office. It was going to be public transport again, because Christian had still not gotten around to sorting out his car. Tom had overheard Christian's call to Lizzie, so he understood why Christian was in such a black mood; it wasn't just the effects of the growing hangover. They stopped for a greasy fried breakfast and some mugs of sweet tea in an attempt to lessen the pain of last night's drinking damage. Little conversation took place over breakfast, but Christian vowed that he would get a meeting with Lord Whitstop as soon as possible.

When they reached the office, Christian called Jinxie and asked him how reliable Whitstop was. Jinxie told him that Whitstop was an all around good egg, very dependable and well liked. He asked Christian if his questions were connected with a possible story, and Christian said yes but was unwilling to say any more, so Jinxie did not press him.

Christian then telephoned Beryl, Lord Whitstop's personal assistant. To his surprise Beryl said she had been expecting his call, and she said that Lord Whitstop was free for lunch tomorrow. She suggested 1.00 p.m. at Simpson's Brasserie because it was one of His Lordship's favourite restaurants. She also added that Lord Whitstop had been looking for someone to write his biography for years. He had set aside tomorrow afternoon for Christian to discuss this. Christian replied that this was indeed of great interest, and he would set aside the afternoon for discussions. Beryl then offered to book the table, and Christian thanked her for all her help.

Christian was still feeling rough, so he made himself a strong mug of coffee, took a couple of headache pills, and drank a can of Coke. After an hour he was feeling a little better, so he tried to call Lizzie again, but he was told she had gone out to a meeting, and so he left a message.

He decided to try to get back in her good books. He rang a florist, ordered a huge bunch of flowers to be delivered to her office, and then sat quietly and composed a fax to her. Her decision not to come home last night scared him—he sensed he was losing her. With his own business on the verge of success, and with his desire not to lose Lizzie, he figured it could be a good time to do something drastic and propose marriage to her before it was too late. She had been hinting that she wanted more commitment for some time now, but in recent months he had shown her less attention than at any other point in their relationship.

Yes, this was time for drastic action. He knew what he needed to do. Lizzie would be bowled over by finally being asked to get married. He sat down and carefully crafted a fax.

Attention: Lizzie
From: Christian
Read This. Call Me. Dinner Tonight. You Choose, I Pay.

I am often wrong,
Too seldom right;
Often selfish,
Quick to fight.

You are my conscience,
My hope in life.
You are my spirit,
My future wife.

Forgive my neglect,
Forgive my sins,
And I will buy you lots of gins.

He knew she would like the crappy ending to the poem; she always liked his daft endings.

As the fax went through, he felt considerably less anxious; everything was going to be all right with him and Lizzie. He would get the story for the magazine. Lizzie would forgive him, and they would get married.

He knew he should have proposed long ago, but it wasn't too late—everything would work out just fine.

*   *   *

Mike wandered past Lizzie's desk in the hopes of finding her there, but he was out of luck. He noticed a huge bunch of flowers sitting by her desk. Mike pulled off the card and read it. 'Sorry, Lizzie, I am an idiot. I love you.—Christian.' He tore up the card, grabbed a piece of paper and wrote simply, 'Lizzie, hope you like the flowers.—Mike.'

As he pinned the message to the flowers, he saw a number of other interesting items on her desk: a fax from Christian and a number of phone messages also.

'Ah a desperate fax and some pleading phone messages from Toss Pot,' he said to himself. 'Well it's off to the toilet for a satisfying early morning crap for me, and I must say it is very decent of Toss Pot to provide me with some loo paper.' With that, Mike marched off to the gents with Christian's fax and the phone messages.

*   *   *

Christian tried telephoning Lizzie a few more times, but he was told that she had not returned from her meeting. He thought it best not to leave any more messages.

'Lunch time, Christian. Fancy a hair of the dog?' said Tom as he poked his head inside Christian's office.

'Sounds good to me.'

They stepped out of the office and fell into the Pig and Whistle. It wasn't a great pub, but it had the benefit of being near the office, and it had a decent selection of records on the jukebox. Tom went to the bar to get the beer order in, and Christian selected a couple of songs from the jukebox. He opted for 'Oliver's Army' by Elvis Costello because it made him think of his forthcoming lunch with Lord Whitstop. Then he played Van Morrison's 'Bright Side of the Road' because it was a favourite of his and Lizzie's. He sat at a table, and Tom came over with the drinks. Christian was in a good mood; the future looked bright.

*   *   *

Jinxie strolled down the Strand to perform his daily ritual at the Wig and Pen Club. As he crossed the road, a car swung out of a turning. He tried to jump out of its path and landed face down on the pavement opposite. An *Evening Standard* newspaper salesman saw what happened and rushed over to help Jinxie.

'You all right, old fellow? Bloody lucky you reacted quickly. I thought that car was going to hit you.'

But Jinxie was not all right. He had escaped being hit by the car, but he was ashen, his breathing was shallow, and he was clutching his chest. The newspaper man said, 'Call an ambulance, someone! I think the old boy is having a heart attack.'

He was right: Jinxie was having a heart attack. An ambulance arrived pretty quickly, but for Jinxie things seemed to be happening in slow motion, and it seemed like he had been waiting for hours. The ambulance crew checked him over and then gently deposited him on a stretcher. They carefully loaded him in to the ambulance and administered oxygen to assist his breathing. They set off for Charring Cross Hospital, and Jinxie felt as if he was slipping away into another world.

*   *   *

Lizzie returned from her meeting, saw the huge bunch of flowers by her desk, and blushed. Then she read the note from Mike and felt guilty about Christian. What had she done? Mike had clearly built up his hopes with her, and Christian knew nothing of last night.

She hid the flowers in her cupboard and decided to sort things out. She would ring Christian and make it up. Then she would talk to Mike and tell him that she had enjoyed last night—but that it could not lead to anything more. She would appeal to his better nature and ask him never to tell anyone what had taken place. That was her plan, and it was certainly the best one available purely on the basis that it was the only one available.

Lizzie phoned Christian's office and was advised that he had gone out to lunch with Tom. She was furious and put the phone down without leaving a message. So much for foolishly thinking he might care for her! Lizzie was very hurt that Christian had not even bothered to call her. Christian was so wrapped up in his own selfish little world. She could not believe that he had not tried to call her again! He should be trying to take her somewhere nice to apologise, or at least send flowers or a card to say sorry. Sure, she felt guilty about last night, but now she felt he bloody deserved it because clearly he did not give a shit.

*   *   *

Christian returned from lunch. No messages from Lizzie. He called her office and was told by the receptionist that she did not wish to take calls from him. He could not understand it. He had sent flowers and a romantic fax—why was she being so difficult?

Maybe the flowers had not arrived yet, and perhaps the fax was still sitting by the machine in her office, and no one had given it to her yet. Yes, that must be it. He would call again later. Once she had his fax and flowers, everything would be fine. She could be moody; he knew that. He had seen her get angry from the dawn of their relationship at university, but she was always quick to forgive.

He remembered the first time he had really pissed her off. They had been going out for a few months, and one evening they went to a party. There were parties nearly every week at university. Up until that point, he had never had the misfortune to bump in to Mike Tyler at a party before. There was no reason why their paths should cross socially because Mike was two years ahead and was doing a different degree course. But that night by unhappy coincidence, they found themselves at the same party.

Mike strolled over to Christian and Lizzie, and to Christian's surprise Mike was really charming at first.

'Hi, Christian, good to see you. And who is this beautiful young woman with you?'

'Er, Mike, meet Lizzie. Lizzie, meet Mike.'

'Lovely to meet you, Lizzie. Christian and I were at the same school together, and now we are at the same university. Of course, I came here two years ahead of him. I guess I must be a role model for him.'

Christian replied, 'Don't think so, Mike. I would sooner model myself on a baboon's bum than you.'

'Well, luckily you succeeded, Christian. You are indeed the absolute personification of a baboon's arse.'

Christian and Mike traded insults for a few more minutes, and then Lizzie walked off.

'Better get going after your girlfriend, baboon bum boy,' Mike said as Christian headed off after Lizzie.

When Christian found her, he said, 'Sorry, Lizzie, he gets right up my nose.'

'Christian, what is wrong with you? He came over and was perfectly civilised until you started insulting him.'

'You don't know him, Lizzie—he is a real wanker. Everyone hated him at school, and I hated him more than most.'

'Christian, these are my friends at this party, and they saw you and Mike trading insults. If you cannot behave, then go join your childish mates down at the pub.'

With that Christian walked off and duly went to the pub. He joined his friends Chris and Russ in the Fighting Cocks in Mosely. Latter they went to the room above the pub to see a new local band, UB40. The band was great, and Christian felt sure they would make it big one day. He vowed he would write up their gig in the university student magazine.

Lizzie left the party in tears after Christian had departed. They had recently moved in together, and when Christian got home, she went berserk. The next day Christian bought some flowers and gave them to her with a sloppy sorry poem, and she forgave him straight away.

The phone rang, and Christian's mind came back to the present. He was sure it was Lizzie phoning to say all was forgiven.

'Mr Christian Davidson?' the voice said.

'Yes.'

'I understand that you are the next of kin to a Mr James Jinks.'

'Well, not exactly, but he is a close friend.'

'Mr Jinks has had a heart attack, and he keeps asking for you. We searched through his wallet and found your business card inside. Can you come and see him in Charring Cross Hospital?'

'Yes, of course, straight away. Is he okay?'

'Yes he will be fine. He just needs a lot of rest and a new lifestyle, that's all.'

Christian rushed out of the office and did not tell anyone where he was going. He hailed the first taxi that he could see.

He arrived at the hospital and asked which ward Jinxie was in, and then he ran down the corridors as quickly as he could to get to his friend. Once outside of the ward, he stopped to catch his breath. He did not want to panic Jinxie by letting him see how concerned and flustered he was. Christian regained his composure and walked calmly over to Jinxie's bed.

'Hello, Jinxie, bad bottle of claret, was it?'

'Ah, dear boy, thank you for coming. There has been a dreadful mistake. I simply rushed to get out of the path of a careless motorist, and in the exertion of the moment, I ran out of puff. No surprise, I suppose, when you smoke as much as I do. Anyway, next thing I know, some idiots are bundling me in to the back of an ambulance, and I wind up in this dreary place. Of course this is all one big mistake, and I should naturally be somewhere else entirely more convivial, having a hearty lunch. For God's sake get me out of here, Dior. You can't smoke, the menu looks dreadful, and there doesn't seem to be a bar.'

'All in good time, Jinxie. You have had a heart attack, and you will get better soon, but right now you are in the best place.'

Then the expression on Jinxie's face darkened, and he suddenly looked very anxious. 'Christian, I need your help.'

'Bloody hell, Jinxie, it must be important—you have never called me Christian before!'

'It's important. Draw up a seat. You need to listen to all I am going to tell you, and then you are going to help me.'

Christian pulled up a plastic chair and sat patiently whilst Jinxie talked. As Jinxie told his story, his normally cheery, gravelly voice became croaky and nervous, and tears rolled slowly down his cheeks.

Jinxie's wife had died some time back following a long, painful, and hopeless battle with cancer. He had loved her very much and worked hard to provide money for a nurse at home to take care of her during the day. In the early stages of the illness, he was able to take care of her through the night. It was an emotional and physical strain for Jinxie, but he bore it well and never showed his wife how much he, too, was suffering.

Towards the last months of his wife's illness, she became totally bedridden. The drugs and the strain on her system meant she was rarely awake, and he was already missing her. In the final stages of the illness the nurse regularly stayed longer and often into the early evening to help Jinxie. The nurse was a great help to him, and although he knew it was wrong, he became fond of her and also quite attracted to her. Jinxie was not overly concerned by his attraction to her, because he knew the love of his wife would keep him from temptation. In any case, she was very unlikely to be interested in an old fool such as him. The nurse was named Siobhan Daley, and she had a gentle disposition and a very charming, soft Irish accent. They became friendly and often used to share jokes as a way of taking their minds off of the strain of treating Jinxie's poor, ailing wife.

One night when his wife was really having a bad time with the effects of the cancer, Siobhan stayed on very late to help out. When Jinxie's wife was finally asleep, he poured himself a large scotch and asked Siobhan if she would like one before leaving. She said yes. They sat and talked for some time, and amazingly they finished off the bottle.

Jinxie admitted to Christian that on that fateful night, he got very drunk, tired, and emotional, and he cried great sobs of tears. Siobhan sat next to him on the sofa, hugged him, and told him she knew what he was going through. Then in her comforting embrace, he found himself kissing her desperately and passionately. They embraced and slid down on to the floor, and within an instant they were indulging in frantic and passionate sex on the carpet.

After they finished, Siobhan suddenly looked embarrassed and got dressed quickly. She took his hand and told him to take heart, and then she hurriedly left.

The next morning Jinxie's wife did not wake up; she had died in her sleep. Jinxie was heartbroken and blamed himself. He could not believe what he had done with Siobhan, and he hated himself for his terrible act of betrayal.

After the funeral, Siobhan tried to contact him, and although Jinxie was fond of her, he could not deal with the guilt and never responded. Then one day over a year later, as he was going through his morning mail, he opened an envelope and pulled out a letter and a photograph. The photograph was of a baby, and on the back it said, 'Julia, aged three months.' He read the letter.

Dear James

 The night we made love was a comfort for both of us during a terrible period of emotional trauma. It did not kill your wife; neither of us was responsible for her death. The time had come for her pain to end. Why did you never return my calls? Were you frightened that I had fallen in love with you? If so, then you hold too high an opinion of yourself.

 I wanted to tell you I was pregnant and that you were the father, because I had not slept with anyone else for more than a year. After calling you on many occasions for a year back without a reply, I vowed to leave you in ignorance about the child. But now she is three months old, and I see no reason why I should bring her up as a single parent and pay for all of her upkeep. I think you should contribute a regular amount per week for your daughter. Please get in touch.

Siobhan Daley

 Jinxie was stunned by the letter. He could not believe that on the night his wife had died, he had created a new life. He wanted to see the child. He had always wanted children, but his wife was unable to have them. He suddenly felt excited and wanted to see his daughter as soon as possible. Jinxie was embarrassed at making the phone call because he knew that he should have returned Siobhan's calls before. He dialled the number, and within two rings it was answered.

 'Eh, Siobhan, this is James. I'm sorry.'

 'Too late for apologies, but not too late to pay your share. Do you agree to contribute?'

 'Yes, of course. When can I see her?'

 'Never. When she is older, I am simply going to tell her that her father died in a car crash.'

 Jinxie argued long and hard with Siobhan, but it was hopeless. Jinxie even threatened to approach Julia when she was older and tell her he was her father. Siobhan explained that he would more than likely be reported to the police as a stalker, because she'd insist that Julia's father had died in a car crash.

Jinxie made regular financial contributions and lived with the terrible knowledge that his daughter would never know him. His only consolation was that he would sometimes see her in the park or just walking down a street. He saw her grow from a baby in to a young woman, but only from a distance.

As Jinxie's story drew to a close, Christian suddenly became aware of something very worrying. 'Jinxie, the Julia that works for me as a production assistant—she's not your daughter, is she? You asked me to contact her and interview her on the pretext that her mother was an old friend. You bloody lied to me, didn't you?'

'No, Christian I never lied to you. Her mother once was an old friend—that much is true. Furthermore, Siobhan phoned me out of the blue a year back and said Julia was interested in getting a job in publishing; she asked if I could help her get an interview. Julia was told by her mother that some old buffer called James Jinks, whose wife she had nursed, had kindly set up an interview with a contact of his as a favour.'

'Are you seriously telling me that to this very day, you have never spoken to Julia? She is still blissfully unaware that her father is alive and is in fact you?'

'Yes, on all counts. Except if I am totally honest, I do not think her father will be alive much longer. I cannot leave this world without letting her meet me. I am her father, for God's sake.'

'So you want me to bring her here under some pretext, and then you can just calmly explain everything.'

'No, no, not here. You think I want her to meet me for the first time like this? I will stay here if I need to for a few more days. Then I want you to check me out of here bright and early on Saturday morning and get me home, where I will do my very best to spruce myself up. In the meantime I want you to invent a reason as to why you want Julia to have lunch with you on Saturday. I want you to book Pontevechio's on the Old Brompton Road for 1.00 p.m. It is a pretty decent Italian place and is not far from my apartment. I will meet you both there, and once we have eaten a little and consumed some wine for Dutch courage, I will tell her all and hope to God she does not hate me.'

'Jinxie, this is a bloody mess. The girl works for me, for God's sake! She will freak out when you spring this surprise on her.'

'Christian, are you going to help me or not?'

'Okay, Jinxie, I will do this for you—but you will really owe me one.'

'Dior, for all the wonderful lunches you have consumed on my expenses, and for all the value of the knowledge that I have imparted to you over the years, you will still be in *my* debt for eternity, even after doing me this favour,' Jinxie joked. He had regained his composure, but nothing could help him regain his youth, for that afternoon he looked really old and very tired. Christian decided it was best to let Jinxie rest, and he departed from the hospital.

CHAPTER 6

CHRISTIAN HEADED BACK to the office and checked for messages. He hoped Lizzie would have called, but she had not. He decided to get Julia into his office to fix lunch for Saturday.

'Julia, you have been with us for a few months now, and I think you are working out fine. I regret that I have not spent much time giving you any training or direction with the job.'

'No problem, everything is fine,' Julia replied. 'You explained the job to me at the start, and it all seems pretty simple. I understand the job, and I'm getting on with it. Everything is great.'

Julia was twenty-two. She had a broad Irish accent and was quite pretty. Christian figured that the looks must have come from her mother—they couldn't possibly have come from Jinxie. She talked a lot, both quickly and nervously, and she always seemed to blush and go a bit pink when she spoke to him. As her boss, Christian guessed he made her nervous.

'Yes, I know you understand the basics of the role, and I know that you are getting on fine. But when you joined, I made a promise to help you to develop a career as a journalist, and I feel I have let you down.'

'Oh no, Christian, I am really very happy. Surely I have not led you to think otherwise.' Julia was now really red in the face and looked incredibly nervous. Christian felt he was frightening her and could not work out what he was doing wrong or even what to do next. He figured if he asked her to lunch now, she would probably pass out in his office from horror.

'Okay, Julia, I'm glad you are happy, and we are happy with you. Thanks for coming into my office.'

Julia left his office and returned to her work. *Well, that was a fuck-up,* he thought. He decided to write her a memo instead.

Memo to Julia Daley, from Christian Davidson

Further to our meeting today, I am of course pleased to understand that you are enjoying your role with the company. However, I do feel that I have not provided you with adequate training to help you develop your journalistic skills for the future. My current difficulty, as I am sure that you will appreciate, is that I am very busy. Therefore although I understand Saturday is a weekend day, I would like to start some training with you this Saturday afternoon. To start the training on a relaxed note, I propose we meet at 1.00 p.m. in the Pontevechio Restaurant on Old Brompton Road for a spot of lunch and an informal discussion about my proposed training programme for you.

Brilliant, that should do the trick, thought Christian. He went to the kitchen and made himself a cup of tea to celebrate. He noticed Julia was away from her desk, so he rushed back to his office, grabbed the memo, raced back to her desk, and placed it carefully next to her telephone. He went back to the kitchen and took his mug of tea back to his office. He was satisfied that he was on the road to fulfilling his promise to Jinxie.

Christian wondered how Julia was going to take the news on Saturday. How would Jinxie feel if she rejected him? Oh God, he was beginning to dread the thought of lunch on Saturday.

Why was Julia always so nervous of Christian? He could not understand it. He thought of himself as a nice, easy going bloke with whom people generally felt comfortable. Perhaps it was just the nerves of dealing with her first boss. He remembered his first job after leaving university: he'd started as a reporter on the *Ealing Weekly News*. It was great training but terrible stories to write about—trivial local news. It was the best job he could get at the time. Every other interview he went to could not believe that he was not going to become a boring economist after having done the degree at university. He could hear them now: 'Take it from me, son, if we give you the job, you will do it for a few months and then will realise you should become an economist after all, and you'll leave.' The only interviewer prepared to believe that he wanted to be a journalist was Jack Reeves, editor in chief of the *Ealing Weekly News*.

He decided to try to call Lizzie again but was told she was away from her desk. He phoned the florist to check on the flowers, and they replied that the flowers had been delivered over three hours ago.

Strange. Why was Lizzie so unresponsive? He had sent flowers, apologised, proposed marriage, and suggested dinner tonight. Apart from going to any further extremes, such as Van Gogh's crazy ear-slicing performance, he was at a loss as to know what to do next.

Lizzie had more luck than Christian, and she landed a job with Lancaster Publishing, a pretty good-quality magazine publisher. It was her fifth interview, and the ad manager who interviewed her for the position of advertising sales executive was none other than Mike Tyler. Mike remembered who she was, and to Lizzie's surprise he offered her the job on the spot. When she told Christian this, he told her not to take the job because Mike Tyler must have had ulterior motives and was not to be trusted.

Lizzie was furious. She had hoped Christian would be happy for her and take her out to celebrate. She presumed that Christian was jealous of her good fortune and totally paranoid without cause about Mike Tyler.

She took the job and settled in very well at Lancaster publishing. Soon she went on to become a senior advertising manager. Fortunately for Christian, she no longer reported to Mike. Mike had progressed to a publisher's position and was running some magazines in a different part of the building from Lizzie. This meant there was little chance of Mike seeing much of Lizzie at work. Christian was really pleased about that.

One thing Christian had never understood was Mike getting him a job at Lancaster Publishing. Much as he hated Mike, he knew that his career was going nowhere on the local rag. Mike helping him to get a job at Lancaster Publishing was a breakthrough, and for a brief period he nearly changed his opinion of Mike.

One year after Lizzie had joined the company, she asked Christian to join her at a pub near her office, where one of her colleagues was having a birthday party. When Christian arrived, Mike wandered over and said, 'Hello, long time no see. How are things in the local newspaper?'

'Pretty dull, as I am sure you are fully aware,' Christian replied.

'There is a job writing for one of our new creative media magazines. Are you interested?'

'Yes, of course—but why would you want to help me?'

'We all have to grow up sometime and forget the past, Christian. Where possible I want to help old boys from the old school. I will talk to the editor tomorrow and get you an interview, if you want it.'

'Cheers, Mike. I really appreciate it. Let me buy you a beer.'

'Sorry, old boy, can't stop. I only popped in for a quick one—I have a hot date tonight and don't want to be late.'

Christian attended the interview and got the job, and everything seemed to be working out fine. The only down side was that Lizzie kept reminding Christian about how Mike had helped him, and she always added that he should be grateful.

Christian did well at Lancaster Publishing: they liked his copy, and his ideas for new sections in the magazines worked out well. Everyone said it was only a matter of time before he came up with his own magazine concept. Finally, when he did come up with his own idea for a new publication, everyone said that they were sure the board would love it and give him a publisher's position.

Mike again stepped in and offered to help Christian present his concept to the directors. Christian appeared before the board with his presentation—and the board shot the idea down in flames, fanned by negative comments from Mike.

Christian felt he had no choice but to resign. The board had said that they saw no chance of his publication working. He left Lancaster Publishing and launched the magazine. Then to his shock and horror, Lancaster announced that they were launching a magazine that matched the concept that he had presented to them! He was now in competition with his old company, pitting his meagre resources against their cash-rich empire.

'Christian, what are you up to?' Tom's voice quickly brought Christian out of his reminiscences. 'I thought you and Lizzie were happy, so why are you inviting our young and impressionable staff member out for lunch on the pretext of an afternoon's training? No one does training on a Saturday afternoon, least of all you. You once told me that you did not believe in training—you said people could only learn the job by actually doing the job.'

'Tom, it's lucky you are not a journalist—you are way off with all your theories. Lizzie and I are in the middle of a huge argument, and sadly I cannot seem to get her to respond to my phone messages, flowers, a faxed marriage proposal, or my invitation to dinner. Furthermore, I am 100 per cent not trying to hit on Julia, who in any case seems to be strangely scared shitless of me. However, I do need to explain something to you about Julia.'

Tom pulled up a seat, and Christian explained what Jinxie had told him. Tom sat in silence until he had been told every last detail. When Christian finished his tale, he said, 'Just tell me one thing, Tom. How did you know that I had invited Julia out for lunch?'

'I heard her phoning a friend. She seemed really excited. She told her friend that you were going to do some training on Saturday afternoon with her, but that you were going to have lunch together first. Julia then said—wait for this one, Christian; it is going to disturb your mind—"What shall I wear? He never seems to notice me in the office, but across a table in a restaurant, he cannot avoid seeing me."'

'Oh shit. If my life gets any more complex, I will have to phone a grand chess master to see if he has any proposals for my next move. I am going to go back to the hospital to see how Jinxie is getting on. Then I am going to find Lizzie to patch things up.'

'Good luck—you need it.'

*   *   *

Lizzie decided she ought to go up to see Mike, thank him for the flowers, and tell him that she was going through a bad patch with Christian but that it wasn't over. She wanted to tell him that she liked him, but she was not searching for a new relationship.

As she approached Mike's office, she could hear him talking to his boss, Frank Stewart. 'No sweat, Frank. Lizzie and Christian are breaking up—I can sense it. I have worked my charm on the little girlie, and by the end of the week she will happily tell me all of Christian's plans for his crappy little magazine. Once we know what the toss pot is planning, we can shit on him from a great height.'

Lizzie could not believe her ears. Christian had been right—Mike was a total bastard! How stupid could she be? She moved away quickly, rushed down the stairs, and returned to her desk. She telephoned

Christian and was told that he was out. Lizzie now felt very desperate. Mike had just used her and did not care for her at all. Sadly, Christian had not bothered to contact her, so clearly he no longer cared anymore. Her life was becoming a mess.

Lizzie was feeling anxious. Her best friend in the office, Fiona, was leaving today, and she was going to have a leaving party in Moriarty's, the pub near the office. Lizzie would have to go, but right now it was the last thing she wanted to do. She decided the only option was to go but then feign sickness and leave early. She also decided that it was time to sort her life out. She phoned Westside Publishing and asked to speak to Bob Evans.

'Hi, Bob, it's Lizzie.'

'Lizzie, don't tell me you have finally decided to accept my proposal and join a real publishing company.'

'Actually, yes.'

'Fuck me! I was only taking the piss, Lizzie. But that is great news!. When can you start?'

'I have loads of holiday owing, and I think my discussions with Lancaster will persuade them to let me leave quickly. So how does next week suit you?'

'Bloody brilliant. Welcome aboard!'

One job done. Lizzie was cleaning up her life. She knew her next decision was to leave Christian; they had been together for ages, but they were going nowhere. He was far more interested in his magazine than her. Besides, if he ever found out that she had slept with Mike, which was inevitable, then he would never forgive her anyway.

* * *

Christian stood by Jinxie's bed side. Jinxie was sleeping and looked frail and very old. Christian felt Jinxie was just hanging on just to explain everything to Julia. He suddenly felt overcome by a huge wave of sadness. Jinxie was not going to be around very much longer, and Christian was going to miss him very much.

He left the hospital and walked in to a public phone box. He tried to reach Lizzie again; it was now just after 5.00 p.m. The receptionist said that everyone had left early for Fiona's leaving party, and she was sure that Lizzie would be at the party. Christian guessed they had gone to Moriarty's—they always went there.

'Can you tell me whether Jackie from circulation has left yet?'

'No, she is still here. Would you like to speak to her?'

'Yes, please.'

When Jackie got on the phone, Christian said, 'Hi, Jackie, it's Christian. Look, I know Lizzie stayed with you last night. Was she okay? Or did she seem upset about something?'

'She didn't stay with me, Christian. So sorry, but I can't help you.'

Christian let the phone fall from his hand. Lizzie had never lied to him like this before. What the hell was going on? *Oh shit—I hope she didn't finally succumb to the charms of Tyler,* he thought. He grabbed a cab and went to Tyler's apartment block. He knew he lived around the corner from Lancaster Publishing. Mike had a flat in a smart building with a doorman downstairs.

Christian wandered in to the lobby and spoke to the doorman. 'Hi, is Mr Tyler home yet?'

'You'll be lucky, mate. It's only just past six, and he doesn't usually get home till after seven at the earliest—and most nights it's after midnight.'

'Oh, a shame. I'm an old friend and wanted to get together with him for a drink.'

'Don't fancy your chances, mate. He's got a new lady friend—saw them leaving a bit late this morning for work, just after nine, I expect he will be out with her again tonight.'

Without warning Christian got the information that he'd dreaded without even having to probe for it.

The doorman continued, oblivious. 'Pretty little thing, she is. Nice blonde hair. I think I heard him calling her Lizzie.'

Christian's heart felt like someone had just plunged a red-hot meat skewer through it. He hated Mike—and now he felt hate and anger for Lizzie, too.

*　　*　　*

Lizzie was sipping her drink and talking to Fiona, wishing her the best for the future, when Jackie walked in. 'Sorry, Lizzie, I think I have just dropped you in it with Christian. He phoned and said he thought you had stayed at my place last night, and I told him that you hadn't.'

Lizzie thought her bowels would collapse. *Oh shit.* She was determined to finish with Christian, but not like this. She had never wanted to hurt him this way.

'Sorry, Fiona, I have to leave,' Lizzie said, and she headed for the door. But before she got to the door, it opened, and there he was—Christian. His face said it all: pain, anger, hatred. Lizzie did not know what to do. She simply wanted to tell him how sorry she was. 'Christian, I'm sorry, I really am . . . ' She put out her arms to hug him.

But Christian pulled away and yelled, 'How could you do it? And with Tyler, of all people! You must really hate me. When you set out to hurt me, you went for it big time! I know I have been neglectful recently, but I don't deserve this. I wanted us to get married, and you just wanted to sleep with my enemy. I feel like such an idiot. Today you ignored my flowers and my messages. How could you have become so cruel? I hate you!'

With that he turned round and burst out of the door and back into the street. He ran as hard as he could, and the tears streamed down his face. Christian had no idea why he was running or to where he was running, but he kept moving.

CHAPTER 7

LIZZIE WAS GLAD that Christian had not come back to the flat that night. She had no idea what to say to him, and she wanted the chance to pack a bag without having to hold an argument at the same time. She called her sister, who readily offered her a spare bed, and Lizzie headed off to her sister's house in Chiswick.

The next morning Lizzie went into Lancaster Publishing and calmly resigned. They didn't argue with her terms—they couldn't—and she left straight away. She couldn't understand why, but she felt very calm, as if everything had happened for a reason and she was now about to start a better and more rewarding chapter of her life. She decided to go shopping because a new chapter deserved a new wardrobe.

*   *   *

Mike Tyler was angry. He had succeeded in destroying Christian's relationship with Lizzie, but he no longer had any chance of getting information on what Christian was up to with his new magazine. Not everything was going to plan, so he needed a new plan.

*   *   *

Christian woke up on the sofa of Tom's flat. There was no getting away from it: he looked like shit and felt like shit. The way his mouth felt, it seemed quite possible that someone had actually shat in it.

What a mess. He had lost Lizzie. Yes, she had slept with Mike, but he had neglected her a lot, and she had probably stopped loving him.

That bastard Tyler must have preyed on her, and for that Christian was certainly going to get revenge.

Tom appeared at the door of the sitting room. 'Bloody hell, Christian, you pick your moments to have a nervous breakdown. What the fuck got into you last night? You arrived at my flat at 2.00 a.m., rang the fuck out of my doorbell, and woke up everyone in the street yelling for me to let you in. Then you stumbled through my front door looking like a tramp, pissed out of your head and talking gibberish. You then drank all my booze and passed out on my sofa. Is there much chance that your crucial lunch with Lord Whitstop today will be a success? If you can indeed regain enough consciousness to be able to hold a conversation with him, it's just possible you might kill him with your breath.'

Christian replied, 'Thanks for the consideration. No "Are you okay, Christian? What happened to you? Can I help in any way?"'

'Christian, we don't have time to indulge in discussing the five hundredth consecutive fight that you and Lizzie had last night.'

'Tom, you need to know Lizzie and I finished last night. She slept with that bastard Tyler. She could not have hurt me more if she had attacked my gonads with a chainsaw.'

'I am really sorry, Christian. I truly am. But if you do not make a success of lunch today, then our magazine is also finished.'

Tom made some toast and brewed some tea. He did the best he could to help Christian to return to the land of living.

* * *

Julia woke early and took a little more care with her choice of clothes and make-up than usual for her day at work. She was feeling good. Julia had only worked for Christian for a few months, but she really admired him. He was still young but had already edited his own magazine at Lancaster Publishing. Now he had launched his own publishing company, and she was sure he was going to be very successful.

It was raining outside, but nothing dampened Julia's spirits as she headed off to the tube station. Julia had been so surprised when she'd read the memo. She was sure she was not reading too much in to it— her friend Anna had agreed with her interpretation of the situation. There was no way her new boss was going to do training on a Saturday afternoon, and he certainly wouldn't do it over lunch in a smart West

London restaurant. She knew his relationship with his girlfriend was in trouble because she had often overheard them arguing on the phone.

She had often hoped that Christian would notice her, but he never seemed to, so it was pretty amazing that he had invited her out now. Perhaps he just wanted a shoulder to cry on; perhaps he was not interested in her. She decided that either way, it was a positive step. If he was inviting her out because he liked her, then that was great. If he just wanted someone to talk to, well, it was a start, and she would be really nice so that he would get to like her.

She had never really understood men, so she hoped she was not getting her hopes up too high. If her father had not died when she was just a baby, then things might have been different. Having a father would have surely helped her feel more comfortable and less nervous around guys she liked.

Julia wished she had known her father. Her mother never spoke of him, and when she asked any questions, all her mother would say was, 'Julia, his loss was a terrible blow to me. Please, let's not discuss your father.'

Julia was a good student at school and at university, and she graduated with a 2.1 in English. She never really had any boyfriends at school, but she did have a two-year relationship at university with one of her lecturers. The other girls said she must have been looking for a father figure because he was in his early forties. He kept saying he was going to leave his wife, but he never did. When she was in her final year, he dumped her for a first-year student.

Julia was heartbroken after the break-up, and she vowed she would never love again, but that had been over a year ago. Today she was sure in her heart that if Christian grew to like her, then he would be the one for her.

She was a sweet girl, and many said she was a bit of a dreamer. Her mother had told her that her father had been a journalist, so perhaps that's why she dreamed of following in his footsteps. She would never know her father because he was dead, but perhaps she could at least live in the same professional field.

She got on the tube and fantasised over what Christian might say to her over lunch. Her mind wandered further, and she began to think about the future. Christian would develop a successful publishing company, and they would fall madly in love. She suddenly realised she had a stupid grin of pleasure and that the old, pervy-looking guy sitting across from her was smiling back at her. Julia suddenly felt very embarrassed and turned bright red. There was no other option—she was still one stop away from her normal stop, but she would have to get out early and walk to the office.

Julia got out and made her way to the office. She had the strange sensation that the pervert was following her, but she knew that this was just paranoia. It was still raining, and she wished she had now stayed on the tube. She looked behind her, and there he was. Julia did not feel frightened; she was simply angry. She marched straight up to him and let rip. 'You fuckin' pervert, what do you mean by following me?'

He looked really shaken and surprised by Julia's verbal assault, and all he could stammer was, 'I'm sorry, so sorry, truly sorry. Please excuse me.' Then he walked away, his shoulders slouched, looking sad and pathetic and quite shaken.

For some strange reason Julia felt really guilty. She had smiled at him unintentionally in her dreamlike fantasy on the tube. Perhaps he was just smiling back politely. Perhaps he was not a pervert at all and was some hard-working father on his way to work. Perhaps he always got off at that stop. Oh God, what had she done? The poor old boy had looked really hurt and upset as she vented her fury on him.

*   *   *

Christian was starting to feel a little more human, but only a little. Tom decided that a ride on the tube would probably kill Christian, so he called a mini cab. This did not turn out to be a good choice. The cab driver had no idea where he was going, and Tom had to direct him constantly. The driver only seemed to be able to select second gear, which meant that the engine constantly emitted screams of pain, and the car either stalled or lurched forward at the traffic lights. By the time they had got to White City Christian had already had to get out twice to be sick—and they had not even covered 30 per cent of the journey!.

*   *   *

Jinxie was also feeling sick. 'Where have you been, Mr Jinks?' the staff nurse asked in a stiff and angry tone. 'You have been missing since at least 6.00 a.m. this morning, and now you come scurrying back in at half past nine, out of breath. The only explanation you are prepared to give is that you have been for a walk.'

Jinxie felt terrible, and the staff nurse was very angry with him. His little trip out of the hospital had not been the success he had dreamed of. He had not managed to slip out and back into the hospital unnoticed— and furthermore, his attempt to follow Julia to work unnoticed had been a complete disaster.

For years he had observed her from a distance, but this time he got too close. He had followed her from her flat in the morning, and he knew she had not seen him. What had possessed him to take the seat directly opposite her on the tube? When he had seen her smiling, he could not help himself, and he smiled back. That was the point he suspected she had noticed him. So why did he get out and follow her? She had sensed his presence, and worse still, she had figured him to be some kind of dirty old man. Christian was not going to be happy. How were they going to have lunch on Saturday now? Jinxie could imagine the introduction.

'Julia, you remember that old pervert that followed you the other day? Well, he is in fact your father, who is actually not dead at all— although currently he probably isn't very far from death.'

*　　*　　*

Christian was feeling pretty close to death. He wondered if Tom had booked the mini cab from hell to pay him back for spoiling his night's sleep. It certainly seemed possible.

*　　*　　*

Lizzie was in Knightsbridge suffering a surge of handbag lust in Harvey Nics. She had always loved handbags, and she had decided that she was going to splash out on a smart designer bag. *There is nothing like retail therapy to make a girl feel good,* she thought to herself as she glided between the displays of bags like a shark through a shoal of fish.

*　　*　　*

Lord Whitstop sat behind his desk and decided that he could not go through with the lunch with the young journalist. He wasn't stupid—he knew what the man was after. He had been indiscreet and had drunk too much the other night, but now he was going to pull back before he said any more. He felt like a silly old fool. What could he hope to gain from this lunch?

He had dreamed that he would achieve two things before he shuffled off the planet. First, he thought he would find someone to write his biography, and second, he thought he might be able to get that same person to run a story to put right a very great wrong. But he knew it now. He was just an old fool. Who would want to read his biography? He had always fallen short of real greatness. The job he had always wanted, prime minister, was never within his grasp. His constant dissent on education, health, and other social services had sidelined him as a troublemaker. They had given him a ministerial position some years back, hoping it would make him toe the line, but it didn't—if anything he became more of an embarrassment, so they'd had no choice but to put him out to grass in the Lords.

In truth he had joined the wrong party. He should have been a Liberal, but he was too hungry to be in government, and he could not see them ever getting enough seats to form a government. Sure, he believed in the free market, but he had a strong social conscience. If only there had been a stronger Liberal party with more national support; then he could have been PM. He was a pretty good speaker, and the press seemed to like him. His choice of party had been forced upon him, but it was never a comfortable one. His colleagues seemed to like him, but, at times they looked upon him as something akin to an anarchist when he spoke out against his own party's policies.

His time in the army had given him a strong sense of honour, and even if his colleagues had been wrong, he could not betray them now. If he told the truth about what he knew, then the scandal would be huge. Ministers would be forced to resign, and many of his friends would end their careers in complete disgrace. If he spoke out, the Falklands veterans would finally find out the truth, but compensation would take years, and most would die before they got a penny.

Lord Whitstop knew that he could not go through with the lunch. He had to cancel—there was no other choice. He called Beryl into his office and asked her to phone Christian and cancel. He told her that he would not take any calls and that he was not to be disturbed by anyone.

*   *   *

Mike Tyler telephoned Bookstall Solutions, the magazine distribution company that handled all distribution of Lancaster Publishing's magazines. They specialised in helping publishers get their magazines stocked by the newsagents. Mike took an educated guess that Christian would ask them to help him get his new title to the newsagents. Christian did not know any other distribution companies, so Mike was sure he was going to be proved right.

'Bill, it's Mike Tyler. How are you doing?'

'Great, Mike. How are things with you?'

'Sadly, not too good. One of our former employees, Christian Davidson, has been causing us quite a few headaches. The directors here are really pissed off with him. Tell me, Bill, you're not going to do the distribution of Christian's magazine, are you?'

'Well, to be honest, yes, we were approached by Christian. We agreed to take his title on our books.'

'Look, just a word of advice. I know you like Christian, and believe me, so do I. But I think you should strongly reconsider doing any work for him. If the powers that be hear that you are going to help him distribute his magazine, then I think you will have a lot of problems renegotiating future contracts with Lancaster Publishing.'

'Understood, Mike. I cannot face telling Christian that we will not be able to help him, so I guess I will have to opt for the coward's route and send him a fax this morning.'

Mike felt very pleased with himself. *That should give Toss Pot a nice headache for the morning,* he thought, and he composed a fax to send Christian later on that day.

> Dear Toss Pot,
>
> I was sorry to hear that you are currently having circulation problems for your proposed magazine. However, I think I have an excellent solution for you. I would suggest that you invest in a giant toilet so that you can flush your crappy little publication into the sewers, where I am sure

it will be very comfortable circulating with other pieces of shit.

Of course he was never going to send the fax, but it amused him enormously to compose it, and he sat back in his chair with tears of laughter streaming down his cheeks.

*   *   *

Christian finally arrived at his office, and he felt truly awful. He was sure things couldn't get much worse. He made himself a coffee and went to his office. He read the phone message from Beryl advising him that Lord Whitstop did not wish to meet for lunch today or any other day. Then he saw the fax from Bookstall Solutions explaining that due to a conflict of interests, they regretted to say that they would be unable to assist him with the distribution of his forthcoming magazine.

Christian was shell-shocked. He stared blankly in front of him at a picture on his office wall of him and Lizzie arm in arm after their university graduation ceremony. He remembered how he felt on that day, ready to go out and conquer the world. But today the world had conquered him. There was nothing left to be done—he was finished. His relationship with Lizzie had died, and now his business was about to die. To make things worse, he felt physically dreadful from his night of alcohol abuse. Tears appeared at the corner of Christian's eyes, small and hardly noticeable at first, but soon great rivers of water flowed down his cheeks as he sat completely motionless and stared into space.

*   *   *

Jinxie sat on his bed with the tears streaming down his face. He wanted to die now—right now. His hands were shaking, and he felt very alone.

*   *   *

Lord Whitstop sat behind his desk and began to cry. He had lost his nerve. He was going to let those poor, young, sick soldiers down.

He bowed his head, and the tears fell onto the wooden floor. His heart felt sick.

* * *

Julia went to the toilet and sat on the closed seat. She had gone there just to find a private place to sit. What was happening to her? She had been horrible to that poor man this morning, and she was living in a fantasy world about Christian. He clearly had no interest in her. She had said good morning to him when he walked in, and he walked straight past her without saying a word.

Julia started to cry, and little tears dripped onto her shoes. She felt heartless and unattractive and wished that she had a father to talk to.

* * *

Lizzie sat down with her coffee and admired her new bag. Then suddenly she began to sob. She believed that she was right to finish with Christian, but she knew that she had broken his heart, and the guilt overwhelmed her. The tears splashed into her coffee, and she felt selfish and heartless.

* * *

The rain splashed down on the pavements all over London and on people whose lives had, at that moment in time, become very connected. Joy and hope seemed to be disappearing in the streams of water running down through the drains and into the sewers below. As the rain continued pouring, Christian, Jinxie, Lizzie, Whitstop, and Julia were sobbing.

However, Mike Tyler was on top of the world; not even the rain was going to spoil his sunny day.

CHAPTER 8

CHRISTIAN CONTINUED TO stare at the picture on his wall. He took a good, hard swallow of all his pride and made up his mind to win back Lizzie. First he had to save his business and get his magazine to succeed. Once this was done, he knew he would be his old, positive self again. He would once again be the upbeat, happy dreamer with whom Lizzie had fallen in love. He wiped away the tears, slugged back his coffee, and strode purposefully out of the office. He was going to see Jinxie.

Christian's father had died when he was very young. He had never had anyone to turn to at the start of his career for advice. Then he met Jinxie, who had proved to be an inspiration and a mentor. Meeting Jinxie had been a fortuitous piece of chance that he would never forget.

Shortly after Christian had joined Lancaster Publishing, he was invited to a publishing awards dinner. Christian dreaded having to go; he was going to have to look ridiculous in a black tie and spend an entire evening sitting next to a bunch of boring old farts that he had never met before.

He arrived at the Ballroom of the Grosvenor House Hotel and gladly accepted a glass of champagne as he entered the foyer. He sidled over to the large board displaying the table plans and the guest list. He found his name on the board and the table number, and he then located his table on the map. Thank God—his table was at the back of the room, so if things got too boring, he could escape without being noticed or greatly missed.

The assembled crew of swaggering dinner suits and preening ball gowns were instructed to go to their tables because dinner was about to be served. Christian knocked back his champagne and swiftly grabbed another full glass before making his way to his table.

As he approached the table, he gazed upon his table companions and figured that it was definitely going to be a painful night. They all looked either close to retirement, retired, or close to death. He bet that they were going to spend most of the night telling boring stories or offering him tips and unwanted career advice.

'So which company has condemned you to an evening with the living dead?' the man to his left asked.

'Lancaster Publishing,' replied Christian.

'Well, I and most of my colleagues here are from a selection of the gutter press. My name is James Jinks, but most people call me Jinxie. What do most people call you?'

'Christian Davidson.'

'Sorry, dear boy, but I have a terrible memory for names, so to make things easy for me, I am going to call you Dior. Childish schoolboy nicknames are far easier to remember.'

Christian really enjoyed sitting next to Jinxie, and the evening flew by. Jinxie told amusing stories about a lot of people who were at the dinner. Christian became aware that Jinxie was providing him with a great wealth of knowledge about British publishing personalities in a really fun way. The evening proved to be both an education and an entertainment at the same time.

As the evening came to a close, Christian rose from the table and said farewell to Jinxie. 'Thank you, Jinxie. I really enjoyed your company and your wonderful stories. I do hope we shall meet again sometime.'

'Dior, you certainly do have the makings of a good journalist. You sounded most convincing when you uttered those kind words.'

'No, Jinxie, I really mean what I said. I was dreading tonight, but you made it fun. Thanks.'

'Dear boy, you have given an old fool a new audience for his dreadful anecdotes. It is me who should be thanking you. In actual fact, if you can stand to be bored some more, you are most welcome to join me for lunch at the Wig and Pen Club.'

'Sounds great. When shall we meet?'

'Does one o'clock this Friday suit you?'

'Sounds great. Look forward to seeing you then.'

And so began a tradition of Christian joining Jinxie for lunch at the Wig and Pen on the third Friday of every month. In time Jinxie managed to get Christian a club membership. Christian liked the club a great deal and started to use it himself, and he would frequently bump in to Jinxie.

Over the years he and Jinxie became good friends. Their ages were far apart, but it didn't worry either of them. In time few people knew Jinxie better than Christian, and few people new Christian better than Jinxie.

Jinxie was like a father to Christian, and he was always keen to hear how Christian's career was progressing and to offer advice. Christian was the son that Jinxie had never had.

Today more than ever, Christian really needed Jinxie's advice, so he made haste to the hospital. As he arrived, he was convinced that he saw Lord Whitstop climb into the back seat of a cab, but he figured his imagination was working overtime. He walked up to Jinxie's bed and found the old man talking to the staff nurse.

'Mr Jinks, you simply cannot disappear for hours on end without telling any of the nursing staff. We have enough to worry about, without you making matters worse. And I simply refuse to believe your story that you just popped out for a stroll. Your current poor physical condition clearly suggests that you are not the walking type. If you ask me, the only time you walk anywhere is to get to a bar.'

Jinxie then proceeded to quote Emily Dickinson to the staff nurse.

> Because I could not stop for Death,
> He kindly stopped for me;
> The Carriage held but just ourselves
> And Immortality.**

The nurse simply said, 'Mr Jinks, quoting poetry and lying to me does not impress. If you have no intention of allowing us to help you recover, then I suggest you vacate this hospital to make way for someone more appreciative of our medical care.' She then departed with a flourish.

** Taken from the poem, *Because I Could Not Stop for Death*, by Emily Dickinson (no relation).

'Seems they wish me to vacate this establishment, Dior. Dear boy, I think you should help me quit this temperance hall and assist me to return home, where Gershwin and Highland spirits can work their magic on my weary soul.'

'Jinxie, you are going to stay here until the weekend, as you agreed, and then I will honour my promise to attempt to acquaint you with your daughter.'

'Too late, Dior. We met today, and I confess the meeting was a disaster. Poor Julia now has me down as some dirty, old pervert who has been stalking her.'

'What the bloody hell have you been up to, Jinxie?'

The ageing schoolboy bravado faded away, and Jinxie suddenly looked terribly pathetic. In a weak and shaky voice, he told Christian how he had followed Julia that morning, and how she had spotted him and then challenged him.

Christian listened in stunned silence and disbelief, and then suddenly he felt their roles reversed. He found himself playing the father figure to Jinxie. It was amazing that Jinxie's weakness had given Christian strength. 'Jinxie, this does not change anything. Sure, you made a fool of yourself this morning, but we are going to have that lunch on Saturday, and you are going to explain everything to Julia. You have no need to worry—I will be there, and I am your friend. Julia is a sweet girl, and once you have told her the truth, she will understand. I am sure everything will work out fine.'

'Christian, how can you be so sure?'

'Do you trust me, Jinxie?'

'Yes.'

'Then there is nothing more to be said. But now I need *your* help and advice.'

With this Jinxie perked up. He enjoyed giving advice to Christian, and he took strength from doing so. 'Tell me all, dear boy, and if an old fool can proffer a young fool some advice, perhaps we two negatives can make a positive.'

Christian told Jinxie how Lord Whitstop had cancelled their lunch appointment. Before he could get into much detail, Jinxie interrupted him with a beaming grin on his face. 'Remember, Christian, that I have always told you that you can never ask enough questions as a journalist. Well, do you recall when you phoned me recently and asked if Whitstop could be relied on, and I told you yes? You never asked how come I was so sure. Christian, I always told you that asking supplementary questions might help you discover the really important facts. You should have asked me why I was so sure that Whitstop was a reliable man. You see, the answer is very simple: we fought together in the Second World War, and we are old friends.'

'Shit, Jinxie. Why didn't you tell me this before?'

'Christian, you seemed to want to be oh so hush-hush about your story. I was sure you had no desire to continue your discussions with me for fear I might get in on your exclusive.'

'Well, you were wrong, Jinxie, and right now I do not need your advice—I just need your help.'

'I know what you are going to ask, dear boy, and I have already fixed it up for you. You will meet Whitstop at seven tonight in his office, after Beryl has gone. I have already written the address down on a piece of paper, just in case you do not already have it.'

'Jinxie, you are a bloody wonder! How did you fix that up?'

'Shortly before you arrived, Whitstop visited me. He heard that his old army chum was at Death's door, and he came to see how I was getting on. We go back a long way, and he also wanted my advice. He was having a problem with his conscience, and he needed an honest broker to tell him the path to tread. Let me play back our meeting for you, and all will become clear.'

Jinxie told Christian how Lord Whitstop had arrived clutching the obligatory bag of grapes and the morning papers. He asked after Jinxie's health and showed all the required concern of an old and trusted friend. But then Lord Whitstop became anxious and told Jinxie that his conscience was in torment and that he really needed his advice. He told Jinxie that he had let his tongue run loose in a bar to a young journalist. The journalist had presumed that he was smarter than Whitstop and had invited him to lunch on the pretext of writing his biography. Whitstop was not so dumb, but nevertheless he decided to go through with the lunch. He had decided at long last tell the truth about why so many young soldiers were now dying years after the Falklands War.

Jinxie asked him why he had not come to him with the story. Whitstop explained that a lot of very important politicians would be forced into dishonourable retirement, and some of them were both his and Jinxie's friends. Disloyalty on such a scale would never be forgiven, and Whitstop had no desire to put Jinxie through this.

Whitstop went on to explain that this morning he had lost his nerve. He was scared of becoming an outcast amongst his friends at this time of his life. There were some he knew who deserved to pay for what they had done, but most had discovered what had happened when things were too late. People would not understand why there was a cover-up, but, if one had been at public school and in the army, as many elder politicians had, then the first rule was never to tell tales on one's colleagues even if one knew they had committed a wrong. That was the culture, and anyone who dared break it was sure to meet with total contempt.

He told Jinxie that he had cancelled his planned lunch with the young journalist, but now he felt really wretched and believed that despite the prospect of living his final years in lonely disgrace, the truth needed to be told. When he had told Beryl to agree to the lunch a few days back, he was scared but had felt as if a terrible burden was starting to lift away from the back of his troubled mind. Then this morning he felt depressed; he, like Jinxie, missed his late wife and didn't have any children. The prospect of losing all his friends in his twilight years conjured up images of a disgraced old man living out his years in lonely misery.

At this point Jinxie decided to tell Whitstop that he knew Christian. He also told him that Christian had in fact called him to ask if Whitstop was a reliable source. Lord Whitstop now looked surprised and asked Jinxie why he had not contacted him following this telephone conversation. Jinxie explained as best as he could.

'Well, John, I guessed that you wanted to tell Christian something big, and as you had not contacted me, it struck me you were finding it hard to let anyone, even an old friend, know the information that you were going to bring into the public domain. I have always admired you; you always spoke your mind even when the consequences held back your own political ambitions. If the reason you are sitting here now is that you want me to help you strengthen your resolve to do the right thing, then I am happy to be of assistance.

'John, you never needed to ask for any advice when you stood up for social justice in the past, and you don't need it now. You know what has to be done—you cannot carry such a secret to your grave. We are old men now, and we must all make our peace in this life before we go to the next one.'

Whitstop smiled. He knew Jinxie was right, and he knew what he had to do. 'You know this young journalist, James. Call him, make sure he has my contact details, and tell him to be at my office at seven tonight. I will be the only one there; Beryl will have left by then.'

After Jinxie finished recounting the visit to Christian, he said, 'So, Dior, you have saved me a phone call, and now you know you shall have your story. But I want you to promise me this: go easy with him tonight. What he has agreed to do will cause him a lot of pain, and you will be his confessional. Take his confession and let him know he is doing the right thing. He has carried the burden of this information for a long time, and releasing it will end his career as he began it—a decent and honest man. But sadly his honesty will bring him dishonour and disgrace.'

Christian was not sure if he felt happy or sad. He was going to get the story that he needed, but his mind could not help thinking of Whitstop living out his final days as an outcast from the political circles in which he had spent most of his life. He thanked Jinxie, and then he once again stiffened Jinxie's resolve to go through with their plan to meet with Julia on Saturday.

Christian left the hospital and headed back to the office to tell Tom.

*   *   *

Tom was not having a good morning. He was not at his best, and failing to get a decent night's sleep did not help things. Tom was very concerned that the magazine project was going to end in disaster. It was Christian who had persuaded him to leave Lancaster Publishing, but Christian now seemed to be losing the plot.

Christian had broken up with Lizzie, was clearly unstable emotionally, and was liable to take his focus off the magazine. With Jinxie in hospital, this was going to disturb Christian even more. But, now things were really bad. Julia sounded more depressed than a Leonard Cohen CD, and when he told her this, she burst into floods of tears. Christian must have something to do with Julia's mood—Tom was sure of that.

Then to his horror he found that Christian had gone out, and no one knew where he had gone. Frustrated and worried, he searched

Christian's desk for some clues as to his whereabouts, only to discover that not only had Lord Whitstop cancelled lunch, but Bookstall Solutions had decided not to distribute the magazine.

Tom stood in Christian's office and screamed, 'Fucking fantastic!. I have my life savings invested in a magazine with an editor who has not only gone mad but has gone missing. Our one staff member has slumped into a depression, our distribution agency has declined to distribute the magazine, and our one chance for a good story has changed his mind. Things just can't get any worse!'

But they could, and they did.

Shortly after Tom returned to his desk, the phone rang: it was Steve Bedding from PQT, a major advertising agency. Tom had spent years developing a good relationship with Steve, which was important because Steve handled the advertising bookings for a number of major blue chip companies. 'Tom I have heard some very disturbing news that gives me no choice but to cancel my clients' bookings with you.'

'I don't understand, Steve. Everything is on schedule with the magazine, and I fully expect it to be a great success.'

'Look, Tom, I am aware that Bookstall Solutions has decided not to distribute your magazine to the newsagents, and my source is reliable. But before you ask me who it is, I am afraid that I am unable to tell you this.'

'No need, Steve. It has to be Mike Tyler.'

Tom tried hard to persuade Steve that they would find another magazine distribution agency, but he failed to convince him. The best he could do was to persuade Steve to reconsider was if Tom could fax him a copy of an agreement with a new distribution agency.

Things were looking very grim. It was only last week that Tom had persuaded Steve to book a whole bunch of his clients into the first issue of the magazine. It was a major booking that included five double-page colour spreads from a leading car manufacturer, an exclusive watchmaker, a top-five bank, a quality men's clothing retail chain, and a major European airline. Steve also confirmed colour page bookings for nine other clients. Tom had in fact managed to persuade Steve to book so much ad space that the booking represented nearly 20 per cent of the total advertising booked for *Style Inc.* It was a terrible blow. Steve had cancelled, and Tom guessed that it was only a matter of time before other clients called to cancel as well.

Where the hell is Christian? Tom thought. This was not the time for him to do a disappearing act. Tom had performed wonders, persuading his clients to make major bookings for a new publication, but now his clients were cancelling, and Tom was scared.

Tom had been an inspirational advertising manager for Lancaster Publishing. His team adored him because Tom led by example and regularly brought in large volumes of advertising. He helped and trained his team, and he was a legend in creative selling techniques.

His first ever lunch with Steve Bedding was famous throughout the publishing industry. Tom was working on a car magazine at the time, and Steve regularly booked ads for a leading sports car manufacturers in a competing publication. Tom repeatedly tried to get Steve to move his ads to his magazine, but Steve insisted that the rival publication offered much lower ad rates and that the marketing director from his client, Derek Jones, was very price sensitive.

Tom persuaded Steve to bring Derek to lunch, and Tom booked a very expensive fish restaurant. When they all sat down at the table, Tom ordered some drinks and then tried to persuade Derek that his magazine appealed to much higher net worth customers. He suggested that the readers of his magazine could afford to buy sports cars, whereas readers from the rival publication could barely afford to buy a pair of roller skates. Derek remained impervious to Tom's arguments.

Then a waiter approached their table with a trolley. Tom asked his guests if he could make a recommendation for their starters, and they readily agreed. 'Okay, on the trolley we have some excellent shrimps, a superb trout pate, fresh oysters, beluga caviar, seafood salad . . . and a bowl of congealed cat food mixed with fish heads. Could I recommend the bowl of congealed cat food mixed with fish heads? It tastes like shit and is totally inappropriate for quality clients such as yourselves with sophisticated tastes—but hey, it's bloody cheap.'

Steve looked horrified, and he stared across at Derek, expecting him to be upset. But Derek started to laugh, and then out of relief Steve laughed with him. Derek agreed to move all his ads to Tom's magazine, and for many years Derek dined out on the story of his lunch with Tom.

Tom was a great team motivator. His staff still remembered the games he used to play with them when they were going through a bad patch. Advertising sales is a tough job, and when a lot of clients say no, it was very hard to find the motivation to continue to make phone calls.

Tom had a variety of games and incentives to keep his team making the calls and enjoying the job.

One such game was 'Say it for me, and drink for free'. Tom would regularly take his team out for drinks after work, and one of the team members would often get to drink for free by winning one of Tom's games. The game was simple. One had to get a difficult phrase into a phone conversation with a client. The first person to succeed was guaranteed free drinks all night, courtesy of Tom.

Tom could still remember one of his better challenges that Tony had managed to win. One morning when things were not going well, Tom wanted his team to keep calling clients, and so he set a challenge. 'Okay, it's time for "Say it for me, and drink for free". And today's words are "pig's snot".'

The team started phoning clients and tried to think of ways of bringing the words 'pig's snot' into their conversations without the client realising it. Tony cracked it when he finished a call with, 'Good, Martin, look forward to seeing you for lunch on Tuesday—and don't worry I will book a good, kosher restaurant where pig's not on the menu.'

Tom had been happy working on the car magazine. He loved the special language that the car dealers spoke. Great phrases sprang back to his mind now. Electric car windows were 'fast glass', and electric wing mirrors were 'electric ears'. One of his favourites was a rear-window wiper washer, a 'bidet'. He also loved the phrase 'it's a monument', which was in fact a car that stayed on the lot and never sold.

Christian and Tom had become good friends at Lancaster Publishing, and they frequently went out drinking together after work. Lancaster Publishing produced an in-house company magazine, and Christian and Tom often used to produce a humorous, alternative version. The company magazine was called *Sound Bite,* and Christian and Tom's version was called *Sounds Shite.* They would often work out their satirical stories together over a few beers; the drunker they got, the more outrageous the stories became.

In the last issue of *Sound Bite,* Lancaster Publishing ran an article about the launch of a new magazine called *4 Wheeler Dealer,* aimed at motor car dealers. The article stated that the magazine was to be a controlled circulation title—in other words, it was to be distributed direct to the readers as opposed to being sold via newsagents. The article boasted that it was a niche market publication that had no competitors.

Tom and Christian wrote their version of the story.

Lungcancer Publishing Is Proud to Announce the Launch of One Wheeler Dealer

This niche market magazine is distributed on a controlled circulation basis to dope pedalling mono cyclists. Our reader, a former circus clown turned dope dealer, is delighted with the magazine. Mr Bobo Goodblow was quoted as saying, 'Now at long last, there is a publication to deal with the key issues related to being a dope-pedalling mono cyclist. A recent article titled "Enjoy your blow whilst on the go—yes or no?" was most illuminating. It carefully reported on my accident last week, when I was mono cycling through a crowd of shoppers whilst bombed out of my brains, and I accidentally cycled over a Rottweiler's leg.

'The dog had been resting outside a shop waiting for its owner to return. I skidded over its left paw, and the dog went berserk and managed to slip its collar. It then proceeded to chase me down the high street. It eventually dragged me to the ground and started mauling me. As usual, on a Monday morning I had a large bag of stash in my pocket, which the dog ate.

'The dog then went very weird and bit a very attractive young lady on her backside. The story was even reported in the *Sun* with the headline "Bombed-out Roti bites red hot totty on botty".

'The article has recommended that people in my profession use the bus when we are bombed out. They are even starting a campaign with a great slogan: "Been toking or sniffing glue? Use the bus—it's safer for you".'

Tom and Christian could sit for hours writing spoof stories, taking it in turns to contribute lines. Once they had completed enough stories for *Sounds Shite,* they would type them all out and create a mock magazine, photocopy it, and distribute it on everyone's desks late at night. It was during one of their sessions creating stories in the bar that Christian said he dreamed of launching his own publishing company one day. Tom said he had the same dream. They agreed that one day they would create a company called ChrisTom Media.

When Christian resigned from Lancaster Publishing, he asked Tom to consider going ahead and setting up ChrisTom Media. Tom had not expected to launch the company so early in his working career, or on such limited resources. Nevertheless, Tom believed in Christian, and so he agreed. He was sure that Christian would make a success of it. But now, he wasn't sure of anything.

CHAPTER 9

LIZZIE HAD LEFT the café more through embarrassment than anything else. The sight of her crying had caused customers and waiting staff to cautiously approach her in a quest to find out if they could help her. She didn't want any help—she just wanted forgiveness. She was saddened by how things had worked out. True, she and Christian had drifted apart, and she was sure that they were not meant to be together, but the relationship had ended very badly.

She dried her eyes, paid her bill, and walked back out into the pouring rain. She was also sorry to have left her job, but she'd had no option but to resign. Lizzie had made a lot of friends at Lancaster Publishing, and she was going to miss them. No one had ever left without having the obligatory piss-up in Moriarty's, and Lizzie decided that she would not be denied hers. She walked into a phone box and called Jackie at Lancaster Publishing. She told her that she wanted to organise a leaving do, and she asked Jackie if she would circulate a memo to a list of staff that Lizzie would like to invite. Jackie agreed and then asked Lizzie if she was free to meet for lunch, because Jackie had something very important that she needed to tell her.

'What is it you need to tell me, Jackie?'

'I can't tell you now—we need to meet. Let's say Drummond's Wine Bar at one?'

Lizzie agreed but was troubled by the nervousness that had come across in Jackie's voice. Drummond's Wine Bar was quite close to Lancaster Publishing, but none of the staff ever went there.

Lizzie left the phone box and hailed a taxi. She decided to pop into Moriarty's on her way, in order to book it up for her leaving party. Twenty minutes later she was sitting in the not very comfortable surroundings of the upstairs of Moriarty's. Eddie, the bar manager, was pleased to see her and gave her a big hug. Then he made her a cup of tea that tasted like drinking creosote. 'Okay, girl, I can do you my special favourite customer party deal. You buy the first hundred quids' worth of booze, along with a guarantee to bring me at least thirty serious drinkers, and in return I will provide a good supply of free pub grub, plus the use of this lovely party room.'

'Sounds fine, Eddie. After my hundred pounds runs out, you can switch to a pay bar. I promise I will have at least thirty of London's heaviest drinkers in my party, and that means you should still be quids in, even after supplying the food and this elegant room.'

'Good, we have a deal. I will get Jean to provide a load of sandwiches, chicken legs, vol-au-vents, sausage rolls, crisps, peanuts, and some other bits and pieces—all on the house.'

'Thanks, Eddie, I appreciate it. Especially at such short notice.'

'So why are you leaving, luv?'

'Too complex to explain, Eddie—and a little too painful.'

But, somehow Lizzie did find herself telling her tale to Eddie, and he was a good listener. She couldn't help wondering why she had told Eddie, but he was a kind man and was easy to talk to.

He said, 'Well, you don't seem to want to get back together with your boyfriend, but you do seem to want his forgiveness. I have to tell you that forgiveness may be hard to find when you have slept with your boyfriend's worst enemy. I think you have got more chance of getting shit out of a rocking horse than getting forgiven.'

'I know that, Eddie, but it can't end like this.'

'No, you are right, luv. What you need to do is to find some way of doing something nice for him. That makes him understand that you are not the deceitful heartless cow he probably thinks you are.'

'Nicely put, Eddie. You know how to make a girl feel good about herself.'

'Just putting it as he must be seeing it.'

'So come on, then—what can I do that Christian will appreciate?'

'Look, luv, there are no sticking plaster solutions. All you can do is wait for an opportunity. At some point, if you remain in his social or working world, you will discover a way to do something good for him. If you can find a way to help him, then whilst he knows it's over with you and him, he will see that you *do* care, and that will count for something.'

'Nice theory, Eddie. Hopefully I can do something good for Christian someday soon. Even if he cannot forgive me, it may at least ease my conscience.'

Lizzie gave Eddie a peck on the cheek and headed off to meet Jackie. She was a little late, and as she entered Drummond's Wine Bar, she was relieved to see Jackie smiling and waving her over to a table. The conversation started lightly, with Lizzie explaining the plans for her leaving party and then repeating her request for Jackie to memo a list of people at Lancaster Publishing. Then Lizzie asked Jackie what it was she needed to talk about.

'It's that bastard Tyler. He's obsessed with destroying Christian's magazine.'

'Well, how is he going to do that?'

'Believe me, Lizzie, any way he can. He has been calling contacts at ad agencies and persuading them to cancel their ad bookings with Tom. He has contacted Bookstall Solutions to persuade them not to distribute Christian's mag.'

'Why is he so keen to destroy Christian?'

'Oh Lizzie, you never could see Mike's hatred for Christian. He only got him the job with Lancaster Publishing in the hope to humiliate him one day.'

'And I guess he only gave me a job in order to sleep with me, to get at Christian. That must be what everyone is thinking of me: stupid bloody tart Lizzie.'

'Lizzie, this is not about you. Perhaps Mike did employ you in the hopes of getting you in to bed. But that's academic—everyone knows you were a brilliant ad manager. Mike's schemes have had no effect on people's regard for you, but they are going to have a terrible effect on Christian's future.'

'Sorry, Jackie, you are right—this is not about me. But what can we do to stop Tyler and to help Christian?'

'I can't do anything—I need my job at Lancaster Publishing, and I have no desire to lose it. But if you still have any feelings for Christian, you can help him with the information that I am going to give you, on condition that you promise never to tell anyone about our meeting.'

Lizzie agreed, and Jackie revealed all she knew. She told Lizzie that in recent years, the Lancaster Publishing board of directors had given Mike Tyler the added responsibility of dealing with Bookstall Solutions and doing some PR on some of the bigger newsagent chains. Bookstall Solutions' role was to get newsagents to put on sale copies of Lancaster's magazines. The general agreements were on a sale or return basis: if a newsagents chain took twenty thousand magazines and returned three thousand unsold, they would pay for the seventeen thousand that they had sold. The sales of magazines could be affected by the position the newsagents gave to the magazines on the shelves. Good eye-catching positions and a greater display of more copies could result in greater sales of a publication. It was Bookstall Solutions' task to get the newsagent to agree to stock the publication and then to try to get the best possible position and amount of displayed copies. With a large amount of magazines available in the market, it was always important to have a good relationship with the newsagents, and Bookstall Solutions was good at doing this.

Bookstall Solutions was aware that Mike Tyler would also do his best to back up their efforts by entertaining directors from major chains of newsagents from time to time, in order to get them to look favourably on magazines from Lancaster Publishing. Mike would also sometimes invite directors of newsagents to parties or launches of publications, to persuade them that a certain publication was worth them stocking and presenting in a good position with plenty of copies. Lancaster Publishing was in a reasonably strong position with the newsagents' chains because they had a number of very popular consumer magazines that regularly sold in big numbers.

Christian was in a very weak position with the newsagents. Only Bookstall Solutions or a similar operation could persuade them to stock Christian's magazine, by using their influence and by presenting the idea of the publication as a future good seller. Christian had been lucky: he had managed to persuade Bookstall Solutions that his magazine would be a good seller, and they liked the concept. They had agreed to handle the distribution and to persuade the newsagents to stock the magazine.

But now Mike had managed to persuade Bookstall Solutions not to distribute Christian's magazine. Mike had applied pressure to them, suggesting that they could damage their relationship with Lancaster Publishing.

Jackie had taken a dislike to Mike Tyler some years back, after he had romanced her briefly, bedded her quickly, and then dumped her like lightning. She could have accepted all of that, except that Mike let it be known around the company how easily and quickly he had managed to get her to go to bed with him.

She had observed him closely over the years, hoping to get her own back someday. Jackie had often felt sorry for Christian; she knew early on that Mike was trying to break him. Now at last she had her chance to revenge herself and to help poor Christian fight back against Mike's devious schemes.

Jackie had learnt some very useful information sometime back. She had picked up her telephone handset, and to her surprise she could hear Mike talking on the line to someone. There was clearly something wrong with the phone system, but she was not going to pass up the chance of listening in to one of Mike's conversations, so she sat and listened. Jackie recounted to Lizzie the call she had overheard.

'Yes, you see, Phil, it's a good arrangement for both of us, and Bookstall Solutions need never hear of it.'

'I totally agree, Mike. I really must thank you—it was a super lunch yesterday and an excellent idea. We should get together more often.'

'Let's have a regular get-together, and if you are finding that you need extra copies of our magazines on a monthly basis, you can call me direct.'

With that the conversation ended, and Jackie found herself trying to guess what Mike was up to. She had a pretty good idea and figured that Mike had agreed to supply a major newsagent direct with extra copies of some of the better selling publications when the newsagent needed them. Mike was bypassing Bookstall Solutions in order to avoid paying them a percentage of the revenue from the sales of these extra copies.

That night Jackie worked late, and when she was sure that there was hardly anyone left in the building, she crept into Mike's office. She leafed through his desk and within minutes found what she was looking for in his out tray. She had been right: Mike had struck a deal with a major newsagent to supply extra copies of magazines direct, thus cutting out Bookstall Solutions. Mike had clearly figured that Bookstall Solutions would never find out because this deal only related to orders beyond the normal requirements of the newsagent. The newsagents' normal requirements would still be handled by Bookstall Solutions, so everything would seem on the level.

Jackie decided to carry on searching through Mike's files, and she was not surprised to find that he had done similar deals with a couple of other major newsagent chains. She was also not surprised to find that Mike had proposed the idea to the board of directors at Lancaster Publishing, and that one of the directors had been stupid enough to tell Mike to go ahead in a memo.

Jackie copied the incriminating documents and hid the copies away under the carpet in her office.

Lizzie sat astonished at what Jackie had told her. Then she asked, 'Will you give me copies of the documents Jackie so that I can help Christian?'

'Of course—I have them here in this blue folder, and when we finish lunch, you can take them away. But I want you to assure me again that no one will ever know that this information came from me.'

'No one will ever know. If anyone ever asks how the documents were obtained, I will be happy and proud to say that I found them.'

*　　*　　*

Tom was in a foul mood when Christian walked into the office, and Tom vented his anger freely as Christian walked towards his desk. 'So, partner, when were you going to tell me that the dream was dead? No big story for the first issue, and no chance of getting the magazine into the newsagents. Plus, even if everything else were okay, Julia looks like someone just tortured her granny to death. And the killer blow: my ads are cancelling quicker than Dr Crippen's patient list. Want to share deeply with me? Or are there any other nasty surprises that you forgot to tell me? Perhaps the office bog is infected with anthrax, or Julia is an escaped manic-depressive serial killer who intends to beat me to death with a binder.'

'Tom, the Whitstop story is on, and I am seeing him tonight. As for Bookstall Solutions, just wait a day or two. When I have the story, I will go see them, and then they will be begging to take on our magazine.'

'You don't see it, do you, Christian? Mike Tyler is out to get you, and my bet is that he's going to win. He has Lancaster Publishing behind him, and all we have is each other. Tyler has persuaded Bookstall Solutions to drop us. Let's face facts: they have too much to lose to change their minds.'

'But they will never want to miss out on distributing the magazine with the scoop of the decade, not even to keep Lancaster happy,' Christian insisted.

'I'm sorry, Christian, but you are wrong. It will take a hell of a lot more than your editorial coup to change their minds, and your story will only ever appear on your PC. We are in deep shit, and you refuse to see it. My advertisers are already aware that we have no way of distributing the title, and there is no way I can hold on to enough ad revenue to cover our print costs. Even if you can find someone else to distribute the magazine, we don't have enough cash to pay for the printing.'

'But Tom, you have to have faith!.'

'Bollocks! I don't have to have faith. I believed in you once, but now I can see how wrong I was. You are not the bloody magazine messiah. Miracles don't happen in the twentieth century. Face up to it: we're fucked.'

Tom stormed out of the office and into the street.

Julia then walked into Christian's office.

Christian said, 'I suppose you heard all of that, Julia.'

'Yes, I wish I hadn't, but I only sit ten feet away from your office, and I am not sure that even putting my fingers in my ears would have helped.'

'Julia, I am really sorry. I think Tom is right. We cannot get through this. Without enough funds to pay for printing, and with no way of distributing the magazine, there can be no future.'

'You selfish bastard! I joined your tiny company because I thought I might learn something from you, and now all I have learnt is that you want to quit before you have even tried.'

'Well, what can we do, Julia? There really is no way forward.'

'Rubbish. We have to get the story, and then we have to go and see every magazine distribution company until one of them finally sees that the magazine is going to be a winner.'

'Nice theory, and admirable loyalty, but it is not going to be as easy as that. Even if we find a distribution company, who is going to pay for the printing?'

'I know a printer who will help me. I will ask him to let us pay our print bill once we have secured enough cash from the magazine copy sales.'

'Julia, printers scare easily. I can't even count the number of printers who have been nearly bankrupted over the years trying to get money from small publishers who cannot pay their bills.'

'If I get you a printer by 5.00 p.m., then you have to promise me two things. First, you have to go ahead with your meeting this evening to get the story. Second, you have to take me to the meeting with Whitstop. I'm tired of writing trivia—I want to get my teeth into a real story.'

'How the hell are you going to find a printer by five? Even if you do, what makes you think you are ready to work on a story like this?'

Julia was firm. 'I will find a printer, and you will let me work with you on this story. Do we have a deal?'

'Secure the printer, and we have a deal. Phone me at the office if you pull off your miracle.'

'I will succeed—just wait for my call.'

With that Julia left the office and caught a tube to Upminster. When she arrived, she walked briskly until she came to a back street where a tatty sign read, 'Brown and Son Quality Printers.' Julia walked in and was struck as always by the terrible noise and the dreadful mess around the place. 'Tommy, are you in?' she called as she approached the back office.

'Bloody hell, Jules. What are you doing here?' Tommy was the same age as Julia, but he looked much older. They had met at university studying English and had become good friends. Tommy's father, Tommy Brown Sr, had come from a long line of printers. His great, great-grandfather had established Brown and Son at the turn of the century. By coincidence every Tommy Brown had produced just one son, and the tradition was that every son was called Tommy and the son eventually took on the business.

Tommy had dreamed of writing books. English was his passion, and there was no doubt that he wrote beautifully. His tutors at university saw a great future for him. He had won writing prizes, and it was widely predicted that he would get a significant first novel into print by his early twenties.

But one day his mother called him to say that his father had suffered a massive stroke. Thankfully his dad had survived, but he was never going to be the same again. In fact Tommy's father became a total invalid, and Tommy's mother was forced to nurse him night and day. There was no one to run the business, and Tommy's mother had to have an income to take care of his father. Tommy did the right thing: he left university and returned to run the family business. But it was in a mess. Tommy discovered from the staff that his father had not been well for some time and that the business was struggling.

Julia was very upset when Tommy had left university; he had so much promise, but now it would probably never be realised. She liked Tommy a lot, but only as a friend.

One evening after lessons, Tommy called Julia on the phone at her flat. 'Julia, it's a nightmare. I am doing the one thing I never wanted to do—and worse than that, the business is in a total state.'

Julia suggested they meet the next day, and Tommy gratefully accepted her shoulder to cry on. They met in a pub near the print works, and Julia said that she had always wanted to do some holiday work at a printers. Of course it wasn't true, and Tommy suspected as much, but he needed her help. It was the last week of term before the summer in Julia's second year at university, so six days later she turned up for work at Brown and Son.

She worked hard all summer, visiting businesses and bringing in orders. Julia also helped with the accounts, and more than anything she gave Tommy emotional support. He was in love with her but knew that it was not mutual. Tommy came to accept that they would never become a couple, and he appreciated the greater value of her friendship.

Now, he saw her sitting in his office again, and he could sense that she was troubled. He had always wanted to do something for her, and although he knew he should not be happy seeing her looking sad, he felt strangely pleased that she had sought him out looking for help.

'Tommy, can you print magazines?' Julia asked.

'Well, Jules, we don't have the latest machines, and we are a bit slow, but yes, we can print magazines.'

'I want you to print a magazine for me, and I need you to accept payment from the magazine sales at a later date. I know it's a risk, and I know things have been hard for you, so I will understand if you say no.'

'This place still looks like a shithole, but don't be fooled—we are doing okay. All being well, we even may buy some new equipment next year. I get most of the print work round here now; I am reliable, and most of all I'm bloody cheap. So the answer is yes—but I will not accept payment later.'

Julia was confused. 'Does that mean you will print for me or not? I don't understand.'

'This is the deal. I will print this magazine for you, but I will never accept one penny in payment. If you ever try to pay me, I will never print anything for you ever again.'

'Tommy, you cannot print the magazine for nothing. You don't even know how big it is or how many copies we want!'

'Actually, you have a point there. If its three hundred pages long and more than two hundred thousand copies, you will bankrupt me.'

'It will be about 148 pages, full colour throughout, and the first print run will be 120,000 copies. We will want to print more if it sells well, but if sales are good, we can certainly pay you some cash then.'

'Jules, this is what I can do for you. I will give you fifty thousand copies free; you pay for the other seventy thousand in two months' time. If you need to reprint, we will talk again. Okay?'

'Tommy, that's fantastic! You have saved our necks.'

'Just one thing, Jules. I hope he is worth it.'

'What do you mean?'

'Well, somebody must have finally stolen your heart to make you come here to persuade me to do this for you. It's just a guess, but with you being fresh out of university, I cannot imagine you have your own publishing company just yet.'

'Tommy, I am not in love with anyone at present. I am working for a small magazine company, and they need a little help getting their first publication off the ground.'

'Whatever you say, Jules. When you are ready to print, call me straight away, and we will book the job.'

Julia got up from her chair, gave Tommy a peck on the cheek, and headed back to the office.

CHAPTER 10

LIZZIE HAD SPENT the afternoon trying to decide what to do next. She could call Christian and tell him to meet her, and she could give him the documents. She could go to Bookstall Solutions herself and tell them what Mike had been doing in the hopes that they would get mad, drop their contracts with Lancaster Publishing, and agree to distribute Christian's magazine. Or she could go to the directors at Lancaster Publishing and blackmail them into calling Bookstall Solutions to say that they would actually like them to distribute Christian's magazine.

In truth, all three options had flaws. If she told Christian, then he would probably see the information as a way to destroy Mike Tyler, which in turn could hurt Lancaster Publishing—which was okay, but this could endanger the jobs of her friends. If she told Bookstall Solutions, then they would be furious, but they would probably use the information to simply negotiate better terms for themselves with Lancaster Publishing.

If she tried to blackmail Lancaster Publishing, then she would be no better than someone like Mike Tyler, and she could not bear to be like him. She was very confused at a time when she knew that she needed to be decisive and act soon. Lancaster Publishing was close to bringing the magazine onto the bookshelves, and if its publication came out first, it would always be seen as the symbol of pioneering eighties publishing. This would kill Christian; the concept had been his idea, and he deserved the credit.

* * *

Mike Tyler was feeling very decisive and pretty pleased with himself. He sat in his office drinking a coffee with Jason, who had just been awarded Lizzie's job. 'Told you, Jason. Stay loyal to me, and you will go places in this company.'

Jason had been a deputy advertisement manager on one of the magazines that Mike ran. Mike had cultivated him and told him on many occasions that Mike would one day be the main guy at Lancaster Publishing.

Mike made a habit of pressing loyalty out of many of his male staff with promises of future promotions and salary increases if they made it their business to always support him. He would often try to get his people more senior jobs in other colleagues' departments so that he could ask his cronies to spy on these people and give him information that could be useful. He had once managed to destroy, Sally his main rival in the race for a junior board position, by finding out that she was a lesbian and breaking the news privately to the main board directors. In truth they would not have fired her for being a lesbian, but Mike persuaded a junior female employee with a salary increase to claim that Sally had been trying to grope her. A number of employees at the time tried to defend Sally, including Christian, saying that the board was being prejudiced, but the sexual harassment allegation left Sally with no option. She accepted being fired as long as no further action was taken.

Mike was now getting one of his star pupils, Jason, into another rival's department, and it pleased him to think that even Lizzie's resignation had done him a favour. He decided to share his recent pieces of genius with Jason because he felt it would serve to make the boy admire and fear him in a way that would guarantee ultimate loyalty. He rocked back in his chair as he howled with laughter, recounting his recent success.

'So you see, Jason, our former colleague Toss Pot now has virtually no ads and no way of even getting his pathetic publication in to the newsagents.'

'You're the man, Mike. I hope I can operate like you do one day. Always one step ahead. No one can catch you.'

'Well, stick with me, and you can learn a lot and enjoy regular promotions each time I get to move further up the tree. Tell you what:

I am in such a good mood that I am going to take you round the corner for a few pints. I feel like celebrating.'

They gathered themselves up and wandered round the corner to Moriarty's, both feeling good about life and the prospect of sinking a few beers.

*   *   *

Tom was still very angry. He had no idea where he was going or what he was going to do when he got there. He had been walking for hours, and his feet were killing him. Then it hit him, as it did most young men with a problem: he needed to get pissed. Trouble was, only losers and weirdoes drank alone. Plus, he felt he wanted to talk to someone. He spied a call box and within a minute had his old colleague, Gary, on the line.

'Gary, it's Tom. Look, I am really pissed off, and I need a drink. What are you doing tonight?'

'Fuck me, Tom, how can I refuse? Sounds like we are going to have a really depressing session. I will bring the rusty razor blades, and you can write the suicide note.'

'Gary, I need a friend. Are you up for a few beers or not?'

'No need to be so sensitive—of course I am. We are mates, aren't we? For good and for bad, as they say. I just hope there might be some good one day.'

'I will see you in Moriarty's just after six. Don't be late, or I will be pissed before you get there.'

*   *   *

Christian looked at his watch: it was 5.05 p.m., and no phone call from Julia. Well he had expected as much. She had guts but sadly no way of finding a solution for their current difficulties. He carried on preparing his list of questions for his meeting with Whitstop. As he wrote each question, he kept wondering if there was any point. He was going to get a great story, but was anyone ever going to read it? Somehow he felt he should keep going; it was always better to be optimistic.

'So when are we heading off to see Lord Whitstop?'

Christian looked up to see Julia standing in front of his desk. 'I take it from that smile on your face that you have some good news for me.'

Julia told Christian what she had agreed with Tommy, and Christian was so happy that he stood up and kissed her on the forehead in a friendly and boisterous manner. To his surprise Julia shuddered, pulled back, and turned bright pink. 'I'm really sorry, Julia. I wasn't making a pass at you—I promise. I just wanted to show you how pleased I am.'

'Don't worry, Christian. You just surprised me, that's all. I won't sue you for sexual harassment. No point anyway—the company doesn't have any money yet!'

'Okay, Julia, a deal's a deal. You are coming with me to interview Whitstop. I just hope the old boy does not get spooked when he sees that you are with me. He is very nervous about telling me his story, and I hope he does not mind you being there.'

'Christian, I am sure you can tell him that I am your assistant and that I am there to take notes.'

'Well, as it happens you *can* take the notes. I want to concentrate on interviewing him. I also want you to take this tape recorder along to record some of the things he says, in case he tries to go back on his story later.'

'Will he agree to be taped?'

'I very much doubt it, but you are going to hide the machine in your nicely oversized handbag.'

*　　*　　*

Jinxie laid in his hospital bed somewhere between boredom and sleep. He was old and tired and lonely. He was aware of his past but very unsure of his future. Was he being selfish by wanting Julia to realise that he was her father before he died? Did he even stand a chance of explaining anything to her now that she had him down as a pervert?

'You don't look too good, James.'

Jinxie looked up, and his heart raced. He thought he might suffer his second heart attack of the week. 'Siobhan?'

'Yes, James, it's me. I expect you never thought you would see me again.'

'Siobhan, why are you here? I thought you never wanted to see me again.'

'The staff nurse that you seem intent on annoying is an old friend of mine. We trained together a long time ago, and we have always kept in touch. We were having some lunch together today round the corner from here, and she was on her break told me about a troublesome old man who had worried her to death this morning, by doing a disappearing act. She said he was a journalist and that when she had challenged him about his conduct, he quoted poetry back at her. I asked her to describe this strange character to me, and afterwards I was sure it was you.'

'So what is this then, Siobhan? A curiosity call? Are you here to see if I am finally going to leave this earth? Then you really can be sure that Julia will never know who her real father was. I could have been a good father to the girl, Siobhan. If I am to die soon, then I will depart this world never really understanding why you would not let me meet her.'

'James, too much time has passed to say that I am sorry or that I made a mistake, but I had my reasons. I was never lucky in love; I always met the bastards. When I was training to be a nurse, I had an affair with a doctor. Predictably, I fell pregnant. He said he loved me but that he could not yet leave his wife. He persuaded me to have an abortion. It was hard for me because I was brought up as a Catholic.

'I had a series of other disastrous relationships, and in time I sensed that for me there never could be a Mr Right. But then I came to nurse your wife through her illness, and I met you. You really loved your wife, and I pitied you as you tried to care for her. I saw the strain it was having on you; you were mentally, physically, and emotionally drained. My heart went out to you, and I wanted to not only help your wife, but I wanted to care for you, too. And then one day it happened. I had fallen in love with you, and I wanted all your pain to go away. I said in my letter to you that I had not fallen in love with you, but that was a lie to cover my wounded pride.

'It was hard for me. I wanted to care for your wife, and I also wanted you. I fought hard against making a fool of myself, and I resisted any urge to tell you how I felt. And then one night it happened between us, and we made love. I had not expected it to happen, and I knew that it should not happen. But it did.

'Your wife died. We didn't kill her—she just couldn't go on anymore. When I tried to contact you, it was to tell you that I was pregnant. I had agonized about telling you or not, but I felt I had to. I was shocked, and I knew you would be feeling guilt after your terrible loss, but I never expected you to ignore me. So I made up my mind never to be hurt by any man again, and I decided to protect Julia as well. I figured that the least you could do was to contribute financially towards her upkeep, but you should never see her because I was sure you would grow bored of her in the end and just hurt her, just like you had hurt me.

'When Julia was struggling to find a career in journalism, I knew you would have contacts that could help her. I hated the idea of contacting you, but it seemed the right thing to do for Julia. But now that I see you here in this hospital bed, I can't help but think that perhaps I had been wrong. Maybe she should know who her real father is. After all these years, I can see now that it wasn't Julia that I was protecting—it was me.

'When I asked my friend your name, and she said James Jinks, I suddenly felt very guilty, knowing that all these years I have not let Julia meet her real father. So many times when she was growing up, she asked to know about her father. All I told her was that he had died in a car crash and that he had been a good man who had loved her very much. If she ever asked for more details, I avoided telling her anything by saying it upset me too much to talk about it.

'You could have died this week, and through my own selfishness I would have denied Julia the chance to meet her father.'

'Well thanks for the *could have died* bit. You have really cheered me up. And yes, I acted wrongly in the past by not returning your calls, but I am sorry to say that you committed the greater wrong to both Julia and me.'

'No lectures, James. What has been done has been done. How are we going to put it right?'

'Well, I am sorry to say that I have moved ahead of you there. I have spent a large chunk of my life observing Julia growing up from a distance, desperate to introduce myself to her on many occasions. This week I thought I might finally die, but it seems not quite yet. The man who employs Julia is my friend; he is much younger than me, and I guess in many ways he's more of a substitute son than a friend. His name is Christian Davidson, and it was he who employed Julia on my recommendation. He did not know she was my daughter when he employed her, but now he does. I asked him to arrange for me to meet Julia with him, and he agreed. However, this morning I seem to have made a bit of a mess of things.' Jinxie told Siobhan about his excursion.

Siobhan said, 'Brilliant, James, you have made things really easy now. I can just imagine the introduction. "Julia, remember the pervert you spotted the other day? Well, the good news is he is in fact your father, who actually isn't dead at all." This is going to be very difficult.'

'Come on, Siobhan, it was never going to be easy. What were you going to tell her? "Julia, I know I told you your dad had died in a car crash. Actually, he didn't. And by the way, he got you your current job." She is going to get the surprise of her life when she is told about me. I only hope she can take it.'

'This meeting your friend agreed to set up—when is it scheduled, and where?'

'Saturday at one, at Pontevechio Restaurant, Old Brompton Road.'

'Well, James, you are going to have another guest for lunch. I will see you there.'

Siobhan left, and Jinxie lay in his bed feeling even more tired and anxious. He patted his heart and said, 'Don't give up now, old boy—you may still have something to live for.'

*   *   *

Mike Tyler sat slurping his beer with his latest disciple. He told embellished stories of the glorious highlights of his career, and Jason hung on to every word. Mike was feeling really good. Things were going well, and it gave him a good feeling to have Jason praise his successes and laugh at his jokes.

Sitting in a corner on the opposite side of Moriarty's sat a young man whose world seemed to have fallen apart. Tom was depressed and really pissed off. Gary was late, and Tom had already drunk two pints and was just about to order his third when Gary finally showed up.

'Where the bloody hell have you been?' Tom demanded.

'No need to get shitty. You called me at short notice. I can't just drop everything. Anyway, I am here now. So tell me what you want to drink, and then you can bend my ear with all your tales of woe.'

Gary went over to the bar and bought the beers. As he was walking back to Tom's table, he suddenly saw Mike Tyler, who by luck did not see him. He said to Tom, 'We really should have picked another bar. Tyler is sitting on the other side. If he sees me with you, he will make a lot of shit for me in the company.'

'Where is he? I am going to murder that hideous fuckwit,' Tom growled.

'Sit down, you dickhead. If you hit him, he will take a legal action against you, and I will lose my job. Let's drink these and then find another pub.'

At that point Eddie the bar manager saw Tom and came over. 'Hello, mate. Not seen you in here for a while.'

'Hi, Eddie, good to see you. Sorry to say we will not be staying much longer—not with that arsehole Mike Tyler sitting over there.'

'Must say, I have never liked him. He always looks down his nose at me and the bar staff, and sometimes when he has had a few, he gets bloody rude and arrogant.'

'Why don't you ban him?' Tom asked.

'I need a better reason than the fact that he gets up my nose to ban him. But we could have some fun with him,' Eddie said with a grin.

'How can we do that?'

'Well, as luck would have it, he has just asked for some menus. I will take the menus over to his table, and you and Gary can nip behind the bar to the kitchen while I block his view.'

They did as Eddie suggested, and within a few minutes Eddie joined them in the kitchen. 'Okay, boys, ever had any cooking lessons?'

'No,' they both replied.

'Good, because Chilli Gone Barmy doesn't require any.'

'What the hell is Chilli Gone Barmy?' Gary asked.

'It's simple: you spoon two portions of chilli con carne from this big pan into these two bowls, and then you add the secret ingredients.'

'What are the secret ingredients?' asked Tom.

'Ah, I knew you would ask that. This is a very complex process. You can only decide on the secret ingredients by seeking divine inspiration.'

'How do we get divine inspiration?' asked Gary.

Eddie walked over to a big fridge, pulled open the door, and pulled out a bottle of vodka from the top frozen compartment. 'Divine inspiration is always best served chilled,' he said. He grabbed three glasses and poured. Eddie then advised them that they all needed to drink five glasses each straight back for the divine inspiration to kick in. They did so, and as with all magic potions, the effects were almost instant.

'Pile Cream,' said Eddie, and he went over to a drawer, pulled out a tube, and squirted some cream into each bowl and stirred it in.'

'Congealed grease,' said Gary, and he grabbed a knife, scraped some grease off the floor, and wiped some into each bowl.

'Cat food,' said Tom, and he picked up the cat's bowl and spooned out a spoonful into the bowls of chilli.

'Flies,' said Gary, and he went over to the bug zapper in the kitchen and spooned up some flies that were lying on the floor below it.

'Blood,' said Tom, and he went over to a tray of liver sitting on a kitchen surface, took the tray, and poured some of the blood in-to each bowl.

'Extra strong laxative syrup,' said Eddie as he poured in the sticky, black liquid to each bowl. 'Okay that should do it. Divine inspiration only allows six ingredients and a preparation time of ten minutes, or the customers start to wonder where their diner has gone to.'

Eddie stirred both bowls, microwaved them for three minutes each, and then stirred the contents again.

'The great thing about Chilli Gone Barmy is that it is pretty much impossible to spot the special ingredients.' Eddie took the bowls with some garlic bread out to Mike and Jason.

'Bloody hell, Edward, you only had to spoon this stuff out of a cauldron. What took you so long?'

'We take pride in our chilli here. It requires those extra special ingredients.'

'Bullshit, Eddie. I bet it came out of a bloody can, which is probably a damn sight safer than one of your cooking experiments. I am sure if you tried your hand at cooking, you would poison the customers.'

Jason laughed as he felt he was expected to do so, and Eddie headed off back to the kitchen trying his best not to laugh himself—but for a very different reason.

Back in the kitchen, Tom and Gary were in hysterics and were demolishing the rest of the vodka.

'Bloody brilliant, Eddie! You have really cheered me up. The thought of Tyler eating that terrible concoction has made my day. Who said revenge is a dish best served cold? This one is piping hot and guaranteed to wreak havoc.' Tom raised his glass to Eddie and knocked back some more vodka.

'Seems to be my day for cheering people up. You boys can sit here with me for a while and have a few more drinks; I am sure my staff can handle the bar for the next few hours. It shouldn't be too long now for that mixture to work on your friends' stomachs, and I am sure you will want to be here when it does.' He paused. 'Before I forget, I am just going to nip out to the gents to lock up the doors to the crapper cubicles and put up the "out of order" signs. When the Chilli Gone Barmy is ready to make a fast exit, our friends will sadly not find any rooms in this inn for their unpleasant deposits.'

Mike continued to impress Jason with his tales of glory, and they polished off their food pretty quickly. They pushed back a few more pints, and then Mike signalled for Sam, one of the bargirls, to come over. 'Sweetheart, do me a favour and get us a couple of large brandies. And tell fat Eddie that we want some of the good stuff, not that bloody drain cleaner that he normally serves.'

Sam went into the kitchen, found Eddie, and told him what Mike had said.

'My God, he really deserves to get the chronic shits tonight. Go and get me two of our oversized brandy balloons and some cheap Spanish brandy.'

She did as requested, and Eddie poured out two large measures. He then went to a cupboard that contained a range of cleaning materials and pulled out a bottle of toilet duck. He put a small measure of toilet duck in each glass and headed off in to the bar. At this point Tom and Gary were on the floor weeping with laughter and close to peeing themselves.

Eddie took the glasses out to Mike. 'Must be a special occasion, Mr Tyler, for you to request my best brandy. This stuff is not cheap, you know—pure Maison Canard, very rare and an acquired taste.'

'Well, Eddie, when you are having a great week and have the combined joys of lots of cash and a refined palate, it is only right to drink the best.'

'I hope you like this one, Mr Tyler. It's a very unusual taste, only appreciated by the real connoisseur.'

'Don't worry about us, Eddie, we are men of distinction. I have every confidence that we will love it.'

Eddie headed back to the kitchen, and Mike swilled the liquid round in his glass, getting it ready for his finely tuned palate. 'Good

God, bloody strange flavour, and quite a kick,' remarked Mike as he took his first slug. 'But I have to say, very good indeed. An excellent digestive—this should clean up our systems.'

And Mike was right. His system started gurgling, and so did Jason's. Their stomachs started to make bizarre noises, and they both found themselves trying hard not to release huge clouds of wind from their posteriors.

Jason looked worse than Mike: his face was contorted, and he had the feeling that he was about to shit his pants. He excused himself and headed off to the gents. Jason did the walk of pain to the gents, clenching his bottom cheeks with all his might as he walked crab-like with gritted teeth to the toilets. He flung the door open with a massive sigh of relief. *Thank God I made it!* he thought to himself. But then the horror: just two cubicles, and both with 'out of order' signs and padlocks on the doors.

No, this couldn't happen to him! He tried to force the nearest cubicle door. His face flushed red, his stomach screamed, air rushed from between his bottom cheeks, and he exploded into his pants.

Mike Tyler sat alone at the table. He could feel what seemed like mustard gas escaping from his backside. It stung his bottom, and the smell started to make his eyes water. People were looking in his direction. Mike wasn't sure if the embarrassment, the smell, or the pain in his guts would get him first.

Where the bloody hell is that little prick, Jason? he thought to himself. Mike needed to get to the toilet, and he needed to get there fast. It was no good—he could not wait any longer for Jason to return and had to head for the bogs. Mike got up carefully, everything clenched and eyes watering. He edged his way towards the gents. His stomach was going bananas; the noise was so loud now that it sounded like a pot of boiling mud. People were staring at him, and he looked as though he was about to give birth.

Finally he reached the door to the gents. He shoved the door and rushed inside. Then he saw the two padlocked cubicle doors. He could also see Jason sitting on the floor and clutching his stomach with tears streaming down his face—and what looked like shit running out the ends of his trouser legs. The smell in the gents was beyond compare, and it was not doing Mike any good at all.

With superhuman effort Mike clenched his buttocks with all his might and headed out of the gents, through the bar, and towards the exit to the street. His guts were killing him, and burning wind was already starting to eke its way out from his troubled backside. Customers waved away the foul air as Mike tried to make his desperate escape from the pub. He knew if he could just make it to the alley at the back of the pub, then he could save his dignity. Not only that, but if he was very lucky, he could crouch out of view and expel the burbling liquid that was desperate to explode in a volcanic plume from his burning arse.

He knew he was seconds away from shitting his pants in full view of the pub's clientele, who largely consisted of his own work colleagues. Luckily he was nearly at the door, and soon he would be able to save his embarrassment, his pants, and his guts by delivering one huge, liquid fart explosion in the privacy of the darkened alley.

*   *   *

Lizzie made her mind up: she was going to see Mike Tyler and let him have it. She would deal him the cruellest blow of all and force him to ask Bookstall Solutions to distribute Christian's magazine in return for her keeping quiet about his dishonest side deals.

She had called his office and his flat, but an educated guess told her she might find him in Moriarty's, and so she headed off to the pub. As Lizzie opened the door, she could see Mike heading towards her. He was clearly on his way out; she had arrived just in time.

Eddie told Tom and Gary to come and sit behind the bar, because he was sure that the fun was about to begin. Sam had reported that Jason had gone off to the toilet sometime back and that customers in the bar were complaining that there was a terrible smell coming from the gents. Apparently they said the smell was like a cross between mustard gas and a sewage farm.

As the boys took their ringside seats, they saw Mike heading towards the street door, and then to their surprise they saw Lizzie open the door.

Mike saw Lizzie and could not believe his misfortune. 'Lizzie, sorry, have to dash—urgent business.'

Lizzie stood in the doorway and spread her arms to block his exit. 'Oh no you don't, Tyler. I need to speak with you now.'

Mike was in desperate pain; the pressure in his guts was at a dangerous level, and he knew that he was going to explode at any second. There was no other option: he was going to have to brush Lizzie out the way. As he tried to push past her, she put both her hands out straight in front of her to push him back into the bar. Her hands pushed into his stomach, and that was the fatal blow!

His face turned purple, his eyes rolled, his knees buckled, and he let out a fart that sounded like a giant lilo being deflated. His buttocks gave up their superhuman clench, and he shat his pants with the full force of a water cannon. The whole pub stared at Mike in shock as a huge, wet stain appeared on the seat of his trousers. He let out a smell that was so powerful that it brought tears to the eyes of everyone in the room. No demon born in hell could have made such an appalling smell.

Mike sank to his knees in pain and humiliation, and he tried again to make his exit. Lizzie stepped back in horror as Mike crawled out into the street on his hands and knees like some wounded animal. Tom and Gary collapsed behind the bar in uncontrollable, high-pitched shrieks of laughter. Tom was feeling a lot better, and the night was still young.

CHAPTER 11

CHRISTIAN AND JULIA stood in front of the building that housed Whitstop's private office. Christian saw Whitstop's name on one of the brass nameplates and pressed the bell. A voice said, 'Push the door and come up to the second floor.' Christian heard a buzz and pushed the door open, and he and Julia made their way up to Whitstop's office. As they approached, they saw him waiting for them framed in the doorway.

'Mr Davidson, I expected to see you alone. I am not sure that this addition to your party is welcome.'

'Lord Whitstop, please do not be alarmed. This is my colleague, Julia. I need her to help take notes whilst you and I have our discussions.'

'Very well, if you think she is needed, then come on through and we shall begin our chat.'

Whitstop led them through in to his study. The room looked exactly as Christian had imagined. Old photographs on the wall of Whitstop with numerous well-known British politicians, and a fair number of photographs of him with some familiar foreign leaders. Few of the pictures were current; most dated back more than twenty years ago, when Whitstop was rated as a political force and a possible candidate for prime minister. The furniture was leather and wood of superior quality and probably antique. A beautiful Persian carpet sat in the centre of the room on polished floorboards. The whole back wall was a huge bookcase filled with old books; many seemed to be biographies of famous political figures from the last two hundred years.

'This is going to be a long night, and for me a particularly difficult one. I frankly need a drink to settle my nerves, and I suggest you both join me to help yourselves relax. I am afraid that I am not a big drinker by nature, so the choice is malt whisky or malt whisky.'

Christian looked at Julia, thinking that she may not find malt whisky to her liking, but he soon realised that despite the fact that he thought of himself as a new man, he was in fact being sexist. She was the one to respond first.

'Ah, Talsisker, one of my favourites,' she said as Whitstop poured three generous measures into the crystal tumblers.

Whitstop smiled at Julia, it had not taken him long to take a liking to her. 'Okay, let us begin,' he said. 'But first I want to do away with all the formalities. We shall be as we were christened: John, Christian, and Julia.'

Then Whitstop began his story.

'As you would expect, our people had been monitoring Argentinean movements on the Falkland Islands for some time before we made our declaration of war and sent the boys out there. We noted all the expected stuff: troop concentrations, land mines, artillery, tanks, armoured vehicles, et cetera. But one thing troubled us. Reports were coming back of large canisters being stockpiled on the islands. We knew by their general size and shape that they were not fuel drums; in any case, we had already seen the establishment of adequate fuel depots at an early stage.

'Intelligence from our team and from our colleagues in the United States had advised us some years back that Argentina had developed a series of military laboratories. We were aware that they had been experimenting with nerve gases for some time. They had been developing the stuff largely through fear of Pinochet in Chile. It was felt that if they could develop reliable nerve gases, then Chile would not want to risk a conflict with Argentina. A more worrying development was that we heard that they were also developing germ warfare capability. The Americans were particularly interested in obtaining data on this; they feared a catastrophe in South America and so expended considerable efforts to obtain data. It seemed that the Argentineans were experimenting with strains of anthrax, but their progress had been slow due to a number of accidents and subsequent deaths at one of their facilities.

'We figured that the canisters accumulating on the islands could possibly contain nerve gas. Our intelligence people advised us that there was nothing to suggest that they were transporting any files of anthrax, particularly because to this point they seemed incapable of dealing with the spores in a safe way that would not risk deaths among their own forces. The start of the conflict went well for us, the nation largely supported the government's position, and a feeling of patriotism swept across Britain. But we were frightened for our boys. Facing gunfire is one thing, but nerve gas is quite a different matter. No one knew quite what to do. We couldn't pull back—the people expected us to go forth and do battle to liberate our distant countrymen.

'Many meetings took place, and at this point not even the prime minister knew about our suspicions. It was just a small group of us who needed to decide what to do with this information, if anything.

Finally we concluded that only a madman would condone the use of nerve gas or anthrax, and we were pretty sure that we were not dealing with madmen. As far as we could make out, the Argentineans had taken the Falklands for three reasons.

'Firstly, they needed a military success and a piece of national pride to prop up the regime. The people of Argentina would see the taking of the Falklands as a great piece of national glory. The story in Buenos Aires was of a great victory; no one knew that they had simply occupied a sparsely populated, inhospitable set of islands primarily occupied by sheep farmers and penguins.

'Secondly, they saw the occupation of the Falklands as a strategic move to give them a military base from which they could protect their coastline. I must say I never really saw the logic in that argument, because the islands are a considerable distance from Argentina's coast.

'Thirdly and possibly most significantly, they felt that if the world could accept Argentina's claim to the Falkland Islands, they may have no problem with Argentina asserting rights to mineral resources thought to be on the verge of discovery in the near vicinity.

'From Britain's stand point we had three strong reasons to defend these islands. We had designs on future possible mineral resources in the area. It was also important for Britain to be seen to be capable of defending its sovereign lands, even if they were thousands of miles away. National security dictated that we had to show that we were still a force to be reckoned with in the world. Finally, I have to admit that despite strong denials at the time, we knew that embarking on such a mission would galvanise the people of Britain behind the government.

'And so after much deliberation, we reached the conclusion that to say nothing about our suspicions was the best and possibly the only available policy. We decided not to tell the PM because her strong resolve might weaken in the ensuing conflict. For my part, I was confused. I had fought in the Second World War and had seen my comrades die, but they had never had to face chemical or biological weapons, and I feared that our boys may not be entering in to a fair fight—if indeed war can ever be thought of as fair. But I was a lone voice, and my colleagues persuaded me to keep quiet for the good of the nation. They assured me that they were confident such terrible weapons would never be used.

'The conflict started pretty well for Britain. We amazed the world with our ability to move men and equipment across thousands of miles of ocean. We quickly gained some victories by sinking some of their ships, and the British people took pride from their country's ability to stand up to the aggressors. When our ship the *Sheffield* was sunk, we feared that people would wake up to the fact that British lives could also be lost and that popularity for the campaign may waver. But the newspapers whipped up even more frenzied support from the people, and nothing short of a quick and total victory was expected.

'We started to land troops on the islands, and they met with little resistance. This surprised us a little, but we figured that our air cover was driving the Argentineans back and that our choice of landing sites had taken them by surprise. A few days in, our lads started to meet with heavier resistance, and the rate of our advance slowed down considerably. With little ground cover, it was hard to make progress in the face of machine gun fire, and the weather conditions made it hard for our helicopters and harriers to knock out their positions.

'For a few days one of our divisions found themselves bogged down and unable to make any progress. It was cold, windy, and damp, but Captain McIntyre kept their spirits high, and they knew that air cover would soon enable them to advance at a greater pace. Then one morning as the dawn broke, they noticed that the mist ahead of them was a slight shade of yellow. The mist around them was normal, but the wind was blowing in their direction, and the yellow vapour was drawing closer. Captain McIntyre instinctively guessed that it must be gas. He issued the order to put on gas masks and forbade them to be removed until he gave the order that it was safe to do so. He was not happy—he knew that his men should have been issued with NBC suits. NBC suits stands for nuclear, biological, and chemical warfare suits. You see, in this modern age we know that protecting the lungs is not enough. Chemicals in gasses can affect the skin, and even penetrate it and enter the system.

'A few hours later, the wind switched around, and the sun burnt off the mist, so McIntyre issued the order to remove the gas masks. To his relief the men seemed fine. Some complained of skin irritation, but they only reported minor discomfort. He had the medical officer inspect them, and he made all the troops change their clothes and wash thoroughly. They were not impressed because it was still bloody cold, but they knew that he was taking the right course of action.

'Over the next few days, air cover was able to successfully pin down the enemy, and the troops were able to make a steady advance. But some of the troops became sick; they experienced vomiting, fatigue, and great fluctuations in temperature and pulse rate. Those who were sick also exhibited skin rashes and heavy mucus deposits from their noses and eyes. Captain McIntyre felt fine, but he knew that these symptoms must have resulted from the gas. He thought his senior officers were bastards; he knew that his troops should have been issued with NBC suits, but he had been told that there was a limit to the amount of equipment that could be hauled around in their advance.

'He took the best decision he could and decided to get the sick men taken away by helicopters to supply and medical ships. The majority of his troops seemed fine, and he continued with his advance on the enemy position. McIntyre and his team distinguished themselves, knocking out the enemy machine guns and forcing the surrender of a small Argentinean garrison. They secured a base at their objective, a small but strategic village where they could set about the creation of a useful supply station for the rest of the conflict ahead.

'Some distance away further south, Captain David Williams was making fast progress across open and windswept fields. After three days of constant advance with no resistance, his team was only one more day's march away from their objective. Their mission was to gain control of large series of farm buildings that were also used as a supply station. The next morning, as their eyes started to make out the shape of the farm buildings in the distance, they could see a very strange and eerie sight. All around them were dead sheep, but not one of them exhibited any signs of having been killed. On closer inspection of one of the sheep, Captain Williams noticed that its eyes were bulging, its stomach was swollen, and there appeared to be trails of mucus around its mouth and posterior.

'He pulled his men back a mile from the field and asked his signals officer to radio a science officer on one of the ships. The officer advised Captain Williams to keep his troops where they were and asked if any of his men had touched any of the sheep. Captain Williams said he would check and get back to him. The science officer said that he would take down their coordinates and try to get flown in by helicopter later in the day.

'Late that afternoon, Science Officer Peters arrived with some colleagues. They proceeded to dress in protective clothing, and then they approached the sheep to take skin, tissue, organ, and mucus samples. When the task was completed, Captain Williams asked Peters if he had any idea what could have caused the deaths of the animals. Peters replied predictably that he was not in a position to speculate, but he would run some tests back on the ship and let him know as soon as possible. Captain Williams confirmed that his men had not touched any of the dead animals, and Peters told him to make camp and to wait for further instructions. Then Peters and his team left by helicopter to return to their ship.

'The next morning, Captain Williams received communication to say that he had new instructions to head for a different location. Again he asked if anyone had a view on what had caused the animals deaths, and again he was told that when they had more information, he would be the first to know. Captain Williams led his men to the newly advised location, another series of farm buildings some ten miles to the west. They met some limited resistance, which they successfully overcame. No one ever came back to him about the sheep, and shortly before the end of conflict, Williams was fatally wounded whilst trying to overcome a machine gun position behind a small ridge.

'As for Captain McIntyre, he returned home a hero and was awarded medals for his bravery and leadership. On his return he heard that some of his troops were still in the hospital undergoing tests. It appeared that the troops who had been evacuated off the island and onto ships during the conflict were not recovering well. He suspected that the yellow gas that they had seen on that morning many months ago during the conflict was responsible for their condition.

'He decided to visit the hospital just a few days after his return to Britain. Five of his men were being treated at the hospital, and he visited each one of them to see how they were doing. He was shocked by what he saw. They all looked old and feeble. Each one complained of headaches, chest pains, breathing difficulties, and general feelings of nausea. They also said that they suffered regular bouts of vomiting and diarrhoea, and that they had difficulties walking due to very bad doses of the shakes. All the men said that they were developing ulcers and cysts, and they experienced almost constant stomach pain. Captain McIntyre asked them what the diagnosis was, and they said that they had been advised that they were suffering from a post-war stress syndrome.

'He went off in search of a doctor to try to discover if everything possible was being done for these men. After some time, he finally found a doctor who was prepared to sit and have a coffee with him in order to discuss the men's conditions. He asked him what the future held for the men. The doctor told him that the men had suffered tremendous mental stress from the war and that their nervous systems had reacted badly, with the consequence that they were suffering numerous physical ailments. Captain McIntyre said that he was surprised at their condition. All the men had seemed relaxed and confident when they'd arrived in the Falklands Islands. They had only met some light resistance when they arrived, and before they had become sick, they had spent a few days without making any further progress at all.

'He recounted the story of the gas attack to the doctor and insisted that this must have something to do with it. The doctor stated that he was aware of the gas attack, and all tests had conclusively proved that it had no bearing on their current condition, except that it may have added to the trauma of the stress that they had started to suffer. Captain McIntyre said that he was shocked by the physical condition of the men and found it hard to believe that they were all suffering similar problems brought on by stress. The doctor assured him that it was quite normal for a major stress condition to produce such complications and that there had been very many similar cases during and after the Second World War. McIntyre remained unconvinced and insisted on seeing the hospital director. He had to wait three hours before getting to meet the director—only to be given exactly the same explanation.

In the coming weeks he continued to visit his former troops at the hospital. None of them seemed any better, and one of them actually seemed worse. Captain McIntyre made an appointment to see his Commanding Officer. He questioned him about the condition of the men. The Commanding Officer said that he was aware of the situation and that he could be sure from his information that they were suffering from a post conflict stress disorder causing their systems to react in bizarre and negative ways.

'Captain McIntyre said that he remained unconvinced and felt that the men should receive further tests at another facility. His commanding officer grew angry and warned him that he was being paranoid and impertinent, and that it would not do him any good to go on with his line of questioning. McIntyre continued to try to question other people whom he thought could provide him with the truth, and in time he was called back to see his commanding officer and was given a written reprimand on his army file. Captain McIntyre decided to drop his investigations, figuring that he only had one more year of service to do. Then he would take up the cause of his former troops again as a private citizen.

'When he left the army, he began almost at once to try to question more people who he felt might know the truth. He visited scientists and described the gas incident and the current physical conditions of his former troops. Some agreed that it was possible that the gas had caused the illnesses of the men; they suspected that the gas might have contained chemicals that were attacking the organs and central nervous systems of the men. However, all agreed that without access to the men, there was no way of confirming their thoughts. Captain McIntyre continued to visit the men, and one day he smuggled Corporal Sussex out of the hospital and drove him to see Professor Chalmers.

'Professor Chalmers and his colleagues examined Corporal Sussex and then ran some tests. Captain McIntyre returned Corporal Sussex back to the medical hospital, where upon arrival he was greeted by a furious hospital director and a major from the military police. Captain McIntyre was questioned and shouted at for having performed such an irresponsible act. He was also informed that the army would be seeking an injunction against him to forbid him from visiting the hospital again.

'Three days later, Professor Chalmers advised that the tests did suggest that Corporal Sussex might well have been exposed to some form of chemical nerve agent. However, the tests were not conclusive, and he needed to see Corporal Sussex again—this time preferably over a period of days. But the army got their injunction forbidding Captain McIntyre to visit the hospital again on the grounds that he was a danger to the well-being of the patients. Captain McIntyre and Professor

Chalmers tried to make representations to the highest authorities that the men needed independent tests, but all requests were declined.

'Just as Captain McIntyre was about to give up hope, he heard a story that drove him to go on. Two years after the Falklands War, he went to a reunion with some of his old comrades. There he heard a story that a John Richardson, one of the men from former Captain David Williams' unit, was trying to draw attention to the mysterious deaths of some of his colleagues during the time of the Falklands War.

'It transpired that a few days after Captain Williams' unit discovered the dead sheep, six of his men became very sick and developed symptoms very similar to pneumonia, except it was more severe. Captain Williams was advised to leave the men camped at a certain point, where they would be collected by helicopter. He was then told to proceed with his mission. Some days later the unit was shocked to hear that their colleagues had died on board one of the medical ships. When they asked about the cause of death, they were told that Captain Williams' earlier observations of pneumonia had been correct. But Captain Williams insisted that pneumonia was unlikely to kill all six strong men in a matter of days; he felt that it must have something to do with the dead sheep that they had all seen. His belief was that they had probably come in contact with a very virulent strain of laboratory-produced anthrax. But Captain Williams was tragically killed before the end of the conflict, and when his unit returned home, they were simply glad to have survived. None of them had the energy to ask questions about the deaths of their colleagues.

'Captain McIntyre knew that he was on to something. He was convinced that the Argentineans had used chemical and biological weapons. He tried to get meetings with civil servants in the Ministry of Defence. Some agreed to see him, but only in order to try to persuade him that he was totally wrong. Others simply refused to see him on the grounds that he was jumping to false conclusions, and they did not have the time to waste in trying to correct his false assumptions. He solicited the help of John Richardson and they both made statements to newspapers and television programmes, but still none of this pressure seemed to influence the government. 'Then one day, he showed up in my office. He looked truly awful, nothing like the pictures in the papers some years ago of the decorated war hero. I agreed to see him. I rather wish I had not. He was like a man possessed and insisted that his theory was correct. He demanded that I come out and tell the truth. Naturally I insisted that he was wrong and told him that for the good of his own sanity and health, he should give it up before he ruined his life with this mad obsession.

'We talked for some time, and I did my level best to convince him to stop his investigations, but he grew more and more angry. He told me that he had always admired me in the past, speaking out for justice in a political party that was not known for possessing a strong sense of social conscience. He said that I had lost my backbone, turned traitor, and sold out for a quiet life and political ambition.

'In truth he was partially right. I had done my years of crusading, and I no longer had any fight left. But as for political ambition, that had died some time back. My refusals to stay silent in my early career had not entitled me to hope for the ultimate job as PM. I had no desire to end my political career in the wilderness or to lose the friendship of my colleagues, who would be betrayed and destined for disgrace if I spoke out.

'And so like everyone else, I sent him away without the truth, without any support, and without a hope in the world. It seemed far better to betray this one decent man than to betray my friends and spend my remaining years lonelier than I already was.'

Whitstop paused at this point and refilled his glass again, as he had already done on at least five occasions in the past hour. Christian and Julia were only on their second glass of malt, but Whitstop had already consumed nearly half the bottle. His hands were trembling, and his old, grey eyes were watery. He looked like a sad and pathetic figure who had finally faced up to something that he knew he should have done for some time. He took a gulp from his tumbler, steadied himself with his hands on the table, and continued.

'I never saw Captain McIntyre again. Of course, I heard reports from colleagues that he was still making a nuisance of himself. Many of the comments were cruel; he looked a wreck, and they nicknamed him Captain Scarecrow. I pitied him, but I admired him for selflessly trying to seek the truth. He was a better man than I, and I felt guilt and shame for refusing to help him. I am an old man now, Christian, and I cannot bear to think that I shall die without clearing my conscience. So you and Julia shall be my conscience, and Captain McIntyre shall discover the truth. I pray to God that my confession in your magazine will give his soul the peace it needs to start a normal life.'

Whitstop's tale came to an end, and he drained his glass again and poured himself another.

Christian said, 'John, do you know what has become of Captain McIntyre now, and how we might be able to contact him?'

'Sorry, Christian, I have no idea. But rest assured, when you print this story, I guarantee you will hear from him. I hope you both have all you need for your article. Now I must ask you to leave me, because I am feeling very tired and I confess a little over emotional. It is not a nice sight to see an old politician cry, so I would prefer it if you make a reasonably swift exit.'

Julia and Christian gathered up their things, drained their glasses, and left. Once out on the street, Christian suggested that they pop into the nearest pub for a drink. Julia gladly agreed; she said she felt a little depressed by Whitstop's story and was not in the mood to head back to her lonely flat.

Christian bought the drinks, and then he set out the plan of action for the next day. He suggested that Julia try to look up old reports on the Falklands War and look for references to Captain McIntyre and Captain Williams, to verify that they existed.

Julia was confused. 'Don't you believe Lord Whitstop's story, Christian?'

'Yes, I do, but old habits die hard. I was always taught to check things out, just in case.' He then suggested that she also try to find any articles about soldiers suffering from post-conflict stress disorders leading to illnesses following the conflict. Christian told her that the best place for looking up old newspaper stories was the British Library, and he proposed that she spend the morning there. Christian told her that these were only limited investigations; if he had more time, he would try to locate McIntyre. However, he still wanted to get his magazine to the newsagents before Lancaster Publishing, so these minimal inquiries were going to have to do.

Christian asked Julia if she had managed to switch on the cassette recorder in her bag, and she confirmed that she had started the recording by delving into her bag for a tissue the minute Whitstop started to speak. The tape was only sixty minutes, but there would be enough material on it to confirm what Whitstop had said.

'Christian, this is a really important story—not just for your magazine, but for many others, including the sick soldiers, Captain McIntyre, and Lord Whitstop. It is important for the country to know the truth. We have to get this story published. It must have been really hard for Lord Whitstop to reveal the truth after all these years. He is right, isn't he? His friends will feel betrayed and turn their backs on him, and all the future holds for him now is public disgrace and years of loneliness.'

Julia looked tearful and moved by the evening's work, and Christian felt the urge to hold her and comfort her. But he feared that she would think that he was making a pass at her, so he simply offered her words of comfort and another large brandy. He reassured her that they were doing the right thing for all concerned.

It was getting late, so they left the pub, and Christian flagged down a taxi for her. He thanked her for all her help, told her he would see her in the office in the afternoon, and gave her a peck on the cheek. Even in the darkness he could see that she had turned bright red. He set off for the tube, confused as to why he always seemed to make her feel uncomfortable.

Julia was not uncomfortable—quite the opposite. She could feel a warm glow about her as the taxi sped towards her flat.

Mike Tyler, on the other hand, was feeling bloody uncomfortable. His evening had been a total humiliation, followed by a desperate half-walk, half-crawl back to his apartment in foul, soiled trousers. And now for the eleventh time since getting home, he found himself expelling foul wind and liquid from his bottom into his toilet.

Tom, Gary, Lizzie, and Eddie were enjoying the delights of after-hours drinking in Moriarty's, and they were also feeling stomach pains, but only from laughing too much.

In three different parts of London, three sad and lonely people were rerunning painful moments of regrets over and over in their heads. It was going to be a long and troubled night for Siobhan, Jinxie, and Lord Whitstop.

Christian was feeling hopeful as his tube drew closer to his destination. There was still much to be done, but something inside him said that things were going to be all right.

CHAPTER 12

LIZZIE TURNED ROUND in her bed as the daylight started to pierce the cracks between the curtains. *Oh shit. This is getting to be a bad habit,* she said to herself as she stared at the face of Tom, who was also starting to wake up.

Tom looked at Lizzie and thought to himself, *Oh shit. Christian will fucking kill me if he ever finds out.*

They both stared at each other for a few moments before Lizzie finally broke the silence. 'I certainly didn't plan on this happening, and I am pretty sure you didn't, either. Whilst I am not a fan of telling lies, I really do not recommend that either of us finds our guilt too hard to live with and makes a confession to Christian.'

'Don't worry about me—I am in no doubt that whilst I had a nice time, what we did was 100 per cent wrong, and telling Christian will not make it any better. Right now if we land this kind of news on him, then only a straitjacket will be able to restrain him from going crazy.'

Lizzie suggested Tom exit to the bathroom while she managed to locate her clothes and get dressed; she would use the bathroom when he was finished getting ready for work. When they were both cleaned up and dressed, they sat in the kitchen and drank some coffee in silence.

Tom had always liked Lizzie, and if he was honest with himself, he had always fancied her. He never let it show because he valued Christian's friendship too much.

Lizzie had always liked Tom, but only as a friend, and she had never had any desire to get involved with other men during her years with Christian. Lizzie had always been loyal and faithful to Christian, and she had only faltered that fateful night with Mike Tyler, but now she had slept with Christian's best friend. What was happening to her? She was losing her once strong grip on morality, and she feared that it would not be long until she lost her sanity. She was a decent girl, and decent girls simply did not do this kind of thing.

Tom's head was completely mixed up. Part of him said, *What a fantastic night.* He had really enjoyed the sex with Lizzie, and he could still replay the good bits back in his mind despite the hangover. But another part of him said that he was a complete shit and bitterly regretted what he had done.

They finished their coffees and agreed to walk to the tube station together. Tom needed to go to work, and Lizzie wanted to go back to where she was staying, to get some more sleep. As they walked along the street, Lizzie broke the silence again.

'Last night was nice, Tom, but it was an aberration. It didn't mean anything to me—it was just a moment of madness.'

'Same, Lizzie. I mean, it was great and all that, but totally mad. It meant nothing to me, either.'

But, they were lying, and they both knew it. They both felt something. They didn't want to, of course. Overwhelmed by guilt and still shocked by what they had done, they knew that they had to deny and suppress any thoughts that said last night had meant anything to either of them. They sat in silence on the tube, and when Lizzie rose from her seat to get off, she only said goodbye. Tom rose from his seat, shook her hand, and simply said goodbye in return. He had always given her a peck on the cheek before, like most friends would, but now an awkwardness had developed, and it had developed because last night had meant something to him—and although he did not know it, Lizzie felt the same way.

Lizzie headed off to her sister's flat to catch some more sleep, and Tom made his way to work.

* * *

Julia woke up early and headed off to the British Library. She was feeling good. Last night's session with Whitstop had made her sad, but she had felt it had brought her and Christian closer together. She knew she had not known Christian for long, and when she had first started working for him, she had tried not to let herself develop a stupid obsession with him, but now she knew that she was in love with him.

She had tried to be sad when he had split up with Lizzie, but she couldn't deny that she had really been pleased.

She went about her research in the library quickly and efficiently. She was looking forward to seeing Christian later in the office.

* * *

Jinxie had been awake for hours even before the sun came up. He had slept very badly; the prospect of telling Julia that he was her father on Saturday was what he wanted more than anything, but the prospect of it scared the shit out of him.

* * *

Nothing could scare the shit out of Mike Tyler, because he didn't have any left. He sat in his office, fuming. The only consolation was that he was no longer fuming from his backside. His hate list had expanded. Christian had once been his sole focus. He had never forgiven Christian for the humiliations that he had exacted upon him when they were young, and he had always taken every opportunity to repay Christian. But now he had three new names for his vendetta list.

He was certainly going to try to screw up that bitch Lizzie. He had already caught sight of a memo to her leaving party tonight. 'Bloody bitch didn't even invite me. But I will be there—she can count on it,' he said to himself.

Mike had caught sight of Tom sitting behind the bar and laughing as Mike had tried to reach the exit to the street. Lucky for Gary, he had been obscured by a pillar, and Mike had not seen him, or else Gary would be looking for a job this morning. 'Well, Thomas the Wank Engine, when I screw Toss Pot's stupid magazine, I will get the extra pleasure of buggering up your life as well,' he grumbled.

Mike had guessed by now that Tom and Eddie must have cooked up the evil scheme to food poison him. Eddie was the final name to join Mike's list of candidates for revenge.

At that moment Jason appeared in Mike's office. 'I am really sorry about last night, Mike. There must have been something wrong with my food—it made me really ill.'

Well, that was a relief: Jason had not discovered what had happened to Mike, so clearly the news of Mike's humiliation had not yet circulated through the entire building. 'No problem, Jason. Some of us are blessed with stronger stomachs. Sorry I had to leave, but I figured that it was best for me to go, to spare your embarrassment in that toilet. As you know I am a smart man, and it is my considered belief that our food was poisoned by that fat excuse for a bar manager, Eddie, and that dimwit ex-employee Tom Stevens. As you are no doubt aware, the bitch that used to hold your job is having a leaving bash in Moriarty's this very evening. Tonight we shall make sure that it goes with a real bang. She was disloyal to Lancaster Publishing, and I am glad that we fired her. Tonight we will give her and her friends a leaving party to remember for many years to come.'

'I thought she resigned,' said Jason.

'Well, we let her tell people that to save her dignity, but since she has left, we have realised that we were too kind to her and that her shabby work did not merit our kindness. If we are lucky, that ex-boyfriend of hers, Christian the Toss Pot, may also be there, and then we may succeed in giving four morons a bad night out.'

*　　*　　*

Christian arrived at the hospital to find Jinxie staring into space. 'How are you doing, Jinxie? You seem to be looking much better,' he said unconvincingly.

'Ah, Dior, nice to see you. Sorry, I was miles away.'

Jinxie told Christian all about his unexpected visitor from last night. He told him that Siobhan wanted to join them at the lunch with Julia and he said that he was pleased because that might make things easier for Julia. Siobhan being present could not only help to confirm the truth, but she could also explain it.

Christian told Jinxie about his meeting with Whitstop.

'Well, Dior, it's a huge story, of that there is no doubt. The consequences of what will happen after it is printed cannot be underestimated. Politicians will be forced to resign their posts. Of course there will be an inquiry, and former soldiers or surviving families of dead soldiers will instigate legal proceedings. Top brass in the military will also come under the spotlight for failing to issue NBC suits, as I am sure the MOD kept them informed of the risks. Your story is going to rock the corridors of power, and it will make you and your magazine famous. But I urge you to check the facts and then check them again, because if your story proves to be wrong, then you are going to find yourself in serious hot water.'

'Jinxie, you know Whitstop, and it was you who told me that he was reliable. So why are you trying to worry me now?'

'I am not trying to scare you, Christian. I do think Whitstop is reliable, but nothing in life is ever certain, and a good journalist always checks out his sources even if they are friends.'

'I hear what you're saying, Jinxie, and you will pleased to know that Julia is doing some checking now on people, dates, and events.'

'This Captain McIntyre that you said Whitstop mentioned—can you trace him?'

'No time, Jinxie. If Julia's research looks good, then we are going to go with it. We spent a long time with Whitstop last night, and he struck me as being totally sincere. He has nothing to gain from me running this story, but he has a lot to lose. We will do some checks, but I must say I am already totally convinced.'

'I hope so, my boy. This is a very big story, and a lot of very powerful people will fall dramatically from grace the day your magazine appears.'

Christian and Jinxie talked some more, and then Christian headed back to his office.

*   *   *

Lizzie tried to catch some sleep at her sister's flat, but she found that a guilty conscience made a very poor bedfellow, and she gave up after one and a half hours. She felt really cheap—in the space of just one week, she had slept with two different men. Worse still, she had slept with Christian's worst enemy and his best friend. What the hell was wrong with her? It was lucky Christian's father was dead, or perhaps she might have found herself sleeping with *him* in a few days time.

The thing that upset her more than most was that she had enjoyed her night and the sex with Tom. She wanted to clean out her mind, but it had clearly become a sordid mass of scrambled brain cells. Poor Christian. If he knew what she had done now, he would probably go insane. She prayed to God that he would never find out. Lizzie took another shower, dressed, and made her mind up that at the very least, she should try to solve Christian's distribution problem for the magazine.

She phoned directory inquiries and managed to get the phone number for Bookstall Solutions. Then she phoned Bookstall Solutions and asked for the name of the managing director. The person on the end of the line never asked why Lizzie wanted the name and simply told her it was Kevin Viner. Lizzie thanked the receptionist and said goodbye.

Ten minutes later, Lizzie phoned again using a very up-market accent and asked to be connected to Kevin Viner. She was then connected to a secretary who asked Lizzie what her call to Mr Viner was concerning. Lizzie explained that she had some very important details to tell Mr Viner about his contract with Lancaster Publishing.

The line went quiet for several minutes, and then a voice said, 'Kevin Viner speaking. What can I do for you?'

Lizzie said that she had some very interesting and reliable documents obtained from Lancaster Publishing that would demonstrate they had been cheating Bookstall Solutions by directly selling extra copies of magazines to major newsagents' chains.

Kevin Viner naturally said that he was shocked and was sure that she must be mistaken. Lizzie suggested that they get together late that morning, and she would show him the documents—which she would let him keep if he accepted her proposal. Kevin Viner said he was happy to meet at 11.30 a.m. in his office, and if it proved to be true and her proposal was reasonable, then he was sure that they could reach an agreement.

*   *   *

Tom was sitting in the office feeling and strangely pretty good. Nothing should have taken place between himself and Lizzie, but it had really boosted his ego. He knew now more than ever that he would really like to have a relationship with her. He felt sorry for Christian, but Lizzie and Christian were over, and things had to move on.

He had decided on a strategy. He would say nothing to anyone about what had happened, and he was sure that Lizzie would do the same. As regards to the future, he would play it cool. In the coming days he would not make any advances towards her, but he would contrive to be in the same places as her as often as possible. Tom was sure that given some time, humour, and kindness, Lizzie would grow to like him. He was also sure that if some time passed, and then they started a relationship, no one could ever accuse them of treading on Christian's feelings—particularly if Christian had a new girlfriend by then. Tom decided he would do all in his power to cultivate romance between Julia and Christian; that would certainly make things easier for his hopes to have a relationship with Lizzie.

He then moved to the next phase in his mind and started fantasising about Lizzie. It did not last long because Christian walked in to the office.

'Christian, I am really sorry about what I said yesterday afternoon. It was the pressure—it was just getting too much for me.'

'No need to apologise, Tom. I got you into this, and it is because of Mike Tyler's hate for me that your hard work in bringing in advertising has been wrecked by the antics of that evil git.'

Christian explained to Tom about his meeting with Whitstop, and Tom was impressed; he could see that the story was going to be big news, and if they were able to get the magazine into the shops, then it was very likely to enjoy major sales. There was a lot to be excited about, and he regretted even more the argument yesterday.

Christian went on to tell Tom about the deal that Julia had made for the printing. Now all that remained was for them to find someone to distribute the magazine, and it seemed more likely than not that they would enjoy success after all.

Tom asked why Julia had not shown up this morning, and Christian explained that she was checking on some details on Whitstop's story. Tom asked the expected question: did Christian had any doubts? Christian assured him that he did not, but it was always better to check out some details.

Then Tom told Christian that he had some tidings of great joy about Mike Tyler, and he recounted the story of the previous night at Moriarty's. Tom struggled to get through the story because he kept breaking into fits of laughter, and Christian found himself in pain from laughing as Tom told the tale with a few embellishments to add to the humour.

As the two young men howled with laughter, Julia walked in and asked what it was that amused them so much. Christian said that they should all go for a spot of lunch. That way Julia could tell them what she had found out, and Tom could retell his story of Mike Tyler's night from hell.

They walked to the pub in high spirits. Upon arrival Julia grabbed a table, Tom went to the bar to get the drinks, and Christian selected 'Bat out of Hell' by Meatloaf on the jukebox in honour of the chilli that had flown out of Tyler's posterior.

Julia told them that a Captain McIntyre had existed and that his bravery had been reported in the papers. Captain Williams had also existed, and he had died in action. Furthermore, there were reports after the conflict of soldiers being hospitalised with what had been described as post-conflict stress disorders that had manifested themselves by creating a variety of physical ailments. She went through a list of other things that she had cross-referenced, and she concluded that she was convinced that Whitstop's story was true. They agreed that ideally they would have liked to have gotten in touch with Captain McIntyre, but there was no time. They agreed that they had every confidence that Whitstop was genuine.

To round off their lunch and to satisfy Julia's curiosity—and Christian's desire to hear of Tyler's misfortune again—Tom told his story of the previous evening. All three howled with laughter like school children, and it seemed that things were really looking up.

*   *   *

Lizzie arrived on time at Bookstall Solutions and was pleased to be shown directly into Kevin Viner's office. Lizzie was offered some coffee, and Kevin told her that her call had intrigued him and that he was anxious to see the documents. She explained to him what Mike Tyler and Lancaster Publishing had been up to, but she said that she was not prepared to give him the documents unless he promised to make an agreement with her.

'If your proposal is reasonable, then of course you have my word that I shall be more than happy to enter into an agreement with you,' Kevin replied.

'Good, then I shall explain my proposal. Your company originally agreed to distribute a magazine for Christian Davidson, and then under pressure from Mike Tyler and Lancaster Publishing, you decided not to honour your agreement. I propose that you meet with the chairman of Lancaster Publishing and that you show him the documents with which I will provide you. You will then get his agreement that Lancaster Publishing will never try to cheat Bookstall Solutions again. Furthermore, to exact a penalty to your benefit, you will demand that they agree to pay Bookstall Solutions an increased percentage of their magazines cover prices for a period of two years. Finally, you will advise him that you do intend to distribute Christian Davidson's publication and that you do not expect him to object. Under no circumstances are you to reveal how you came into possession of the documents.'

'Your proposal seems fine to me. But what makes you think he will agree to all this?'

'He really has no choice. Lancaster cannot fire Bookstall because you will take a court action against them for acting outside of your existing agreement with them. In the current circumstances, your terms are not unreasonable, and therefore he would be foolish to refuse.'

'I have to admit, what you say is true. But why shouldn't I just sue them anyway?'

'Because if you do not agree to what I say, you will never get the documents, and without proof you have no case. If you agree, as I am sure you will, then I am prepared to wait while your secretary types a letter to me, to be signed by you, that summarises our confidential agreement.'

Viner agreed, and within ten minutes Lizzie had her letter. He also agreed to send a new fax to Christian within the hour to advise him that Bookstall Solutions was sorry about the earlier fax and was indeed happy to distribute *Style Inc.*

Lizzie had acted with total confidence in the meeting, but inside she had felt very nervous, and she was very relieved when she stepped out of the building with the letter in her bag.

*   *   *

Mike Tyler and his prodigy, Jason, united in crime from their hideous bottom-exploding experiences, were busily scheming. They had code-named their campaign for Lizzie's leaving do as 'Party of the Plague'. They were feeling much better physically and emotionally because their ideas were giving them much to laugh about.

*   *   *

Christian, Tom, and Julia returned from their pub lunch in good spirits and were greeted by yet another dose of welcome news. Christian could not believe his eyes when he saw the fax from Bookstall Solutions, and at first he thought that it was some cruel joke from Mike Tyler.

He called them to check and was pleased to find that the fax was genuine. He asked why there was a change of heart but was simply told that Bookstall Solutions regretted the previous fax and felt that it was only right and professional to honour the original agreement with Christian.

Tom didn't waste a moment and started calling advertisers, but he was not so lucky; most said that once they saw the first issue in the newsagents and obtained some figures on copy sales, they would consider booking into future issues. However, Tom's spirits were not dampened, and he kept on making the calls.

Christian started to write up Whitstop's story and was absorbed for hours in what he felt may become his finest ever article. Julia started collecting all the other pages together to get them ready to be made into films for the printer. All three colleagues were united in their efforts to produce a great first issue, and they felt very positive about the future. No one spoke as they worked on through the afternoon, but they felt part of a great little team. Things were certainly looking up.

CHAPTER 13

LATE THAT AFTERNOON, Lizzie phoned Christian and invited him to her leaving do. She was relieved to find that Christian was no longer angry, just philosophical about her lapse with Mike Tyler. He accepted that he had become absorbed with his new magazine and that after all these years, their relationship had come to a dead-end. They both accepted blame for their break-up, and it was agreed that they would at least stay friends. It was strange for them to both reach such a comfortable and non-confrontational closure to their relationship, but it seemed right. They were happy to accept that there was no sense in them going on.

Christian said that he would be happy to come to her leaving party, and she told him to ask Tom to come as well. He asked if Julia could come, and Lizzie said she was most welcome. They talked for a while, and Christian told her about the recent progress with the magazine and how well everything was going. He told her how Mike Tyler had tried to wreck his plans, and she told him that she had finally discovered what an evil bastard Mike was. She managed to feign surprise when he told her how Bookstall Solutions had recently said that they would not distribute the magazine, but today they had said that they would do it; he was impressed with their sense of honour. She wanted to laugh at this point, but she simply agreed with his observation.

When their conversation was over, they both felt a huge sense of relief. They were no longer together, but they were parting with dignity and the prospect of a lifelong, solid friendship.

Christian had hated Lizzie when he'd discovered that she had slept with Tyler, but for days afterwards he had wanted to win her back. Now he realised that their relationship had dried up, the fun had died, and neither of them was able to relight the flame.

He was looking forward to Lizzie's leaving party. It was going to signal their mature acceptance of a dead relationship, but it was also going to herald a new and comfortable friendship. Christian was also looking forward to seeing some of his old colleagues from Lancaster Publishing. He was certain it was going to be a good night.

*   *   *

Mike Tyler was certain that it was going to be good night for him, but certainly not for Christian, Lizzie, Tom, and Eddie. He had very good reasons to believe this because he and Jason had arranged a compendium of evil surprises for the night ahead.

*   *   *

Eddie had spent a lot of the day laughing to himself about the events of the previous evening, however, he was regretting what he had done. Mike Tyler was objectionable, but he wasn't stupid, and he was bound to realise that Eddie had played a major role in his humiliating, public, bottom explosion.

Mike Tyler was bound to want revenge. Eddie depended heavily on custom from the staff of Lancaster Publishing, and he suspected that the staff might be told that Moriarty's was off limits. He was sure that Tyler would probably go even further and make a complaint to the brewery, or persuade health inspectors that the bar should be closed down. As the day went on, he became more and more concerned that Mike would exact a terrible revenge, and he was extremely worried.

*   *   *

Jinxie was bored out of his brains. He was fed up with wandering around the hospital, he hated TV and couldn't bear to watch it, and he was even growing tired of reading. He decided to go shopping. On the face of it, it was a strange choice of activity for him because he hated the frivolity of shopping as much as he hated TV. Jinxie had largely lost interest in clothes many years back; his wardrobe was very dated, to say the least. A lot of his colleagues at the newspaper had often joked that his wardrobe was locked in a time vacuum from the 1960s.

He was sure that Julia's presumption that he was a pervert had not just come from the fact that he had followed her; his clothes had probably not helped, either. Jinxie was going to get a new outfit for Saturday. The only problem was he hadn't a clue what passed for stylish these days.

Jinxie called up Nick Hughes, one of the young, dynamic advertising salespeople from the newspaper. 'Nick, it's James Jinks here. I need you to do me a favour. When you finish work in the next half-hour, I want you to meet me outside of Selfridges on Oxford Street. I want you to help me to select a new suit, shirt, tie, and shoes, and in return I will buy you a suit of your choice. Do we have a deal?'

Nick agreed; it was a good deal. He was very fashion conscious and liked to spend money on clothes. This was an offer too good to pass up, even if it was going to mean he had to start his Friday night drinking a bit later than expected.

At 6.35 p.m. Nick spotted Jinxie standing outside of Selfridges, and he took Jinxie down the street to one of his favourite designer stores. 'Okay, Mr Jinks, what kind of suit are you after?'

'I am in your hands, young man. Everyone says you are the best-dressed man in the office, so I have absolute faith in your choice.'

Nick looked at a rail of dark blue Cerruti suits, and a shop assistant came over and spoke to Jinxie. 'Would your son like to try something on, sir?' he said.

Nick laughed, and Jinxie looked a little uncomfortable as he replied, 'Actually, the suit is for me, and this young man here is a work colleague who has kindly agreed to help me chose something fashionable but tasteful.'

'Well, sir, you are clearly in good hands. Cerruti use excellent fabrics; their suits are very well cut and always the height of fashion. If you tell me your size, I will select one for you, and you can try it on to see how it looks.'

Jinxie confessed that he had not bought a suit for a very long time, and he had no idea what his size was. The shop assistant brought over a tape measure, and with the measurements taken, he selected the appropriate size from the rail.

Nick liked the suits as well, so they both disappeared into the changing cubicles. Once dressed, they came out of the cubicles and inspected each other.

'Spot on, Mr Jinks. It really looks good on you. I think you should take it!'

'Thank you, Nick. I think I will. And in case you were wondering, I think the suit looks really smart on you as well, so as agreed I shall purchase it as a reward for your consultancy services. But before we are finished, I just need your help to select a tie, some shoes, and a shirt.'

The shop assistant inspected Jinxie and agreed that the suit was perfect for him. It was a little long in the legs, but the shop assistant advised that it could be altered and collected in two days. Jinxie said that he had to have the suit now. At first the assistant said that it was impossible, but when Jinxie offered an incredible one hundred pounds for the alterations fee, the assistant sent a younger colleague off with the suit and said that it would be back in half an hour.

Nick helped Jinxie select the rest of the outfit. The shoes were straightforward black brogues, the shirt was light blue with French cuffs, and the tie was an Italian thick silk with dark blue and purple stripes. Jinxie was a little surprised by Nick's combination of such dark colours, but Nick assured him that the overall effect would make him the very pinnacle of cool.

Jinxie paid for all the clothes and then told Nick that his job was done. Jinxie would wait for his suit to come back with the alterations. Nick was a genuinely nice guy, and although he was anxious to join his friends for the traditional Friday night piss-up, he turned to Jinxie and said, 'No rush, Mr Jinks. I think there is one more job that needs doing: your hair.'

It was true that Jinxie had not had a haircut for a while; normally he went to a very old-fashioned barber. Nick led him down the street and selected a trendy unisex salon, where most of the staff looked like rejects from pop groups. At first they were not sure if they could fit him in, but Jinxie offered considerably more than the going rate, and they were more than happy to accommodate him. Nick issued directions for the cut, and Jinxie hoped to God that he was not going to end up looking anything like the hairdressers. When it was all over, he was very pleasantly surprised. His hair looked very smart indeed, and even the gel, about which he had been sceptical, added positively to the overall effect.

They returned to the shop, and the suit was ready. Jinxie thanked Nick for his help, and Nick thanked Jinxie for the suit. Nick was desperate to ask Jinxie what all of this was in aid of, but Jinxie had not offered any information, and so Nick felt it polite not to press him for details. In any case, Nick guessed that it had to be for a woman, and he smiled to himself as he walked down the street and thought, *Good old Jinxie—he certainly can't be past it yet!*

Jinxie had quite enjoyed his early evening shopping and thought he might try it again sometime soon. He returned to the hospital to find the staff nurse who had told him off before standing in his room and waiting to give him another lecture. She looked very angry and let Jinxie know exactly how she felt. 'Let me see, now, were you the man that came in here a few days ago with the heart attack? Or are you the man suffering from invisibility disorder, a strange and immensely irritating illness that causes the patient to disappear with an alarming degree of frequency? What is it with you, Mr Jinks? This is a busy and stressful hospital. Do you completely lack all consideration for the rest of the human race?'

Jinxie did it again: he quoted poetry and really upset her.

> You may shoot me with your words,
> You may cut me with your eyes,
> You may kill me with your hatefulness,
> But still, like air, I'll rise.[***]

The staff nurse was now very angry. 'Mr Jinks, I want to know where you have been and why you decided to wander off without telling anyone.'

'I have been shopping, my dear.'

'I can see that, but it does not answer my question.'

'If you must know, I have been to Oxford Street, and if I had told you that I wished to pop out, you would have said no.'

'Of course I would have said no! But that is no reason for you to just disappear. We have enough to do round here without having to worry about where you have got to. All I can say is that I hope the doctor passes you fit to leave tomorrow morning, because I for one will not be sad to see you go.'

[***] Taken from the poem *Still I Rise* by Maya Angelou.

But Jinxie's spirits were not dented; he was actually feeling pretty optimistic. Siobhan would be there tomorrow to help break the news to Julia, and he was going to look smart and presentable. He was sure that although Julia was bound to be shocked, she would accept him as her real father. At last he would be able to have the relationship with his daughter for which he had yearned for so many years.

* * *

Lizzie was sitting with Eddie in the upstairs bar of Moriarty's. Eddie had gone to a lot of effort for her, and the food, whilst simple, looked great. Eddie had even put some balloons and flowers in the room; she was certainly getting the VIP treatment. Lizzie was looking forward to her party: she was going to get the chance to say goodbye to some work colleagues of whom she was fond. She had really enjoyed some good times with many of them over the years, and she was going to miss them.

She was pleased that she had solved Christian's magazine distribution problem—at least it made up for some of the recent wrongs she had done to him. Lizzie was also pleased that Christian had agreed to come; she felt that the end of their relationship was now closing in a decent, friendly manner, and this was more than she could have hoped for a few days back.

There were some nervous thoughts in the back of her mind. She hoped Tom would stick to their bargain and that no one would ever hear about what had taken place between them. If things had been different, she would have been pleased to start a relationship with Tom. She had always liked him, but it really did not do to sleep with your boyfriend's enemy and then start dating his best friend and business partner.

Eddie was also a little nervous. He was still wondering when he might be on the receiving end of Mike Tyler's revenge. It was just a matter of time before something unpleasant would happen.

* * *

Mike Tyler was not nervous at all. He was too preoccupied preparing for the Party of Plagues, and he was rather enjoying himself. He had spent virtually the whole day in his office scheming and coming up with ideas to make sure that Lizzie's leaving party was a total disaster. It also proved to be Mike's good fortune that Jason's boss was away on vacation, because now Mike was also able to send Jason all over London on errands to collect some of the surprises.

Jason was also enjoying himself. Mike had loaned him his BMW, and Jason was enjoying driving it. Last night had been a rotten experience for him, and he was more than a little pleased to be helping Mike with the Party of Plagues.

Just after 6.00 p.m., Mike and Jason had concluded their plans. 'Well, Jason, it is going to be a great night for us, but sadly not for Fat Eddie, Thomas the Wank Engine, and Lizzie the Bitch. Tonight they are going to wish that they had never crossed Mike Tyler. I simply cannot wait to see the looks on their faces when the Party of Plagues gets underway.'

'But Mike, we are not invited. How on earth are we going to get in?'

'Do you honestly think we are going to miss out on the party of the year? You are in the company of the master now—just follow me and learn.'

Jason followed Mike, and to his amazement they headed off to Moriarty's. Mike walked in and ordered some drinks. Eddie had left Lizzie upstairs and had gone down to the main bar to watch the early evening Friday night trade coming in. Then Eddie saw Mike and nearly panicked. Eddie held it together and walked as coolly as possible over to where Mike was standing.

'Mr Tyler, how nice to see you. I really am most terribly sorry that you were taken ill last night. I can't think what must have happened. Either there was something up with that batch of chilli, or that old brandy must have fermented in the bottle. I hope that you are now fully recovered; please be my guest tonight. All the drinks this evening for you and your colleague are on the house, and if you are feeling hungry, please order anything you like—on me.'

'That's very decent of you, Eddie, but we were thinking of moving on to champagne after these beers—it's been a pretty good week.'

'If it is champagne you want, then you shall have champagne, and I will tell my staff that they are not to take a penny from you for the whole night.'

'Most decent of you, Eddie. We accept your most generous compensation. I give you my personal guarantee that you will not hear another word about our discomfort from our evening here last night.'

Eddie was relieved by the turn of events. 'Very fair of you, Mr Tyler. I am so pleased that you are such a decent and reasonable man.' And with that he headed off to get some champagne.

Mike turned to Jason and said, 'Stupid blubbery git. I shall enjoy drinking copious quantities of his champagne whilst we visit the Party of Plagues on him and his idiot friends.'

Eddie returned with the Champagne, and Mike asked him, 'So when does Lizzie's party begin?'

'Oh, no set time—people will just wander upstairs when they arrive.'

Mike could see some of the Lancaster Publishing staff already arriving and making their way upstairs. 'Well, I guess Jason and I should make our way upstairs soon, then.'

Eddie did not respond; he was pretty sure that Lizzie would not have invited Mike, but he was too scared to point out that fact. Eddie decided to pop upstairs quickly and to warn Lizzie. 'Lizzie, Mike Tyler is downstairs, and he is planning to come up to your leaving party.'

'Well, let him—he won't get a warm welcome, and he is not going to worry me. I am not scared of him. Besides, he will get a shock when he sees Christian later, and from all the games he has been trying to play on Christian, he should be pretty scared of how Christian may react.'

'Bloody hell, Lizzie, I hope they don't start fighting—I have my licence to think about.'

'Don't worry. I will keep Christian on the lead. I expect they will just trade insults, and I am used to that.'

At that point Mike and Jason appeared upstairs. Mike said, 'Lizzie, great to see you. Silly girl Jackie forgot to send me the memo about your party, but luckily some of the Lancaster staff told me, so here I am to come and wish you the very best for the future.'

'Well that is a stroke of luck, Mike—for you, but not for me. What makes you think I would want you to come here tonight with your pet clone?'

'Lizzie, that's not nice, especially after our very recent night of passion.'

'Stay if you want, Mike, but please don't soil your pants again in front of my guests—they may be offended.'

And with that Lizzie walked off to chat with some of her old colleagues. Mike was boiling inside. He was now looking forward more than ever to the surprises in store for later that night. The stupid bitch was going to regret what she had said, and he was going to enjoy every moment of her misery.

*　　*　　*

Twenty minutes later Christian, Tom, and Julia arrived. 'Ah, here comes Piss Pot Publishing,' quipped Mike to Jason.

Christian wandered over to Lizzie and gave her a peck on the cheek. Tom shook her hand. Christian was a bit surprised by Tom's formality but put it down to it being a long and difficult week.

Christian asked Lizzie what Mike Tyler was doing there, and she told him that he had invited himself. She said she knew how much Christian hated Mike, and she would rather he had not come, but she asked that Christian ignore Mike for the sake of her guests, and he readily agreed.

The room was filling out nicely, and despite the presence of Mike and Jason, the atmosphere was good. Lizzie was pleased and was sure that it was going to be a good evening.

Mike stood with Jason, quaffing his champagne. He was in a very good mood and was certain that it was going to be a really super evening for him and Jason.

Chapter 14

The party was going very well, and at 9.00 p.m. Jackie asked for silence to make a small presentation to Lizzie. Jackie stood in the middle of the room and told stories of Lizzie's time with Lancaster Publishing. At that time, Jason left the room and disappeared downstairs and out of the bar. Jackie made quite a good speech. She talked about some of Lizzie's great achievements, made some jokes about some of Lizzie's more embarrassing moments, and concluded with nice comments about Lizzie and how much everyone was going to miss her.

Then Lizzie was called upon to respond before she got to open the big present box and the oversized card. Lizzie gave a really relaxed speech full of humour about her days at the company and some affectionate and humorous comments about her colleagues. She concluded as expected by saying how much she was going to miss working with them, but she was never going to lose touch. It's funny, really, how people always start their speeches with the truth and, even with good intentions, finish on a promise that they will never keep.

Everyone applauded loudly and raised their glasses in a toast to Lizzie. Then they all chanted, 'Open the box, open the box!' Lizzie said okay and took her position behind the huge box to unwrap her surprise.

Little did they know that Mike had spotted the box in Jackie's office earlier in the day, and he had read the good-luck card to Lizzie. This immediately gave him an idea to create the ultimate leaving gift. He called Jason's extension and instructed him to go to a local pet shop to buy what had recently become the fashionable pet to own—a rat. He told Jason, 'Hey, it is a big occasion—let's splash out and be generous. Get ten rats.'

As soon as Jason returned with the box of rats, Mike managed to carefully unwrap the present box, remove the contents, and dump in the rats. He took great pleasure in hurling the original gift, an espresso machine, into the skip at the back of the office building.

Jason told Mike that he had found the pet shop quite interesting because it specialized in rare pets. The animals on display included such creatures as locusts, tropical frogs, lizards, and even a wide selection of snakes. This set Mike thinking, and in a sudden flash of inspiration he decided to create the leaving party of the year with a unique biblical theme. He would present Lizzie with three plagues for her party: rats, locusts, and frogs. The name 'Party of Plagues' was born. Mike kept Jason busy and sent him back to the pet shop to make the other purchases, a box of frogs and a box of locusts.

Lizzie now started to open her box as the chorus shrieked louder and louder for her to open the box. She tore away the paper and then proceeded to open the flaps on the box. Lizzie was still removing the paper when Jason returned with two more boxes. No one noticed him walk in because they were all facing Lizzie in the centre of the room, giving her their full attention. As she started to open her box, Jason also opened his boxes at the rear of the room, unseen and unsuspected by any of the other guests.

Lizzie stared inside her box and suddenly pulled back and shrieked with horror as she spied the rats moving around within. Suddenly, as if by magic, the room was swarming with locusts and frogs, and the rats began to escape from the box and onto the table.

The partygoers screamed and panicked, and mayhem broke out in the room as people knocked over trays of food and drinks in their haste to try to escape from the plague of animals that Mike Tyler had visited upon Lizzie's leaving party. No one had noticed that Mike and Jason had already made their exit.

As many of the guests rushed downstairs into the main bar, they were met by further strange sights. Mike had not forgotten Eddie and the painful experience that he had inflicted upon his rear end the previous night. The bar was filled to the brim with what looked like tramps. But the tramps were not the only newcomers to the bar, and Eddie was surrounded by a small group of very angry people who were shouting loudly about Moriarty's being a den of animal cruelty.

Jason had not particularly enjoyed himself at the back end of the afternoon, delivering fake Salvation Army invitations to tramps around the Victoria bus station and inviting them for free food and drinks courtesy of Moriarty's. Nevertheless, his bum was still stinging with pain from the previous evening's assault on his digestive system and, he was as keen as Mike to make life unpleasant for Eddie.

Mike had performed the final task of the day himself. A few hours back he had phoned in the anonymous tip off to an animal rights group. He had informed them that the publican of Moriarty's a man by the name of Eddie shared a predilection for inflicting cruelty on animals for the pleasure of himself and some of his friends.

Suddenly the animal rights activists became acutely aware of the screams emanating from the upstairs bar, and they could not help but notice a number of shocked people rushing down the stairs in panic. They ceased shouting at Eddie and rushed towards the stairs, anxious to engage in combat with the perpetrators of what they were guessing was some hideous spectacle of animal cruelty.

Upstairs, Christian and Tom were trying to return the rats, locusts, and frogs to their original boxes with some of the other more level-headed guests. As the animal rights activists reached the upstairs bar, they could not believe their eyes as they watched what to them seemed like a bunch of frenzied people chasing a variety of helpless creatures around a small room. They dived in and started to brawl with what they could only imagine were a group of sick and unnatural perverts who got their kicks from getting drunk and chasing small creatures around a room for their own cruel amusement.

Downstairs, the tramps had decided to take matters into their own hands and were helping themselves to drinks and food left behind by customers who had fled the pub upon hearing the screaming coming from the room upstairs. Eddie was trying hard to recover his composure after having been yelled at furiously by the animal rights campaigners. He was now engaged in a desperate attempt to shoo the tramps out of the bar. However, they were having none of it as they greedily tucked into the remains of hastily abandoned meals and drinks.

Mike and Jason squeezed their way out into the street, delighted with their night's efforts. They returned to Lancaster Publishing and Mike's office, where Mike produced a bottle of scotch and some mugs.

He filled the mugs and toasted their success, and then he phoned the police to add the final piece of misery to the Party of Plagues.

Minutes later the sounds of sirens could be heard as vanloads of officers arrived at Moriarty's. The pub was in chaos as the bar staff tried in vain to eject the tramps from the bar, and in turn the tramps began to get louder and more obstinate.

The noise from the upstairs bar was unbelievable: screams and noises of furniture splintering and crockery breaking made the police aware that a full riot was in progress on the upper floor. They radioed for more support as they tried desperately to clear the tramps from the downstairs bar.

By the time the police had finally cleared enough people out of the downstairs bar to make an assault on the upper level, the noise seemed to have died down. Christian had managed to persuade the man who appeared to be the leader of the activists to stop. He had guessed that Billy might be the leader because he was constantly shouting instructions to his comrades about being careful not to harm the animals as they made their attack on the remaining partygoers. Christian had also correctly guessed that the attackers must be from some type of animal lovers group, because Billy and his mates were clearly far more concerned about the animals than they were about the human beings in the room.

Christian held up a rat up by its tail in front of Billy and threatened to beat it to a pulp unless the fighting stopped. Billy immediately shouted to his colleagues to stop, and then Christian at last had everyone's undivided attention. He explained that he believed they were all victims of a cruel, practical joke. He said that he and his friends were actually supposed to be at a leaving party for the woman in the far corner of the room, who was currently sitting in the corner in hysterical floods of tears. Following a few more conciliatory and well-chosen words, he made Billy understand that neither he nor any of his friends had any intention of harming the animals and that their only wish was to return them to the boxes for their safety. He then proceeded to place the rat gently in the box on the table and suggested that everyone in the room should help to repatriate the frightened animals to the safety of their original boxes.

When the police finally reached the upstairs bar, they could scarcely believe their eyes. No one was fighting anymore, but a large group of people scurried around the room trying to catch rodents and frogs and put them into boxes. The locusts were sadly no longer a major problem because they were mainly squashed in a soggy mess of food and broken glasses on the carpet.

Once the animals had finally been restored to their boxes and order had been restored to the room, the officer in charge set about the task of getting his team to take statements.

As they made their way downstairs, the senior officer was relieved to see that the bar had been totally cleared of tramps; the only people that remained were some of his officers and the bar staff.

Eddie was told by Sergeant Wilson, the officer in charge, that he wanted to take down some statements to make a report. Eddie called Sam over and asked her to set up some tables and make some tea to help the police perform their task.

Sergeant Wilson asked who they thought could have been the instigator of these cruel practical jokes, and Lizzie and Eddie both stated that they felt it was highly likely to be a man called Mike Tyler.

It took them some considerable time, helped by Christian and Tom, to explain their reasons for believing that tonight's strange events were orchestrated by Mike, but in the end Sergeant Wilson was satisfied that they should try to get hold of Tyler to interview him.

Lizzie was happy to oblige by furnishing him with the address of Lancaster Publishing and Mike's home address, and she secretly hoped that Mike would be brought to account for his evil games.

*   *   *

Meanwhile, Mike and Jason were in Lorrenzo's, a very nice little Italian restaurant not far away. Sergeant Wilson sent a couple of his officers to Lancaster Publishing to see if Mike and Jason were there, but the building was empty. He also sent a couple of officers to Mike's apartment building, but the doorman said that Mr Tyler had not yet returned home. The policemen left a note for Mike to contact them at the station.

Mike and Jason were enjoying their meal very much. 'It was brilliant, Mike. I really can learn so much from you.'

'Well, I also owe a thank you to you, Jason. You did a great job, and I will not forget it. You are a loyal and capable man, and one day when

I am running Lancaster Publishing, you will be my number two. Now, I propose a toast to the Party of Plagues, and to future glory.'

They both raised their glasses and toasted each other. It had been a great night and a fantastic piece of revenge.

*   *   *

At about 11.10 p.m. Sergeant Wilson and his officers finished interviewing everyone, and he started to send people home. By 11.30 only Lizzie, Billy, Christian, Tom, Julia, Eddie, and Sam remained.

Eddie looked badly shaken and was clearly worried about the news of this disturbance reaching the brewery. 'I will lose my job for this,' he said. 'And I really bloody love this pub. I have been happy here. It's not just my job, you know—it's my life and my home.'

Sergeant Wilson surprised all of them at this point when he showed enormous sensitivity by cheering up Eddie. He told him not to be concerned. Sergeant Wilson would produce a report that would go to the brewery and clearly show that Eddie had done an outstanding job in a difficult situation. Eddie pointed out that he had in fact done nothing at all except nearly have a nervous breakdown. Nevertheless, Sergeant Wilson said that his report would make Eddie look like a hero who had managed to stop customers becoming endangered, and he had prevented the bar from suffering too much damage.

Eddie was very grateful and was quite cheered up by the sergeant. The brewery certainly could not sack a hero. He offered the sergeant a drink, but he declined and pointed out that he was still on duty and it was after hours. Eddie felt foolish for making such a suggestion and apologised. Sergeant Wilson simply smiled and told him that he would owe him a decent send-off at the pub when his retirement day from the force finally arrived. Eddie, who was now in much brighter spirits, declared that no police officer in the whole of London would ever be thrown a better party than the one that Eddie would plan for Sergeant Wilson.

The police finally departed, and Eddie invited Christian, Lizzie, Tom, and Julia back to his living area for a drink. He even invited Billy, who gladly accepted. They all needed a few drinks to calm their nerves, and they sat around for some hours talking.

*   *   *

Christian and Billy got on really well, and when Billy discovered that Christian had his own magazine, he became very animated. Billy told him how he had been trying to investigate a high-profile Labour MP who had an interest in a cosmetics firm that did experiments on animals. Of course the MP had denied any association with the firm, and furthermore the MP had actually given speeches against vivisection.

Billy nevertheless said he had a plan to get proof of the MP's involvement in the firm. He already had video and photographs to prove that the testing on the animals was cruel and very inhumane. All he now needed to do was to prove the MP's involvement.

Christian was fascinated and said that he would like to talk further with Billy about doing a story for the second issue of his magazine. Billy told him that he was close to completing his investigations and writing the story. He said that when it was finished, he had thought about taking it to a newspaper, but he had a deep-rooted mistrust of newspaper journalists, so if Christian was genuinely interested, Billy would be happy to consider letting Christian run the story in his second issue.

Billy had studied history at university, and during his time there he had become a member of an animal rights group. Since leaving university, the campaign had become his life; it had been a hard existence, living on state benefits and staying in low-grade, cheap accommodations.

As the night turned into morning and they had all consumed quite a lot more alcohol, Christian came up with an idea. 'Look, Billy, I cannot afford to pay you at the moment, but if you think you can write, why don't you come to our office a few days a week and try your hand at some stories? If your stuff turns out to be decent and we make some reasonable cash from the success of the first issue, then Tom and I will look at taking you on—as long as Tom has no objection.'

Tom was pretty drunk and in good spirits, and he said that he thought it was a great idea. Julia felt a little uncomfortable at the thought of someone else writing on the magazine, because it was her hope to progress from less mundane tasks to full-time writing, but, she said nothing.

Christian sensed Julia's anxiety, and he quickly told Billy that he had to understand that if he was taken on, he would also have to do quite a bit of the production work because Julia would be working full-time on her own stories within the near future. Julia was relieved and went back to thinking about her lunch tomorrow and the romantic possibilities of some time alone with Christian.

Lizzie was doing her best to reassure Eddie that everything would be okay, and Tom spent most of his time saying nothing, staring at Lizzie, and agreeing with anything Christian suggested.

*　*　*

Not far away Jason was still hanging on Mike Tyler's every word as their stories of glory grew to gigantic proportions in direct relation to the enormous bill that they were clocking up in the restaurant. Lorrenzo, the restaurant owner, was keen to get to bed because all his other customers had left long ago. However, Mike was ordering the most expensive cognacs and downing them like water, so he figured it was far more profitable to keep serving.

*　*　*

Jinxie was finding it difficult to sleep; he was like a young boy who was about to start his first day of secondary school the next morning. He was constantly getting out of bed to inspect his new outfit just like a schoolboy checking his smart new uniform.

He was looking forward to checking out of the hospital tomorrow because he was sure that the doctor would pass him as fit. Most of all, he was looking forward to finally being able to talk to his daughter after all these terrible years of silence.

His heart raced a bit, but he was not worried and knew that it was just the excitement. He had everything to live for now.

CHAPTER 15

A GOOD PERCENTAGE of Londoners spent Saturday morning in search of their tried and trusted hangover cures that in reality never seemed to work. Lizzie was drinking Coca-Cola, eating chocolate, and constantly splashing cold water over her face. She felt bloody awful, but at least this time she had slept alone.

Eddie had spent most of the early hours being sick; he had carried on drinking after everyone left. He was now drinking raw egg mixed with vinegar and sugar, and he hoped that this would have some effect on the way he was feeling. It did in fact have quite a big effect: ten seconds later, he projectile vomited the vile cocktail all over the kitchen wall.

Tom was sitting in a greasy café, eating a huge fry up, and drinking a mug of very sweet tea. It wasn't making him feel much better, but he thoroughly enjoyed the meal nevertheless.

Julia had already drunk about three litres of water and was trying to get through her fourth. She had been to the toilet so many times that she was certain her liver and kidneys must be clean by now. She had eaten a few headache pills and taken every vitamin known to modern science, but she was still not feeling a lot better.

Mike Tyler felt really bloody awful. The rich food and enormous quantities of brandy had played havoc with his stomach. He was certainly not as delicate as he had been the previous night, but nonetheless he still had a pretty bad dose of the shits. He took some tablets to calm his stomach and made himself a large omelette in the hopes that it might bind his guts. He vainly hoped that a good dose of sugar would reduce his head pain, so he drank a couple of bottles of Lucozade, which only served to build up a vast reservoir of gas in his stomach, causing him to spend another twenty minutes on the toilet expelling noxious, watery wind.

Christian had not stocked his fridge for a while, so he was eating anything he could find that was not covered with mould and that could be slapped between slices of toasted stale bread. He had started with a couple of slices covered in salad cream; he was now trying a toast with the last scrapings from the peanut butter jar. He had saved the remains of the marmite jar for the last two slices; he was sure that marmite had revitalising qualities. The milkman had delivered his milk, two pints, and he drank both of them straight down.

Christian not only felt fragile but also quite bloated. He rather wished that he had not eaten so much toast and drunk so much milk. He tried as best as he could to get his act together and headed off to meet Jinxie at the hospital.

Jinxie had got up really early, anxious to see the doctor and to be given a clean bill of health to go home. So sure was he that he would not have to stay another day that he had already showered and dressed in his new suit. His favourite staff nurse was on duty again that morning, and she could not resist commenting on Jinxie's new look.

'Thinking of joining the Mafia, are we, Mr Jinks? Old men and sharp suits always look a bit sinister to me.'

He was not amused; he had thought he had looked just the part to meet Julia for lunch, and now she had dented his confidence. The rotten hospital breakfast had given him indigestion, and his poor night's sleep had left him feeling tired. Jinxie was really hoping the doctor would come soon—he was getting a bit worried that if he had to wait too long, he may not seem fit enough to go.

Jinxie decided to take a walk around the ward in the hopes that it might make him feel a bit better. He also hoped he might be able to break in his new shoes because they were pinching his feet, and the shiny leather soles certainly needed some wear to stop them sliding around the floor.

Not long now. Only a few more hours until he was going to see Julia. He felt quite calm about it now; the walk was doing him some good. He rehearsed in his mind the things he wanted to say to her. Jinxie was lost in his own world, miles away, and he did not see the mop lying on the floor.

It all happened in seconds. He caught his foot on the mop and tripped, his head caught against a metal trolley, and he tore away a large chunk of flesh just over his right eye. His body folded into a heap on the floor, and as he hit the ground, he clawed at his chest, gasping for air. He tried desperately to catch his breath, and pain rushed through his chest and down his left arm. Jinxie knew it was over. In an instant his life had ended.

Nurses heard the commotion and rushed to his side. They tried desperately to resuscitate him, but it was useless—his breathing had ceased and his pulse was dead. They put his old, crumpled body on a trolley and tried to jump-start his heart with electric shocks, but it was all over. Jinxie was dead.

*   *   *

Minutes later Christian arrived. He broke down when he saw Jinxie's lifeless body. Jinxie's shirt was torn away from where they had tried to access his chest, but, Christian could tell that Jinxie had dressed especially for today, and it made the sight of his dead friend even more painful. Jinxie lay there, a lifeless body in a brand-new suit, with blood caked to the left side of his face. Christian was inconsolable. 'How the hell did this happen?' he asked, shaking with tears.

A nurse informed him that Jinxie had tripped and hurt himself. She explained that his heart was not strong enough to take the trauma of the fall and the blow to his head that he received when he hit the trolley. The nurse could see that Christian was in shock, and she took him away to a waiting room, where she gave him some hot sweet tea and tried her best to comfort him. 'Are you his son?' she asked.

'No, but he always seemed like a father to me. He was my friend and my mentor. No one will ever be able to fill the gap he is going to leave in my life.'

Christian hung around the hospital for a few hours. He did not really know what to do, but the hospital staff was kind and helped him sort out the formalities. They gave him the names of some funeral directors, and Christian said that he would make the necessary arrangements.

When they asked him who Jinxie's next of kin was, he at first said that he did not have any, and then he corrected himself and said that he had a daughter. A nurse asked if Christian wanted to contact her, and he said that he would.

Christian was now not only filled with sorrow for the loss of his friend, but he was also filled with fear at what he would say to Julia.

How the hell was he going to tell her that her father had not died years ago in a car crash, but that he had in fact died today? Worse still, how on earth was he going to tell her that but for a cruel twist of fate, she would have met him at lunch today? Should he tell her that the pervert she had verbally abused was in fact her now dead father? And if he did tell her all of this, would she then want to see the body and freak out when she realised that it was in fact the man whom she had scolded a few days back?

The situation was truly ghastly. His friend was dead, and Jinxie's daughter, the current sole employee of ChrisTom Media, was going to be thrust into a pit of despair and confusion. *What a fucking hideous mess,* he thought. How was Julia going to react? Then she was going to work out that she had probably only got her job because the father she had never known was Christian's friend. Julia was going to need therapy after she discovered all the facts. The prospect of having to reveal them made Christian feel that he might require some counselling himself.

The hospital was not prepared for Christian to take away Jinxie's wallet and apartment keys despite his pleas; they insisted that his personal property could only be taken by his next of kin. This set up more complications in Christian's mind because Julia did not even share Jinxie's last name, so he doubted she would have much luck obtaining the possessions, either.

Christian knew that arrangements would have to be made for a funeral. How would he even be able to obtain approval for an undertaker to remove the body? How would he be able to get into Jinxie's flat to look through his address book and invite his friends to the funeral? How would he be able to settle Jinxie's affairs without any kind of authority, and with a next of kin that may not even be able to prove that she *was* next of kin?

He did not want to think it, but another big question also pushed its way into his mind. How was he going to bring out his magazine with all this going on? Then add the prospect of his one member of staff suffering an emotional crisis. It was a tragedy and a disaster rolled into one.

Then there was Siobhan. He had no idea how to contact her; all he knew was that she was going to be expecting to see Jinxie in the Pontevechio Restaurant just before 1.00 p.m., slightly ahead of Julia's arrival. He had no choice: he would have to go through with the lunch, but without the leading man. It was going to be like a scene from a very bizarre and emotionally uncomfortable play.

Christian looked at his watch: 12.35. He felt sick and panicked. He had no choice and had to get to the restaurant as soon as possible. He rushed out to the street and jumped into a taxi. The Saturday traffic was light, and ten minutes later he arrived at the restaurant.

But now a further complication struck him: how was he going to recognise Siobhan? Fate intervened. It did not actually give him a helping hand, but it neatly delivered the equivalent of a very unhelpful kick in the bollocks. Julia was early, and he watched transfixed, unable to move as he saw her approach what he guessed must be her mother. Christian stood rooted to the spot, staring through the window as he saw Julia stop by a table in the window and start to speak to the woman who bore a strong resemblance to Julia. He pulled himself together and sprinted into the restaurant, sliding past waiters and narrowly avoiding sending their balanced dishes flying.

'Ah, Christian, I would like you to meet my mother,' Julia said as he skidded to a halt by her side. 'Isn't it a coincidence that she should be about to have lunch in the same restaurant as us?'

Christian stammered, 'Er, well, not quite. Actually, to be precise, in a manner of speaking, it's no real coincidence . . . I need a drink.' Panic had a strange way of making people lose their command of language, and Christian was certainly in a panic. He managed to regain some of his composure, and with enormous willpower he tried to put enough words in the right order to persuade Julia to join him at Siobhan's table.

Siobhan was looking anxious. She was also feeling more than a little confused. She could not understand why James had not arrived with Christian. Had he lost his nerve, or was the hospital keeping him in for a bit longer? If either of the two were correct, then why hadn't he called her? She had made a point of giving him her phone number at the hospital.

Julia sat next to Christian as requested. She was desperate to know why Christian seemed nervous and unable to communicate properly; his eyes were also very red, as if he had been crying.

Christian signalled to the waiter by impersonating a human windmill, and it certainly had the desired effect. The waiter asked if they would like a menu and an aperitif, and Christian asked if they could just have three very large cognacs for the time being. The waiter could sense Christian's anxiety and made no sign that the request seemed odd; he simply went off and returned with the drinks within a very short space of time.

Both Siobhan and Julia were now becoming very anxious. Christian's behaviour seemed distinctly odd, and neither of them had wanted a cognac. Christian had still not spoken one word of explanation as he proceeded to drain his glass in one gulp.

Julia broke the silence first. 'Why are you in such a state, Christian? Why have you ordered us these brandies? And why are we having lunch with my mother?'

'Yes, yes, sorry. You do need an explanation—both of you, that is—but first I really think you should drink your brandies.'

Both women said that whatever the news, they did not wish to knock back a cognac. But Christian did, and he grabbed both of them and knocked them back one after the other, spilling half the contents of the last one down his shirt in his haste. He felt a bit more decisive now and asked Julia if she could do him an enormous favour and go for a walk round the block for fifteen minutes. She was surprised but eventually agreed and left Christian sitting alone with Siobhan.

'He's dead, Siobhan,' Christian blurted out.

After so much thinking time and cognac, it was a terrible opening line, and Siobhan was totally stunned. She did not cry, but, the shock registered in her face.

Christian explained the circumstances of Jinxie's tragic death whilst Siobhan listened in total silence. He did not spare her feelings and let her know what a terrible mistake that she had made by keeping Julia in the dark about her real father's existence for so long. Now it was too late. Jinxie had died without ever getting to know his daughter, and Siobhan had robbed him of this opportunity. She had denied her daughter the chance to know her father.

She knew she had done wrong, and this more than anything made her start to cry. The tears ran down her face, streaking her make-up and bouncing off the table, but she did not utter a single word.

The waiter, a sensitive soul by nature, arrived at the table with two large cognacs, as if he possessed the powers of telepathy. This time Siobhan drank the warming liquid as she tried to inhale the fumes to clear her senses.

The fifteen minutes elapsed, and Julia took her place again at the table. 'Is this some odd tradition of yours, Christian, for new recruits? You invite them to lunch with their mother and then proceed to drink like a maniac and make their mother cry?'

No one laughed, and Julia regretted her quip. She simply wanted someone to tell her what was going on. Just when she expected Christian to explain, her mother spoke.

'Oh Julia, I have done something really terrible, and I beg you to forgive me.'

For one terrible moment, Julia thought her mother was going to confess to having had a long and steamy affair with Christian. Well, if she wanted forgiveness for that, no bloody chance—even if her mother had persuaded Christian to give Julia a job.

Siobhan spoke as the tears rolled down her face, and she started to bite her lip in fear of Julia's reaction. It was Julia's turn to be silent as her mother told her the whole story. Julia was too shocked to react at first; it was too much to take in. She was stunned that for all these years, her mother had prevented her from knowing about or seeing her real father, who until this morning had still been alive.

Christian took up the story and told her how Jinxie had been desperate to meet her, and how he had watched her from a distance as she was growing up. He told her how he had recently followed her and that he was indeed the man that she had mistaken for a pervert. Christian even admitted that he had given her the job because of Jinxie—but that Christian was delighted to have her working for him. Then he told her how her father had died all dressed up in a new suit, in anticipation of meeting the daughter he had always wanted to meet.

Julia exploded and rose from the table, her face filled with rage. 'You total bloody bitch!' she screamed at her mother. She grabbed the glass of cognac that Christian had failed to down and threw the contents into her mother's face. The whole restaurant went silent as she stormed out to the street.

'Go after her, Christian—she needs you now. She is not going to speak with me for some time. Help her, please,' Siobhan said. Christian never heard the rest of the sentence because he was already on his feet and chasing after Julia.

Julia raced down the road, and as Christian set off in pursuit, he could feel the cognac trying to make a break for freedom as it burned its way back up his throat and into his mouth. He gulped it back, and to his horror it was a lot hotter the second time it went down. Christian was surprised at how fast Julia was running, and although he had always fancied himself as a good runner, he was not convinced that he was going to catch her. She did not look back, but Christian was sure that she was aware that he was in pursuit, as she seemed to be trying to run even faster.

After about ten minutes Christian was at last beginning to gain on her, but if she continued much longer, he was convinced that he would have to stop to be sick. As Julia turned a corner and stepped off of a curb, she lost her balance and flew forward in to the middle of the road. Luckily there was no traffic coming, and by the time she had raised herself to her feet, Christian was standing next to her.

Julia had torn her dress. Her arms, knees, and hands were all grazed, but she seemed more upset about the dress than her injuries, and Christian guessed that she must have bought it for their lunch today. Ironic, really—father and daughter would have both met today for the first time kitted out in new outfits that they ended up spoiling.

She was angry with Christian and asked him if she still had a job now that the father she never knew was dead. He told her not to be foolish because he was really pleased to have her as his one and only member of staff. Julia asked him why he had not had the decency to tell her who her father was, and Christian explained that he had only known for a few days. The whole purpose of today's lunch was to inform her.

Julia swore that she was never going to speak to her mother again, and then finally her lip quivered, and she broke down in tears. She looked like a helpless child with her torn dress, her grazes, and her flood of tears. Christian pulled her towards him and hugged her, and she did not resist. She buried her head in his chest and sobbed. They stood there for some minutes, and then Christian suggested that they take a walk.

They walked for hours, eventually finding themselves walking through Hyde Park. Julia wanted to learn as much as possible about the father she had never known, and Christian was happy to furnish her with as much as he knew about Jinxie. Talking about Jinxie helped Christian with his own grief, and he was surprised at how much information he was able to tell her about Jinxie's life.

Christian had never realised before just how much information that Jinxie had confided in him; even Julia was surprised at how much

Christian knew about her father. She was particularly surprised at how Christian was able to tell her about Jinxie and her mother, and she was deeply touched when Christian suggested that Jinxie must have shopped for a new outfit to meet Julia today.

Julia wished she had not been denied the chance of knowing her father. He sounded like a great character, and she was sure that she was never going to forgive her mother for her selfish deceit. Although Christian had felt that Siobhan had been totally wrong, he wanted Julia to feel better, so, he did his best to explain Julia's mother's reasons for keeping Jinxie's existence a secret.

Christian went on to explain how Julia's mother did regret keeping Jinxie away from Julia, and her presence at today's lunch was her attempt to right some of the wrong. Julia was not impressed and continued to insist that her mother had acted unforgivably.

Suddenly Christian woke up to the fact that someone needed to do something about getting in touch with an undertaker. They could not leave Jinxie lying there in the hospital. Christian explained to Julia that they needed to find a way of proving that she was Jinxie's next of kin. He suggested that she contact her mother to help them, but Julia refused. Instead, she gave Christian the phone number and told him that she expected her mother would have returned home by now, and that he should call her.

Christian went to a call box. He felt uncomfortable making the call, but he did it. Siobhan answered the phone immediately; she must have been sitting by the phone and hoping that Julia would call. She questioned Christian straight away about Julia, wanting to know if Julia was okay. Siobhan asked to speak with Julia, and Christian tried to coax her to the phone, but Julia refused.

Siobhan was upset but understood. When Christian asked if she had any details that could prove that Jinxie was Julia's father, she said yes, but she wanted to know for what reason he needed them. Christian explained, and so Siobhan agreed to meet him at the hospital within an hour.

Fifty minutes later all three were together at the hospital. Julia glared at her mother and refused to communicate with her. They went through the formalities, and Siobhan produced Julia's birth certificate, with mother Siobhan Daley and father James Jinks. Julia was furious— why had her mother told her that she had lost the birth certificate? No wonder her mother had offered to deal with her passport application when she was a teenager.

They eventually completed the formalities and obtained a death certificate. The hospital agreed to release Jinxie's possessions and permission to instruct an undertaker to collect the body. Siobhan left them at this point, with Julia still refusing to talk to her. Christian promised that he would call Siobhan about the funeral, and Julia said she was surprised that her mother was interested.

The afternoon was drawing to a close, and Christian was anxious to contact an undertaker; he could not bear to think of Jinxie continuing to lie in the hospital mortuary. He decided not to contact the undertakers that the hospital had suggested—instead, he decided to go off to Gloucester Road to find the nearest undertaker to Jinxie's flat. Somehow it seemed more fitting to choose an undertaker from near where Jinxie lived. He could not explain why, but it seemed a more personal touch.

Some forty minutes later, after the cab journey and walking round some side streets, they found an undertaker. Inside they discussed the arrangements for the funeral. The funeral director asked Christian if he was the son of the bereaved, and for the second time that day he explained that he was not, but that Jinxie had seemed at times like a father to him. He told him that Julia was the daughter of the deceased. The funeral director said he was sorry for her loss, and Julia just accepted the comment, although her real sorrow was that she had never been able to know her father.

The funeral director asked Julia if the deceased had wished to be buried or cremated, and Julia looked across at Christian for help. Christian hesitated, but then he said, 'Cremated.' They set the day for the funeral to be Tuesday; it was probably enough days away for them to go to Jinxie's apartment and leaf through his address book to phone up all his friends.

They left the funeral parlour, and Julia asked if Christian could take her to Jinxie's apartment, because she wanted to see how he had lived. Christian was a bit nervous about this because he was not sure if Jinxie's years of being a widower would have made him particularly house proud. He knew that Jinxie lived just off the Gloucester Road, but he had to check the contents of his wallet to find an address. He had known Jinxie for years, but he had never seen where the man had lived.

After some minutes and asking some shopkeepers, they worked out the address location and found themselves climbing up a few flights of stairs, because the old brass cage lift, elegant as it was, did not seem to be working. As they walked up the stairs Julia asked Christian why he had told the funeral director that her father wished to be cremated. Christian admitted that at first when the question had been asked and Julia looked to him for help, he did not have a clue. But then a voice inside his head from a lunch long ago at the Wig and Pen club said, 'Dior, dear boy, promise me that when I finally leave this world, you will make sure that I am cremated. I want my ashes sprinkled from the top of the Mirror Building in the direction of Fleet Street, so that the wind may take my remains once more through the street where I spent the greater part of my life plying my trade.'

Julia was touched by what Christian said. She touched his arm and said, 'Christian, you are the only person who can tell me about my father. Please help me through this.'

Christian told her not to be daft, because she could count on him to paint the picture of the man that he had loved and now missed very much.

They entered the apartment, and to Christian's pleasant surprise it looked very neat and presentable. They wandered around the few rooms for a short time, and then Christian settled himself down at a desk, where the telephone sat in the corner of the sitting room. There he found Jinxie's telephone address book as he had hoped. He put it in his pocket and planned to call the few entries in it the next day, to tell them about the funeral.

Julia was looking at the photographs around the room, and then she started to cry again because she noticed a gallery of shots of her, from a small child to quite recently, laid out across the top shelf of a bookcase. Christian comforted her again, although right now he also felt in desperate need of comfort for the loss of his old friend.

Christian hoped that the funeral director had kept to his promise to collect the body that evening; he did not want to spend tonight thinking of Jinxie's body in the cold hospital mortuary. He telephoned to check and was advised that a car had already left with Julia's signed authorisation to collect the deceased. Christian was relieved and suggested that they leave the apartment, because there was nothing more to be done tonight.

Both of them were in need of something to eat, and Christian also felt he needed a drink or two to steady his nerves.

* * *

Mike Tyler also felt he needed a drink to steady his nerves. He had spent most of the day at the police station, having agreed to go there of his own free will to answer some questions. He felt that he had no choice because the police may come calling at Lancaster Publishing later in the week. Mike had given them Jason's full name so they could also collect him.

Mike was advised that both he and Jason were suspected of causing the disturbance at Moriarty's on Friday night. If proven, they would be charged with a number of offences that could include disturbance of the peace and incitement to riot. Neither of them asked about having a solicitor present because they were told that they were not being charged at this point in the investigation. As the day drew to a close, Sergeant Wilson sat with Mike himself.

'It is only a matter of time before we are able to find some evidence linking you and your colleague to last night's disturbance, Mr Tyler. You may think that the events of yesterday evening were one big practical joke, but a lot of people could have been seriously hurt, and furthermore the damage to the public house is considerable.'

'Sergeant, I am sure that a number of people would love to lay the blame on me for what took place yesterday, but I can assure you that I am not in the habit of indulging in such childish pranks as you have described to me today. I have been totally cooperative with you and your colleagues, and when you finally catch the culprits, I do expect you to make a full apology to me for spoiling my weekend.'

'Mr Tyler, one thing you can be very sure of is that if I am not able to link you with the events of yesterday evening, then I will be amazed, and you shall have your apology. However, I would like to warn you that if you admit responsibility for last night's chaos now, it will be a lot easier for you than if I am able to prove your involvement at a later date.'

Mike was scared, but he did not show it. He simply repeated that he was surprised at the groundless suggestions and looked forward to having his apology.

When Mike finally got back to his apartment, he was also in need of a stiff drink.

*   *   *

Jason sat alone in his flat and knocked back some scotch. He had been very badly shaken by the experience and was starting to wonder if his faith in Mike was misplaced. He had stuck by Mike at the police station and said that he had nothing to do with the chaos at the pub. However, it struck him for the first time what a foolish and dangerous set of events they had put into operation the night before.

Jason reflected on his last few days. He had suffered his most chronic dose of the shits in his entire life on Thursday night, he had contributed to causing a considerable number of people to having a truly appalling evening on Friday, and he had spent most of Saturday terrified out of his wits answering questions in a police station. He had made his mind up: he was no longer going to be Mike Tyler's willing accomplice—it was too dangerous for his future liberty, his nerves, and his stomach.

*   *   *

Christian and Julia took the tube to Ealing and walked to the Grange pub. It was a nice evening, and they sat out in the bar garden, ordered some food, and had a few much-needed drinks. They attracted a few strange looks as Julia sat there in her torn dress with her cuts and bruises visible from her earlier fall, but neither of them seemed to notice.

Julia was still keen to find out more information about her father, and Christian was happy to oblige because it seemed to help him keep Jinxie alive in his mind by telling as much as he knew about the old man's life. Time passed quickly, and before they knew it the bar was calling last orders. They ordered a last drink, and then it struck Christian that Julia was going to have to make her way home soon, and he was concerned about her going home on her own in her current state.

'Julia, this is not a pick-up line or anything, but I think you should spend the night at my place. I can sleep on the sofa, and you can take my bed.'

Julia was tired and did not relish the prospect of travelling home on her own. She did not want to inconvenience Christian, so at first she said she was fine, but eventually she gratefully agreed to stay over.

They walked to Christian's flat and bought some milk from a late-night store on the way back, because Christian had remembered that he had polished off all the milk that morning. When they arrived,

Christian made some coffee. He could see that Julia looked very tired, and he suggested that he show her to his bedroom and find her one of his shirts to wear in bed. She was very tired and was happy to agree.

Julia stood at the entrance to the bedroom while Christian looked in his wardrobe for a shirt. She noticed a picture of a black tie dinner, with Christian sitting next to what she guessed must be her father; the man bore a strong resemblance to the man that she had accused of being a pervert a few days back. Julia wanted to get a closer look and walked towards the picture, which was positioned close to wardrobe. As she walked forward and stared at the picture, she stubbed her toe on the edge of the wardrobe, lost her balance and fell forward.

Christian turned straight away to catch her, but as he did, she fell too fast and caught her right eyebrow on his lip, which sent both of them crashing to the ground. Julia's head had caused Christian to split his lip on his teeth, and Christian's teeth had caused a gash above Julia's eye. They were both bleeding quite a bit and had no choice but to call a mini cab and to go to Ealing Hospital. They sat for hours amongst the Saturday night drunks and druggies before Julia could get stitched up. Christian was okay because his lip had stopped bleeding, but, he was disturbed by insinuations from people in the hospital that he had caused Julia's injuries. Most people assumed that he and Julia were married and that, following a night out and lots of booze, they had concluded their evening with an argument, and that he had become physically aggressive with her. Her torn dress, cuts, and bruises and the wound above her eye certainly made it look that way. Christian was developing a strong aversion to hospitals. He had spent a lot of the last few days in them in unpleasant circumstances, and he hoped that this would be his last visit to one for some time.

*   *   *

Mike Tyler was developing a strong aversion to toilets. His nerves, lack of food, and the scotch he had consumed that evening had played havoc with his delicate stomach. Mike was now sitting for his eighth time that night passing hot liquid, and he was sure that he was developing piles. If he continued at this rate, he would end up being hospitalised with a very serious bottom disorder, and one of the few things that he and Christian shared in common was that he was not particularly keen on hospitals.

CHAPTER 16

CHRISTIAN WOKE UP quite early on Sunday morning; he had not slept well because he had spent most of the night thinking about Jinxie. He felt really miserable and already missed his friend.

He could not hear any sounds of Julia stirring, so he took a walk round the corner and bought some things for breakfast. Christian filled his basket with eggs, bacon, sausages, baked beans, white stodgy bread, and some butter. Ten minutes later he was back in the kitchen frying up the bacon and drinking a much-needed cup of coffee.

Julia appeared in the kitchen doorway looking groggy. Christian noticed her; she looked quite sweet standing there in one of his old shirts. He turned his eyes back to his frying—he felt guilty, and he should not be having any impure thoughts about her. What was happening to him? He had just split up with Lizzie and had just lost one of his dearest friends, but now he was eyeing up his only employee who was also Jinxie's daughter. Christian was ashamed of himself.

'Dress up, Julia. Breakfast will be ready in five minutes,' he said very formally to cover his shame.

Julia, still half-asleep, obediently went off in search of the bathroom. Under different circumstances the scene she had just seen of Christian cooking up some breakfast for her would have been one of her fantasies and would have delighted her. One week ago it was her dearest wish to find herself about to have breakfast with Christian after spending the night in his flat.

They ate breakfast in silence, and then Christian suggested that they go through Jinxie's address book and try to phone people about the funeral. The funeral director had booked the crematorium while

Christian and Julia were with him the day before. The time for the funeral would be 11.20 a.m. on Tuesday.

Julia was a bit drowsy throughout the morning and made occasional cups of tea. Christian did his best to make his way through the address book. There were not a lot of entries, and some of those he called stated that the person he was after had moved away years ago. Christian was growing despondent—he did not want Jinxie to end up with a sad send-off with a tiny gathering.

As he came towards the back end of the book under the letter Q, he came to an entry that read, 'Quackers (Gordon Duck).' Christian had always wondered what Quackers' real name was. He had met Quackers a few times in the Wig and Pen club. Like Jinxie, Quackers was a great character full of interesting stories and good humour.

Christians dialled the number, and it rang for at least fifteen rings. Just as Christian was about to give up and put the phone down, a very deep and hoarse voice answered, followed by a long, coughing fit. 'Gordon Duck speaking. To whom do I owe this pleasure of an interruption to my lunch preparations?'

Christian remembered that Quackers was also a widower like Jinxie, but somehow he imagined that he was a little less domesticated. 'Quakers, it's Christian, Jinxie's friend.'

'Good God, Christian, how on earth did you get my number? And why on earth are you calling me on a Sunday morning? I hope Jinxie is not still in that wretched hospital.'

'No, Quackers, he is no longer in the hospital. I am really sorry to tell you that he passed away yesterday morning.'

There was silence on the line for a few moments and Christian hoped that he had not given Quackers a heart attack. Christian had always thought that Quackers looked as if he was about to cough himself into an early grave. Quackers eventually responded, and the shock clearly registered in his voice as he asked what had happened. Christian did his best to explain the details of the tragic accident. Quackers was greatly saddened by the loss of his old friend—and he also very aware of his own sense of mortality. He commented that he was one of the last of the old guard left in Fleet Street, and he was sure that his end was coming soon.

Christian felt sorry for Quackers, but he did his best to get him to focus on the task ahead: ensure that Jinxie had a decent turnout for his funeral. Quackers told him not to worry—he would guarantee that there was a good representation from the gentlemen of the press.

'Christian did he ever tell you that he wanted his ashes sprinkled from the top of the Mirror Building?'

'Yes, he did, but I have no idea how we can pull this off for him.'

'Leave that one to me. I propose that following the cremation, we adjourn to the Wig and Pen club with a small group of the faithful, where we shall eat heartily and then drink as many toasts as possible in fond farewell to Jinxie. We shall drink long into the evening, and when we have consumed enough to have truly honoured Jinxie's life, we shall go to the roof of the Mirror Building. I am very friendly with one of the evening security officers, so there will be no problem getting everyone in. Once on the roof we, shall open some bottles I have been saving of some of the finest malt whisky, and we shall fill our glasses. You, dear boy, will say a few well-chosen words, and then I shall take the urn and sprinkle the ashes of my great friend into the night sky.'

Christian agreed to the plan and thanked Quackers for helping him to organise the perfect send-off for Jinxie. He then told Julia about the plan, and she seemed a little less convinced that it was a good idea, but nevertheless she had to admit that Christian was far more likely to know what her father would have wished.

Julia and Christian walked to the tube station, and he told her to take the rest of the week off. Julia said she needed to work to take her mind off the loss of the father she had never known. She also did not want to dwell even more on the wrong that she felt her mother had done.

Julia walked off in to the tube station, and Christian headed off back home. He had one more promise that he had to keep for Jinxie, and this was going to be the hardest one of all. Christian sat in his living room, drinking endless cups of coffee and trying to write his farewell to his friend. There could be no humour in this poem, only sadness, because for once in his life he was compelled to write something decent.

The time dragged slowly leading up to Jinxie's funeral, but Christian buried himself in his work and finished the Whitstop story. It lacked the power in the words that he had hoped for, but he was certain that the story was good enough to provide the power to sell his magazine on the bookstalls.

Tom managed to bring in some more advertising revenue, but it was not a lot. They were very lucky that Julia had secured a brilliant deal with her friends printing firm. Julia decided not to take any time off and worked on the production of the magazine to get it ready for print. Billy took up Christian's offer and turned up for work at the office, helping Julia as best he could as he tried to learn the ropes. The magazine was making good progress, and it seemed that they would probably be able to go to print on Thursday.

Tuesday morning finally came, and only Christian and Julia followed the coffin in a black car from the funeral directors. Neither spoke as they made their slow and painful way to the crematorium. On arrival they were met by Quackers and a small group of what must have been Jinxie's friends. Christian was disappointed: it was a very small turnout for a man who had lived such a full and interesting life. He had hoped that Quackers would rally a few more people, and he was starting to wonder if there was much hope of Jinxie getting to have his wish of having his ashes sprinkled from the top of the Mirror Building.

Christian had visited Jinxie's flat again late on the Sunday night, and he had discovered that Jinxie was Church of England from an ancient marriage certificate in a box of papers. He had visited a church near to Jinxie's apartment, and a vicar had agreed to say some words at the cremation despite the late notice and other commitments. He had asked Christian if he was Jinxie's son, and Christian began to wonder how many more times he would have to explain things before he just lied and said yes.

The small band filed into the crematorium chapel as the pallbearers took Jinxie's coffin in and placed it on the covered rollers in front of the back wall. Christian stood at the front with Julia and Quackers as the vicar delivered a short speech about Jinxie's life from the notes that Christian had given him the previous day. The vicar asked them to stand and sing a hymn about a green hill far away without a city wall, and then they all sat down again as Christian was signalled to come up and say a few words. He had told Julia on Monday that Jinxie had asked him to write something for his funeral, and that he had spent most of Sunday trying to come up with something worthy of his friend.

Christian rose to his feet and made his way to the lectern. He spoke with affection about Jinxie and recounted some funny and some sensitive stories of how Jinxie had mentored him. He spoke of his sadness for Julia at losing her father before she had even had the chance of finding him. Then he delivered a piece of poetry. It was not his own composition, but it was one that he knew was a personal favourite of his departed mentor.

> Under the wide and starry sky
> Dig the grave and let me lie:
> Glad did I live and gladly die
> And I laid me down with a will
> This be the verse you grave for me:
> Here he lies where he long'd to be;
> Home is the sailor, home from the sea,
> And the hunter home from the hill.****

Christian explained that Jinxie loved poetry, and this was one of his favourite pieces. Julia guessed that Christian had not been able to find the confidence to deliver his own words, and she cried for her father and for Christian's loss of a friend and mentor.

Christian stepped down from the lectern, and the vicar asked them all to join him in Psalm 23, the Lord's Prayer. He told them that Christian had said that whilst Jinxie could not be described as a particularly religious man, he was deeply fond of Psalm 23 and felt that it was one of the most beautiful pieces ever written. They all bowed their heads and recited.

> The Lord is my shepherd; I shall not want.
> He maketh me to lie down in green pastures,
> He leadeth me beside the still waters.
> He restoreth my soul.
> He leadeth me in the paths of righteousness for his name's sake.
> Yea, though I walk through the valley of the shadow of death,

I will fear no evil.

> For thou art with me,
> Thy rod and thy staff they comfort me.
> Thou preparest a table before me in the presence of mine enemies.
> Thou anointest my head with oil,

**** Taken from *Requiem* by Robert Louis Stevenson.

And my cup runneth over.
Surely goodness and mercy shall follow me all the days of my life.
And I will dwell in the house of the Lord for ever and ever.
Amen.*

* Psalm 23 known as The Lord's Prayer.

By the end of the prayer, everyone was crying gentle, silent tears as they stared at the coffin. As the coffin slid away, an instrumental version of what Jinxie had told Christian he thought to be a very fine piece of modern music played in the background. It was 'Waterloo Sunset' by the Kinks, and it really did seem to be the right choice for the occasion. As the music played and the coffin slid out of view, Christian was finally aware that Jinxie was never going to share his wonderful stories with him ever again.

Julia hugged Christian as he shook with tears and grief, and Quackers wrapped his arms around both of them. They signed the book of remembrance and stood outside for some time, talking with the small group of mourners. Christian thanked the vicar, and after some time Julia signed for the ashes to be placed in an urn; it was agreed that she could collect the urn at the end of the day. She had told the crematorium that she was leaving for the United States the next morning for good, and so she was allowed to collect the ashes early. They had offered to courier them to her, but she insisted that she wanted to take them with her today.

Julia had not wanted to join the people at the Wig and Pen; she wanted time on her own. However, she agreed that she would collect the ashes at the end of the day and deliver them to Christian at the Wig and Pen in the early evening.

Christian, Quackers, and two of the other mourners headed off to the Wig and Pen, and before leaving Christian gave Julia a peck on the cheek and asked her if she was going to be okay. She told him not to worry and told him to make sure that he and Quackers did not get too drunk.

In the car, Quackers said that Jinxie would be pleased to know that his daughter had taken up with Christian. Christian had spent the last five days trying to tell people that he was not Jinxie's son, and now life was getting even more complicated. He found himself having to explain that he was not dating Jinxie's daughter.

On arrival at the Wig and Pen, Quackers was greeted by a large number of people who had all come to honour Jinxie in the place that they had clearly felt was most appropriate. It was a good turnout, with well over thirty people there. Most were either journalists or retired journalists, and all had some good stories to tell about Jinxie.

Christian wondered why Lord Whitstop had not come. Christian had called him and invited him to the crematorium and to the Wig and Pen, but the old man had not shown up at either. When Christian had called, Whitstop had been genuinely shocked and saddened, and Christian had been sure that he would come.

The mourners took their tables, and all had steak and kidney pud in memory of Jinxie's favourite fare. They consumed vast quantities of red wine and then moved on to malt whiskies to toast the passing of a great man. Many got to their feet and told some excellent stories, many of which Christian had never heard before.

Then Quackers stood up somewhat unsteadily and told a very funny tale. He reminisced how he and Jinxie had gate-crashed a *Daily Mirror* sports celebrity party and laced all the drinks, causing numerous well-known football players to clash with a load of darts players in a massive food fight during the speeches. They had managed to get a colleague to run a headline in the next day's paper that Jinxie had dreamed up during the party: 'Footies and Fatties in Frenzied Food Fight Fiasco'.

Far from being a sad afternoon, it was one of good humour and fond memories, and Christian knew that this is how Jinxie would have wanted it.

*   *   *

Not far away, Mike Tyler was enjoying the launch party for *Alpha Male*. The magazine had arrived in the newsagents that morning as planned, and the response to it was very good. Lancaster Publishing had organised a launch party at the Savoy to coincide with the appearance of the publication in the newsagents.

The guest list had included a large number of top advertising agency directors, as well as a large number of senior marketing staff from leading brand names in men's fashion, fragrances, watches, cars, and other businesses that either had already decided to advertise or could advertise in the magazine in the future. Mike had given a pre-lunch presentation that had gone very well, and he was now enjoying standing in the centre of the room having his hand shaken constantly by guests congratulating him on the success of the publication.

Christian was blissfully unaware that Lancaster Publishing had beaten him to getting their magazine produced first. At that moment it was true that ignorance was bliss. Mike was overjoyed: his publication had received an excellent reaction, and he knew that he had done what he said he would do—he had managed to beat Christian.

Mike was certainly going to celebrate today; he had earned it. He had proven that he was an excellent publisher and that he was a better man than Christian. He was also feeling randy; one of his guests, Linda Chance, had been sitting at his table over lunch and constantly smiling at him. Mike was certain that if he played his cards right, he was certainly going to be shagging the lovely Linda later on that night.

*   *   *

Just after 7.00 p.m., Julia arrived at the Wig and Pen with the urn containing Jinxie's ashes. She had felt very odd travelling across town with the urn; it had been a weird experience, holding in her hands a pot containing the remains of the father she had never known.

A small group was left drinking with Christian and Quackers, and she could tell that they had consumed a lot of alcohol during their afternoon session. She handed the urn to Christian and asked him if he was seriously going to scatter the ashes from the top of the Mirror Building. He told her that he felt it was his duty to fulfil Jinxie's wish, and everything had been arranged. Christian asked her to stay for a drink, but she declined.

Christian stowed away the urn behind the bar and ordered another round of drinks. He told of how he had first met Jinxie and how he had so often confided in him like a father. Christian recalled that when he had first left Lancaster Publishing, he told Jinxie that he was concerned that Mike Tyler would try to spoil his new magazine venture, and that he was sure that Tyler would try to blacken his reputation in publishing circles. He recalled Jinxie's words.

'Dior, dear boy, if that idiot ever tries to blacken your reputation, I shall blacken his face.'

Christian told his fellow mourners, 'Funny, really, to think of old Jinxie trying to take on Mike Tyler, but you know I do believe that if he had ever thought Tyler was trying to hurt me, he would have done it.'

*   *   *

Mike Tyler had not been wrong about Linda Chance—she was certainly keen because she immediately agreed to have a few drinks with him after the launch party. He suggested Knights Bar in Simpsons on the Strand, and she agreed that it was an excellent choice. Knights Bar was not far from the Savoy, and by coincidence it was quite close to the Wig and Pen. Knights Bar was smart and swanky, the perfect setting for Mike to continue his seduction of Linda, who certainly seemed very up for it. She had told him that she had an apartment in the Barbican Centre, which was not far away, so he was sure that if he plied her with enough cocktails, she would invite him back for a nightcap.

Mike laid on the charm to a level that would have made most people eject the contents of their stomachs, but Linda seemed to enjoy every moment of it. By the end of the evening, he started to solicit an invitation for a nightcap with as much subtlety as a dog having a pee against a tree, but Linda simply seemed captivated by Mike's shallow conversation. He told her how much he had always wanted to look inside one of the flats at the Barbican, and without hesitation she suggested he come back for a last drink.

Mike wanted to take a taxi, but Linda said that she loved walking in London late at night and insisted that they walk to her apartment. This was frustrating for Mike because he could not wait to get her back to her flat to try to worm his way into her bed. Linda wanted to be romantic and linked arms with Mike as they strolled along the Strand. Mike decided to make the best of it and smiled sweetly at her, and she squeezed his arm affectionately. *Well, it is going to be a bloody long walk, but I am definitely on for shag,* he thought.

*   *   *

Meanwhile, Christian, Quackers, and the last of the hardened drinkers had made it onto the roof of the Mirror Building, with a warning from Quackers friend in security not to make too much of a bloody racket or he would get the chop. They gathered on the roof with some bottles of aged malt whisky that Quackers had been saving. The Wig and Pen had given them some glasses for the whisky, and Quackers now poured out some generous measures to toast their dearly departed friend. They were already extremely inebriated, but that was not going to stop them raising a few more glasses in honour of Jinxie.

Christian now felt more confident about reciting the poem he had prepared. He had not had the confidence to say it at the crematorium for fear that people would laugh at his literary efforts. But now his audience was very drunk, and in their current state they would probably applaud the recital of a baked beans commercial.

Christian told them that he had promised Jinxie to write a poem in his honour, and he now proposed to read it out loud as his parting tribute to the great man. As expected they all cheered and urged him to read it, and so with his confidence boosted he started.

Mentor

I was his moth.
He was my flame.
       In his light I shall remain.

I loved his stories,
       For they were gold,
     Fondly said and freely told.

He filled my soul,
He gave me sight.
     He touched my heart with rays of light.
His body gone,
He lives no more.
But in my mind his words endure.[*****]

The audience all stood with watery eyes as Quackers praised Christian's words. 'He would have been proud of you, my boy. Jinxie always said that there was a poet inside of you.'

*****   Poem Mentor by Geoff Dickinson

Quackers raised his glass and toasted Christian, and then he told Christian that it was time to let Jinxie's soul take flight along Fleet Street. They moved to the back of the building to face the direction of Fleet Street and the Thames. The wind was blowing from behind them, and therefore the direction was perfect.

Quackers suggested that Christian should be the one to empty the ashes into the sky as Quackers said a few well-chosen words. Despite the chill at the top of the building, they all had a warm feeling inside from their special ceremony—and of course from the whisky.

*   *   *

Down below, Mike Tyler was getting a warm feeling in his groin. Mike and Linda had stopped in the doorway of an office building on New Fetter Lane. They were a few hundred yards away, down the road from the Mirror Building. Linda was planting passionate kisses on Mike's lips, and he was sure it was going to be a great night. She was very drunk and getting very amorous and romantic. Suddenly she pulled away from him and gazed dreamily up at the stars above. Mike was not big on romance but figured he should stare up in to the sky as well, to keep her thinking he was a sensitive soul.

*   *   *

Up above, Quackers was finishing his speech, which Christian took as his signal to start pouring out the ashes.

> And now, Jinxie, we say farewell
> As your ashes take their flight.
> And as your spirit heads for Fleet Street,
> So we say goodnight.
>
> And as you fly in to the wind,
> So we say farewell . . .

Christian started to pour out Jinxie's ashes as Quackers words rang out into the night. Suddenly the wind seemed to drop down, and the ashes fell like a stone, only travelling a small distance forward but descending fast.

*   *   *

Mike stared dreamily in to the heavens, sure in the knowledge that this would further guarantee his chances of getting into Linda's pants. He looked like a crazed evangelist preacher as he stared beaming into the sky above. There he was, the perfect target—and Jinxie's ashes hit him full in the face.

'Fucking bollocks, what the shit was that? My eyes are fucking burning!' yelped Mike as he furiously tried to rub away the huge cloud of black dust that had mysteriously flown into his face. He flapped around in agony, unable to see whilst Linda stared at him in amazement.

'Mike, you are spoiling the moment,' she whined.

'Shut up, you stupid fucking bitch! I'm in bloody agony over here.'

'Fuck you!' she said, and she stormed off, leaving him stumbling around half blind with pain shooting through his eyeballs.

*   *   *

Up on the roof, Quackers was feeling very emotional. 'Jinxie would have been proud that we have given him the perfect send-off, and now his ashes are exactly where he would have wanted them to be.'

*   *   *

And Quackers was absolutely right.

Mike staggered away rubbing at his blackened face, wondering what kind of an evil bastard throws a huge load of black dust into a man's face.

And so it was that Jinxie really had managed to blacken Mike Tyler's face.

CHAPTER 17

CHRISTIAN WONDERED IF one ever got used to having hangovers. He seemed to be having them almost every day lately. Funny—really he never seemed to suffer too badly from them a few years back. Either his resistance was weakening, or he was drinking a lot more than usual.

It had been a good send-off for Jinxie, and despite Christian's sadness, he was pleased that it had all gone as Jinxie would have wanted. He looked at his watch; it was 9.10 a.m. He was going to get to the office very late once again.

Tom, Julia, and Billy were already hard at work. They had expected Christian to be late; they knew that Jinxie's funeral day was going to be a major drinking spree. The magazine was nearly finished, and they knew that they should be able to get it to the printer on Thursday. Lizzie rang and asked to speak to Christian, but Julia said that he was not in yet, so she asked to speak to Tom.

'What do you think of Lancaster Publishing's *Alpha Male*?' she asked.

'Why do you ask? Have you seen an advance copy, Lizzie?'

'Tom, where have you been? The magazine went on sale yesterday— they even had a launch party at the Savoy.'

'Oh shit! Christian will be mortified.'

An hour later, Christian arrived at the office. Upon hearing the news, he was indeed mortified. How could he have let it happen? He had taken too much time to produce the magazine, and now Lancaster Publishing would take all the credit for a breakthrough in the magazine industry. No one would see his title as original or groundbreaking when it finally appeared. People would think that he had copied Lancaster Publishing, when in fact they had actually copied *his* idea.

When he heard that they'd even had a major launch party, he felt really sick. He could just imagine Mike Tyler strutting around and taking handshakes of congratulations with a smug, self-satisfied, cheesy grin on his face. He bet Mike was sitting in his office right now with a huge smile.

*   *   *

Mike Tyler *was* sitting in his office, but he was grimacing and staring up at the ceiling as he put some eye drops into his red and painful eyes. He would love to find the bastard that had nearly blinded him last night. He bet it was either some lazy office cleaner emptying a Hoover bag out of a window, or a bunch of stupid kids having some moronic fun. He was going to try to find out who it was at some point, and by God he was going to get his revenge.

His shit list of people destined for evil retribution was growing. Not only had some bastard fucked up his eyes, but he had lost his chance of shagging Linda Chance.

Mike was in a foul mood, so he decided to send Christian a fax to cheer himself up.

Attention: Christian Davidson

Dear Christian,

How does it feel to come second? Actually, correction. How does it feel to fail? Bad luck, Toss Pot. No girlfriend, no magazine, no future, no hope.
See you around, loser.

From your pal, Mike

Mike felt better after sending the fax.

*   *   *

Christian was predictably upset by Mike's fax. He wished he could talk to Jinxie. He smiled at the memory of Jinxie saying that he would blacken Mike's face—always highly unlikely, and now totally impossible. Anyway, it was a nice thought from Jinxie even if it was never going to happen.

Julia walked into his office with a cup of coffee for him. 'Looks like you need this,' she said.

Christian looked up at Julia, and now that he thought about it, she did bear a slight resemblance to Jinxie in some of her features. 'We lost the race, Julia, and there are no prizes for coming in second.'

'Christian, stop feeling sorry for yourself. I bought you a copy of *Alpha Male*. It's good, but there are no really big stories in it. We have a sensational story, and when our magazine hits the bookstalls, it will outsell Lancaster's by ten to one, just you wait and see'.

'True, our cover story is good, but I so very much wanted to be the first; it meant a lot to me. I wanted to bring out something new. I wanted to be remembered for having created a new sector in consumer publishing.'

'Christian, you are too young to start thinking about how you are going to be remembered. You are not about to retire, and I am pretty sure that you are not about to die on us. You have a lot of your career ahead of you, and there is still time to leave your mark on the publishing world. Mike Tyler is determined to beat you, and if you let his fax get to you, then yes, he has won. We have a busy day ahead of us. We need to go through the designs and page layouts that the team at our magazine designer, Grafix D Sign, has come up with. I suggest all of us get together and start to go through everything now.'

Julia was right, and there was no sense in arguing. The best medicine was to get on with the job in hand. His magazine might be second in to the market, but it was going to be the best.

Julia said she would get Tom. Christian said why not involve Billy as well—it would be a nice gesture to involve their unpaid helper in going through the pages.

As Julia stepped out of his office, he flicked through *Alpha Male*. It was good; there was no getting away from it. The publication had very high production values. It was very obvious that Lancaster Publishing had spent a lot of money on photography. The pictures were really good, beautifully shot with warm and vibrant colours, making every page attractive to the eye. It looked like a male version of one of the upmarket women's magazines. They had used his original content plan that he had proposed to the Lancaster Publishing Board. There were car reviews, articles on fashion and male grooming, some sports news, music industry gossip, and comments on new album releases. There were a few stories on some male icons from the world of music, sport, and business, as well as a section on happening bars and clubs from around the country.

The magazine was well put together, but it lacked real substance. There was no big story and no originality in the layout or design. One could tell that Lancaster Publishing had looked at some of the best of the women's magazines and simply produced an equivalent, mirror-image magazine for men.

Tom had also been flicking through a copy of *Alpha Male* as he sat sipping his coffee at his desk. He was pissed off; a lot of his major clients who had cancelled their bookings with him were advertising in *Alpha Male*. Lancaster had gone after the same advertisers for cars, watches, men's designer clothes labels, booze companies, men's fragrances, and other male-orientated lifestyle products.

He was impressed and had to admit that they had done well. There was a high volume of quality advertising. He was upset that he had not managed to get more ads for *Style Inc*, but that bastard Tyler had not helped. Tom really hated Mike Tyler for telling his clients that *Style Inc* had no way of getting into the newsagents. Tom had lost a lot of advertisers because of this—and worse still, they had switched their bookings to *Alpha Male*.

*   *   *

Lizzie had started at Westside Publishing earlier in the week and had spent the last couple of days doing very little. Bob Evans had offered her the job because he had always thought highly of her, but in truth there was no current position available. Bob himself had formerly worked at Lancaster Publishing and had been impressed by Lizzie; he had always hoped to persuade her to follow him to Westside Publishing, but now he had not got a clue what to do with her.

Bob sat in his office and flicked through a copy of *Alpha Male*. He liked it and thought it was a very well put together. He felt that it would probably sell to the thirty-year-old plus male bracket, but it would not be trendy enough to pick up younger readers. Bob was sure that there was room for a younger male publication in the market and figured that it was worth researching, so he dialled Lizzie's extension and told her to come to his office because he had an important project for her.

* * *

Faxes of congratulations were arriving at Mike's office, and he enjoyed reading every page. People hailed him as a great innovator in the publishing world. He was certainly feeling on top of that particular world. When the chairman called him in to see him, Mike was sure that he was going to be in for some more praise—and perhaps a pay rise and a promotion.

He walked to the chairman's office with a swagger and was looking forward to being commended for a job well down. Mike confidently took a seat, waiting for the mountains of praise and the offers of future glory that he so richly deserved.

'What the fucking hell have you been up to, you bloody imbecile?' the chairman bawled at him. Mike was stunned—he had not expected this at all. Sir George continued to speak. 'I've just had the most appalling meeting with Kevin Viner. He has just shown me some confidential memos that clearly came from your office detailing our private agreements with some major newsagents. Kevin has informed me that he is shocked that we have entered into some side agreements to sell quantities of our publications direct to the newsagents. Naturally, he has said that our actions have gone totally against our legally binding contract with Bookstall Solutions. Of course he could take us to court. and no doubt I am sure he would win. However, he has proposed that we sign a new contract with Bookstall Solutions, giving them a higher percentage of our cover prices for the next two years. Although I hated his proposal, I had no option but to agree to his terms.

'Your bloody carelessness has cost us a fortune, and I am seriously thinking of cutting your salary.'

'I have no idea how, Kevin Viner got his hands on the memos!' Mike protested. 'I can only assume that somebody must have rifled through my office.'

'Well my view is that your inability to keep highly sensitive information locked away has led a friend of Christian Davidson to get his hands on some very important documents. God only knows what other information he has.'

'But sir, why do you think it is connected with Christian Davidson?'

'Well, here is the final cruel blow because of you, you cretin. Viner's final condition was that he was going to go ahead and distribute Davidson's magazine, and he did not expect me to object. I asked him why he wanted to add this peculiar extra condition, and he refused to explain. This leaves me no other conclusion than Davidson or one of his associates must have furnished Viner with copies of the memos.'

Mike figured that Sir George was correct in his assumption, but who in the building had managed to go through his office in order to get their hands on sensitive documents? Was the person still working at Lancaster Publishing? If so, he needed to find out who it was and fire them straight away. Whoever they were, they must be someone loyal to Christian, and firing them was going to be too small a punishment.

Mike apologised profusely and hoped that Sir George had finished bawling him out, but he was wrong.

'Your ridiculous little feud with Davidson is not only becoming expensive, but it threatens to become a major embarrassment to this company. I do not enjoy having early morning meetings with the police!'

Oh shit, thought Mike. He had never imagined that Sergeant Wilson would continue with his investigations, and he certainly had not expected him to call on Sir George.

'Tyler, I have just covered your arse this morning. But be assured that I did not do it for you—I did it to save this company from unwanted negative publicity. A Sergeant Wilson, whom you already have had the pleasure of meeting, came to see me first thing this morning. He said that he suspected you and an employee named Jason of causing a near riot at Moriarty's public house last Friday evening. He told me about the mayhem that had been caused and said that he was determined to catch the culprits. Wilson left me in no doubt that he is convinced that the troublemakers are in fact you and this Jason. I told him that his suggestion was ridiculous, but I am inclined to believe that he is correct.

'He requested that when we get our telephone bills, he should be given copies because he wants to check on some phone calls that he suspects were made from your office last Friday evening. Wilson believes that the call to the police to go to Moriarty's came from *your* office. Lucky for you, Wilson does not have enough evidence to force British

Telecom to furnish him with these details, and I refused to give him confidential company information based on groundless allegations. Sergeant Wilson was most unhappy, claiming that he could not accept that I viewed our telephone bills as confidential information. I told him that we took data protection very seriously and were not prepared to give anyone phone bills that contained private phone numbers of some very important people that our editorial staff often had the privilege to interview. Of course he did not believe me, but he cannot force me to cooperate without more evidence. For your sake, Tyler, let's hope he does not obtain further evidence!'

'But Sir George, what makes you think I was involved?'

'Wilson told me the names of some of the people who were in the bar on that night and suffered from your childish practical jokes. When he mentioned Christian Davidson, the man that you have always seemed hell-bent on ruining, I knew that you must have been behind these vindictive acts of stupidity.'

There was no sense in Mike continuing to protest his innocence. Sir George was very angry, and it seemed that nothing would convince him that Mike had not been behind the events of last Friday night. He also knew that Sir George only had to look at the telephone bills when they arrived to see that Mike had indeed telephoned the police from his office on the night in question.

Sir George made him promise to stop his obsessive feud with Christian, and Mike said that he would. But now more than ever, Mike wanted to destroy Christian and all his stupid friends.

*   *   *

Tom walked in to Christian's office, and he was clearly in a bad mood. He was holding his copy of *Alpha Male*. 'That bloody bastard Tyler—look at this! He's stolen all my fucking advertisers!'

'Tom, calm down. You will get them back with us once we get our magazine in the shops. Look on the bright side: we have our big story, we have a distribution agreement, and we have the best print deal in the market. Once our magazine hits the streets, we will outsell the competition, and your advertisers will be queuing up to book space with you.'

Julia was pleased Christian had recovered his fight. It was a good thing that Tom was angry and depressed—it was forcing Christian to get his act together and motivate his friend.

Christian, Tom, Julia, and Billy gathered around Christian's desk to look at the page proofs for *Style Inc*. The design agency had done a great job, and their magazine was going to look much more original than *Alpha Male*. The front cover sported a bold 'S Inc', and the words 'Style Inc, Issue 1' appeared only in small type in the top left-hand corner. They all agreed that 'S Inc' would give the magazine a much cooler name and was likely to catch on as an almost designer brand name for the publication.

The pages were grainy and quirky in their layout, and they had a much more laidback and fashionable image than *Alpha Male*. Photographs were set at angles with mock picture frames around them, and they seemed almost three-dimensional. The text switched between different sizes, colours, and typefaces, and the overall effect was of something stylish and avant-garde.

They were very pleased with the treatment from Grafix D Sign, and they knew that they were ready to go to press tomorrow. The process of going through the magazine pages had a positive effect on all of them. They liked the designs a lot, and they now felt sure that the magazine's look, combined with its content and Lord Whitstop's story, would bring them successful copy sales in the coming weeks.

*   *   *

Lizzie had finished her meeting with Bob Evans. She had agreed to research a magazine aimed at men in their twenties. She did not tell Bob that of all the possible publishing projects, researching another magazine for men was the last thing on which she wanted to work. Neither did she tell him that Christian was soon to bring out the second lifestyle magazine aimed at men within a matter of days.

Lizzie had been so surprised at Bob's proposal that she had not told him anything to persuade him that this was not something she was comfortable doing. Now, as she sat behind her desk in her back office, she had wished that she had not said yes. She needed her new job, and she knew that Bob had done his best to think up a project to provide a role for her. If she went back to him now and refused the project, she would come across as difficult and ungrateful for his offering her a job so quickly. Lizzie was very anxious and confused. She needed someone to talk to, and she did not feel that Christian was the right person to call after all the recent events.

*   *   *

Tom was back behind his desk and feeling more positive about the future. He had noticed how close Julia and Christian seemed to be during the meeting, and he really hoped that they might get it together soon. If Julia and Christian were to start a relationship, then this would leave him clear to try to start something with Lizzie. His mind drifted back to the night he had slept with Lizzie, and he hoped that he would be able to do it again, but he was sure that this was a totally forlorn and unrealistic hope.

The phone on Tom's desk rang, and he picked it up. He was surprised and began to believe that Lizzie was telepathic.

'Tom, I need to see you tonight. I have something that I really need to discuss with you. Are you free this evening?' Lizzie asked.

'Yes, of course. Where would you like to meet?'

'Let's get together in the Crusting Pipe wine bar in Covent Garden, and we can get something to eat and share a bottle of plonk.'

Tom agreed and suggested that they meet at seven. After he put the phone down, he could not help but think that things were starting to head in the right direction, and he was feeling even more cheerful now.

*   *   *

Billy was enjoying himself at ChrisTom Media. He had not had a clue what he wanted to do when he left university, and he had spent his time since living on the dole and campaigning for animal rights. He had got to the point where he had convinced himself that no company would want anyone who had not gone straight into a job after his studies.

Billy did not care that he was not getting paid; he was still collecting his dole money, and he was sure that if the magazine went well and if he impressed Tom and Christian, they would soon offer him salaried employment.

He had been uncertain how to dress for work. Tom always wore very smart suits, because he often had to go and see clients. Christian was inconsistent: sometimes he dressed in casual clothes, and sometimes he wore a suit if he was going to interview important people. Julia seemed to have it easy because she could wear a dress or a suit or trousers, and it did not really matter which because she always looked nice.

Billy had bought a suit from Oxfam, just in case he was asked to go to anything important. The suit was in excellent condition, and no one would have known from where he had got it. He had not yet had any opportunity to wear it, which was a relief to him because he felt very uncomfortable in it. He was also scared that should he have to wear it, one of his friends was bound to see him and take the piss out of him.

Billy had opted to dress in smart chinos and a proper work-style shirt. He managed to look neat and tidy but still reasonably casual. He had also had his hair cut; this had really been a hard decision to make, and he finally decided to do it on Tuesday at lunch, when he had made his mind up that now more than anything, he wanted this job.

Julia had taken to Billy and no longer saw him as a threat; in fact she hoped that they would employ him because he could do all the mundane stuff and leave her free to spend all her time writing articles for *S Inc.* She knew that she lacked editorial experience, but her writing skills were strong, and she was sure that Christian would guide her.

Julia had shown Billy the ropes, and he had been a great help around the office. She had encouraged him a lot, and he was very grateful to her. Billy spent some of his time working on his own story. He was convinced that he could link the Labour MP he had told Christian about to a cosmetics factory that used animals in testing.

Tom and Christian agreed that Billy could follow up his story, and if it proved to be true, then they would almost certainly use it in the second issue of *S Inc.* One of Billy's friends, Wendy, had managed to get herself a job at the cosmetics factory as a secretary. She had seen the tests and confirmed that she had been sickened by the cruelty. Animals were having substances smeared on their eyes to check for sensitivity, and when they were almost blind, they were being switched to other tests on their skin that caused chronic infections. The cosmetics firm had been experimenting on make-up that would last longer through the day and night, and the tests were not going well. The make-up was definitely causing problems, and the animals were paying the price. Rabbits were used for most of the tests because they could be bred quickly.

As an owner of a pet rabbit herself, Wendy did not want to spend much more time working at the factory lab. She had managed to discover that Michael Freeman, the Labour MP of whom Billy had spoken, was indeed planning an early evening meeting with the other board directors of Cosmet Sensicare to discuss the company's financial problems that evening. Wendy had already provided Billy with video and pictures of the animals in the laboratory, along with a number of copies of confidential documents linking Michael Freeman with Cosmet Sensicare.

Wendy called Billy and told him about Michael Freeman's proposed visit to the factory. Billy was very excited and knew that if he could get some good photos of Freeman at the company, then that was going to nail the bastard.

Billy was so excited that he had to tell someone, and so he told Julia about Wendy's call and explained that she was going to meet him later to help him gain access to the facility tonight. The plan was that Wendy was going to drive away at 6.00 p.m. and then pick up Billy. She would then drive back fifteen minutes later to the factory lab, claiming she had left behind her handbag. The security guard on the gate never checked her car, so she would be able to sneak Billy into the lab in the boot of her car.

Wendy knew where all the security cameras were, and she knew that if she reversed her car up next to the back door of the ground-floor office section, she could sneak in Billy. All she had to do was stand to the left side of the car, open the boot sideways on, and block any camera view. Billy could then climb out of the boot and crouch on the floor unseen. The back office door would be to the left of her, and if she moved sideways to open the door, she could block the view to the door as Billy crawled through. There was always a large plastic bin full of lab coats for the laundry sitting by the back door, and Billy could sneak in behind this as he crawled into the building.

The camera in the corridor moved on a pivot to scan the corridor back and forth. When it was facing away from the door, Billy would stand up and start talking to Wendy. He would already be wearing a lab coat, lab hat, and lab facemask that Wendy left in the boot of the car for him. He would chat to Wendy about having to spend another late night in the lab, and then he would wander off down the corridor and head for the lab. In his pocket he would have a tiny camera without a flash; the pictures should be okay because he had been told that the boardroom was very brightly lit.

Wendy had coached him many times on the layout of the building, which was pretty simple. Once he reached the lab, he was to keep walking past it and head towards the front entrance of the building. Just before the front entrance of the building, there was a set of stairs leading to the first floor. He was to go up the stairs and head straight for the boardroom, which was four doors down on the right.

The meeting would be in progress, and Billy would have to rush in and take some very fast pictures. He would then run as fast as he could and head off down the corridor and back down the stairs. Billy was to run towards the back door and then head into the ladies toilets; once there, he would drop the camera into the waste bin of paper towels.

He should then pretend to hide in one of the cubicles and await his capture by security. Once he was caught, they would search him for the camera. In his pocket would be a second camera that had been deliberately broken so that the film inside was jammed.

The directors of Cosmet Sensicare would naturally be given the camera and would be delighted to find that it was broken. They would then call the police and have Billy arrested. When it was all clear, Wendy would retrieve the real camera from the bin in the ladies toilet and leave the factory.

Julia was impressed by the plan, but she was convinced that something would go wrong. She was also very concerned for Billy because he was going to be arrested either way. He said that he was pretty sure that he would simply be taken to the nearest police station and questioned for some time. The police would probably advise him that charges would be brought against him for trespassing, and he would most likely get a fine and a warning from the judge. She hoped Billy was not underestimating the seriousness of what could happen to him, but she sensed that there was no possibility of persuading him not to go through with it.

*   *   *

Mike Tyler was planning some trespassing of his own. He knew where Christian's office was, and tonight he was going to do some breaking and entering of his own. A friend of his at university, Brian Peters, had once claimed that he could open any door in less than ten minutes. Brian had proved it to Mike on quite a few occasions when they had broken into the university bar a few times and helped themselves to a few bottles.

Brian was now a broker in the city, and Mike was sure that he would help him out for old times' sake.

Christian, Julia, Tom, and Billy agreed that they would meet at the printer the next morning to see the historic first issues of *Style Inc* come off the press. Christian suggested that they go for a drink together tonight, but Billy said he had to leave early, and Tom said he had to meet an old friend. Julia was happy to agree, so they said they would go to the Pig and Whistle and then perhaps get a curry later.

Christian and Julia did not leave the office until after 7.00 p.m. By this time Billy had already achieved his plan, and he was now sitting in a police station answering questions.

Wendy had headed off with the camera containing the pictures, and although she was concerned about Billy, she was happy that she was never going to go back to Cosmet Sensicare ever again. Tom had met Lizzie in the Crusting Pipe as agreed, and she started to explain her dilemma.

As Julia sat at the table with Christian, she started to fret about Billy, but she kept her promise not to say anything. Christian was excited about getting his first magazine printed in the morning, and he was happy to be having a drink with Julia to talk about his dreams.

Eddie was reopening Moriarty's for the first night since the near riot in his bar. The brewery had been impressed by Sergeant Wilson's letter to them, and they had praised Eddie for his skilful handling of a difficult situation. They had quickly put into action the repairs needed, and the bar looked almost as good as before.

Eddie was not sure that the builders had done a particularly brilliant job, but at least it had been quick. He was looking forward to a good night and was pleased to see that he had an excellent crowd in to see the bar reopen.

Lord Whitstop was sitting in his private office with a bottle of expensive malt whiskey and a journalist from a well-known popular newspaper.

Mike Tyler had got together with his old chum Brian Peters and was in the process of buying him dinner in one of his favourite haunts, Rules.

Tonight was going to affect a lot of people's dreams, but as yet none of them knew it.

CHAPTER 18

JULIA AND CHRISTIAN sat in the bar for hours, chatting away. Christian told her how her father should have written books, and how he had always regretted never having had the courage to try to write a novel. Jinxie had told Christian to give up journalism and to write a novel or some serious poetry, rather than live with regret as he had done. Christian had always asked Jinxie how he thought Christian was going to pay his bills, and Jinxie had said that he would be happy to support him until he became a successful writer.

Julia said that she was pleased that Christian had been her father's friend and that he knew so much about him. 'Perhaps you should write that book one day. You could base it on my father—he seems to have been a great character.'

'Yes, he was. You would have liked him. If I ever do write a book, then I could never find a better subject than Jinxie.'

*　　*　　*

Tom told Lizzie that there was no harm in her researching another men's lifestyle publication, because it would probably take her quite a few weeks to finish the project. By the time she finished the research, *Style Inc* would hopefully have sold a lot of copies. Westside Publishing would probably realise that with two good publications to compete with in the market, their chances of success were limited, and they would probably drop the project. If they still showed some enthusiasm, he was sure that Lizzie could persuade them to give up.

Lizzie said that was all well and good, but what about her? She needed something to work on because Bob would eventually have to get rid of her if he could not find something for her to do. Tom saw her point and admitted he did not have an answer. It was possible that after a few weeks, some advertising manager was bound to decide to leave Westside Publishing, and that would then provide a slot for Lizzie. But they both new that was just wishful thinking. Tom knew Bob pretty well from his days at Lancaster Publishing, and he told Lizzie that she knew that Bob was a good guy and would work out something.

They talked for some time longer on the subject, and then Lizzie finally agreed that Tom was probably right. She would take his advice and do the research. She was sure that they would drop the idea, by which point Bob was almost sure to find another opportunity for her.

* * *

Mike and Brian were enjoying talking about old times at university, and Brian said that he would be able to get Mike into Christian's office with no trouble later on that evening.

'I hope you remembered to buy some gloves, Mike.'

'Two brand-new pairs of gloves are sitting ready for use in my briefcase, and I cannot wait to put them to work. Let's drink a toast to terminal illness, because tonight Christian's computer terminals are going to develop a very nasty illness.'

They both raised their glasses and knocked back some wine.

'Mike, let me make one thing clear: once you are inside the office, you are on your own. I have a huge salary and benefits, and I am not going to risk it for your vendetta. I will leave as soon as you are in.'

Mike said he understood and was grateful to his old university chum for agreeing to put his special talent to good use.

* * *

Eddie was really enjoying himself. Moriarty's was packed out. Many of his loyal customers were remarking how pleased they were that he had managed to perform a miracle and reopen so quickly. He had hoped that Lizzie, Tom, and Christian would pop in, but he had not seen any sign of them yet. Eddie was pleased that the bar was open again, and he was sure that the upstairs room would be ready for functions again in a few more days.

*　*　*

Billy was still at the police station answering their questions. He had declined to have a solicitor present, and he had been charged with trespassing. The interviewing officer was making a few jokes at his expense about the broken camera. When Billy asked to go to the toilet, the officer told him he hoped that not all his equipment was broken. Billy smiled at the joke and said nothing; he knew it was better to be smart than to just think one was smart.

It was a frustrating evening at the station. Billy had admitted to trespassing, and they had eyewitness statements and video footage, so he really could not understand why they wanted to detain him so long. They were just being bloody-minded and trying to spoil his evening.

Finally they let him go with a warning not to attempt to go back to Cosmet Sensicare, and they told him that he would receive notification of his court hearing soon. He was desperate to get in touch with Wendy to see if she had managed to get his friend Eric to develop the photographs. Billy set off to meet Wendy at the Lamb and Flag near Covent Garden. He had told her earlier in the day that he would meet her there at 10.00 p.m., and it was 9.30 already, so he needed to hurry.

Wendy had been told to get Eric to develop several sets of the photographs, as a precaution. Eric was to keep one set for himself, give one set to Wendy, and post a third set to Christian at the office.

Billy finally arrived at the pub just after ten, and Wendy was looking anxious. She was pleased to see Billy and offered to buy him a beer, which he gratefully accepted. He asked if the pictures had come out oaky, and she produced an envelope from her handbag. Billy had only managed to click off two pictures before people started rising from the boardroom table to get him. He looked at the pictures: his first shot was fine, but the second was blurred. But that was enough—he just needed the one good shot, and he had it.

Wendy squeezed Billy's hand. 'You did well, Billy, really well. How are you feeling?'

'From the time that we entered Sensicare to the time that I left the police station, I have to admit that I was pretty scared, but now I know it was all worth it. I feel really great.'

Billy knew that with the picture, he had all he needed to expose Michael Freeman. A lot of people had asked Billy why he had not simply used the pictures of the animals in the Cosmet Sensicare laboratory, exposing the cruelty of the company and trying to get them closed down. But Billy insisted that if they also connected Michael Freeman to Cosmet Sensicare, the story would be much bigger, and public attention on the evils of vivisection would be much greater.

Wendy told Billy that she had taken a number of documents connecting Freeman with the company that same day, so Billy had everything he needed. Wendy had hated working at Cosmet Sensicare, and tonight's events had also made her feel very frightened, but she knew that Billy had been right. She admired Billy's conviction and courage, and she was proud to have played a major role in exposing Michael Freeman.

Billy and Wendy were going to celebrate tonight. Their feelings of success and their enormous relief that it was all over made them feel intoxicated before they had even finished their first drink of the evening.

* * *

Michael Freeman was pleased that the camera that he assumed Billy had used was broken, but nevertheless he was still disturbed by the thought that Billy had seen him in the boardroom and was bound to speak out. He had sat for ages with the other directors watching the security videos and trying to work out how Billy had entered Sensicare without being detected.

It did not take long for them to realise that from the security footage that the laboratory technician talking to Wendy in the corridor was Billy. They concluded correctly that she must have had a hand in this, and they planned to interview her in the morning to try to find out more. Should she fail to show up for work in the morning, then they had her address on file and would send someone to her home.

Michael Freeman had wanted to have someone waiting outside the police station to follow Billy when he was released, but his colleagues had persuaded him that Billy may have accomplices that would be watching and waiting for this, and so it was not a good idea. As it happened, they were wrong. Worse still for Michael Freeman, they were not going to see Wendy at work tomorrow, and she was not going to return to her home address for another six weeks.

The police had been advised that Cosmet Sensicare were considering a private prosecution against Billy for trying to steal confidential documents from the boardroom. This was not true, but they felt that this would help them to obtain Billy's address.

But Billy was also not going to return to his address for six weeks, and although Michael Freeman did not yet know it, his political career was soon going to come to a very dramatic end.

Billy was smart and one day he was going to become a highly respected investigative journalist, but tonight he did not know that and was happy to have done something for his cause—and to be sitting with Wendy.

*   *   *

Mike Tyler was also pleased to be doing something more for his cause, namely the destruction of Christian's dreams. It was a little after ten when he and Brian entered the building that housed Christian's office. The building was old, with a big wooden door that looked like a front door to a large house. Next to the door there were a series of dimly lit name cards under plastic covers, and next to each name there was a button to ring a buzzer in each office. Mike studied the name cards and found it quite hard to read them. He saw ChrisTom Media and the office number, 302. *How bloody amateur,* he thought. *They don't even have professionally made company name cards for this building.*

Mike was glad to have found the name card. He knew that this was the building that housed Christian's office, but until now he had not known the office number. He had once spotted Christian walking near Holborn Viaduct some weeks back, and he had followed him out of curiosity to see where he was going. Scared of being noticed, Mike had kept back some distance and stopped for a while when Christian had entered the building. Mike had waited for some time and then he had gone to the back of the building to see if he could see if there were any car parking spaces, and if Christian was still driving his old Volkswagen Golf. He was pleased to see that the car was indeed there. This confirmed to him that it was Christian's office building. Mike decided to inflict some instant inconvenience on Christian. He pulled out his key ring penknife and punctured all the tyres on the car, before finally snapping off the valves. He smiled to himself at that happy memory of that day.

Then his mind returned back to the job at hand, and he realized that he was nervous. He hoped that Brian would get them inside the building quickly, before anyone noticed. It seemed to take forever for Brian to get the door open, but in fact it only took a little over four minutes. They climbed the dark stairs to the third level, with Mike using a small pen-sized torch to light their way. There were only four doors on the third floor, and all were numbered. Only door 304 had a company sign; the rest were all blank. Mike was glad of the numbers to use as a reference. The light was poor and the numbers were old and damaged, but, they both felt sure they had located number 302.

Brian worked his magic on door what he assumed to be office 302 and told Mike that he was on his own from now on. Mike entered the office and kept the lights off because he did not want anyone in the street to see him through the windows. He used his pencil-sized torch to feel his way around. He opened his briefcase and produced a small, heavy metal hammer and a tin of very caustic cleaning fluid. He knew exactly what he was going to do: he was going to tilt the computer drives and pour in some fluid, and then he was going to crack the screens to each computer monitor with the hammer.

*   *   *

Jack Beecham had not had a good day. His train back from his meeting in Manchester had been heavily delayed by problems on the lines. He had expected to get back at 5.00 p.m., but instead he was having to go back to his office late at night to get the documents that he would need for tomorrow's meeting, and to pick up his car.

As he approached his building, he could swear that he saw a faint trace of light dart across his office window. He let himself quietly in to the building and silently made his way up the stairs. Jack ran his own private security company, providing bodyguards for the rich and famous. He was in his early forties but was still very fit and strong. Jack had been in the paras and knew how to look after himself.

Mike decided to switch off his torch because there were no blinds on the windows, and he was scared of being detected. He felt okay in the semi-darkness because he could make out the outlines of desks and other office furniture from the glow of the streetlights down below. One thing he could not make out, however, was that the documents on the desks were in fact on headed notepaper that said Beecham Personal Security Services. Mike stopped at the first desk and tilted the computer drive as he poured in some of his caustic cleaning fluid.

Jack was now outside his office door and was sure he could hear someone moving about inside.

Mike took his little hammer in his hand and whacked the screen of the computer monitor and to his delight the screen cracked.

That was it—Jack heard the noise and knew he had an intruder. Jack slipped his key into the lock.

Mike heard the key turn, and at first he froze with panic. He then quickly decided to make a run at the door, surprise the person entering the office, and make a break for it. Mike rushed at the shape in the doorway, swinging his briefcase violently as he tried to make his escape.

Jack raised his hands in the air, took a grip on the door frame above his head, and swung himself forward with his legs outstretched. He kicked Mike hard in the chest with the full force of his body.

Mike flew across the office as if he had been hit by a cannon ball. His body collided with a desk, and he collapsed in a heap on the floor. Jack strode across the office and as Mike tried to raise himself to his feet. Jack belted him straight across the head with a metal waste bin. Mike slumped back on to the carpet and drifted out of consciousness.

Jack went over to the office light switches and turned them all on. He noticed fluid coming out of the disk drives of one of his computers, and he noticed that the monitor screen had been cracked. He was furious, but he could see that he had been lucky to get back when he had, because nothing else seemed to have been damaged. He went over to Mike Tyler and rolled him over on to his back. He took a good look at Mike but did not recognise him. *Must be from one of my competitors,* he thought to himself. He went through Mike's jacket pockets and pulled out his wallet. Inside were a number of business cards for a Mike Tyler from a company called Lancaster Publishing.

Now Jack was really confused. Who the bloody hell was Mike Tyler, and who the fuck was Lancaster Publishing? And more important, why had this idiot been trying to break his computers? He could only guess that Lancaster Publishing must have some petty vendetta against him for perhaps being a bit too physical in fending off one of their reporters when he was guarding one of his celebrity clients.

Well, Jack was not going to stand for this. He was going to send a warning back to Lancaster Publishing not to mess with him. He got some tape out of his drawer and taped up Mike's eyes and mouth, and then he found some cord and tied Mike's arms behind his back and his legs together. He decided he was going to deliver Mike back to Lancaster Publishing with a message of his own.

Jack took hold of Mike and dragged him bodily down the stairs. As he got towards the bottom Mike started to come round, and so Jack delivered a nice hammer punch to his temple and knocked him out again. He dragged Mike out of the back door of the building and over to his car in the rear parking area. Jack opened the boot and manhandled Mike into it. Jack went back up to his office and retrieved Mike's briefcase, hammer, and the can of caustic cleaning fluid.

Jack got into his car and looked at the address on the business card for Lancaster Publishing. He knew the street and drove off to make his delivery. He reached the street and the building some twenty minutes later. Jack was not happy; it was quite a large building on a very well lit street. How was he going to get in without being noticed?

He decided to drive round the block to see if there was a back entrance from the street behind. He found that behind the street, there was a small, narrow street going behind the buildings. Trouble was, how was he going to calculate which building was the rear entrance for Lancaster Publishing? But luck was on his side tonight, because one of the buildings sported a sign saying, 'Deliveries for Lancaster Publishing.' He stopped the car and inspected the back of the building.

Some steps led down to a basement, with a door with some glass panels on the top half. Jack wondered if the door had an alarm, but he decided to be bold and to break one of the panels of glass. If an alarm went off, he would leg it back to the car and drive off. He went back to the car, retrieved some gloves from the glove box, and returned to the door, he punched one of the glass panels. To his relief, no alarm sounded, not even when he opened the door. Jack returned to his car to get Mike.

The small street above was totally dead—not a soul in sight, and no lights from any windows. Things could not have been better. He opened the boot of his car and saw Mike squirming about, so he bent over and punched him into unconsciousness for the third time that evening. He retrieved some rope from the boot of his car and hung it round his neck.

He figured the rope might come in handy to stop Mike from leaving the building when he woke up later.

He dragged Mike's body down the steps and through the door. The basement area seemed to be used for outgoing mailings and sorting the incoming post. Jack let Mike's body fall to the floor, and he used Mike's torch to take a brief look around him. Jack could see some plastic boxes for incoming post with names on them. He read the names. 'Ground Floor: Advertising Sales Depts.' 'Level 1: Editorial Depts. and Publishers Offices.' 'Level 2: Directors Offices.' 'Level 3: Accounts Dept.' 'Level 4: Promotions and Marketing.'

Jack made up his mind. He was going to deliver Mike to the most senior director's office that he could find on level two. He just hoped there was a lift. He dragged Mike down the corridor, and to his relief he came to a lift. Jack took the lift up to level two and dragged Mike along the corridor. Then he saw a nameplate on one of the doors that read 'Chairman's Office'. He let Mike drop and tried the handle. It really was his night—the door was not locked.

Once inside the grand office, Jack knew that he had to decide pretty quickly what to do with Mike. He knew he should not hang around too long in case he was discovered. He removed Mike's jacket and tie, and then with a pair of scissors he found on the desk, he cut away Mike's shirt, trousers, and boxer shorts. Just for good measure and out of spite, he cut Mike's jacket into pieces.

He sat Mike in the big, leather-bound chair that was positioned behind the desk, and he took the rope off from round his neck and proceeded to tie Mike to the chair.

Jack did not know it, but the sensors in the building had alerted the local police station, and two cars were already on their way. An officer checked the file for the contact person for the building and telephoned Sir George to advise him that they believed that there was an intruder in his office premises. Sir George had been reading in his study when he got the news. He was very concerned and decided that he would drive over to the office to meet the police there.

Jack took Mike's hammer from his pocket and fractured the screen on the computer on Sir George's desk. He then took out Mike's can of caustic cleaning fluid, tilted the computer drive, and poured in some fluid. That was it, job done. They were not going to fuck with Jack again! Mike was still out cold when Jack then removed the tape from his eyes and mouth.

Jack headed back to the lift and returned to the basement. He exited the building, got into his car, and drove away. Little did he know that he had left just in time—three minutes later, a police car pulled up to the front of the building, and a second pulled up at the back delivery entrance.

Mike was coming round. His head hurt like hell, he was freezing, and he could not move. It was dark in the room, but from the light from the street lights outside, he began to recognize some familiar furnishings in the room. Then it hit him, and he realised where he was. Mike was sitting in Sir George's office tied to his chair, wearing nothing but his socks! He knew he had to try to break free and get out quickly or his career was going to be finished.

The police officers communicated by radio. They established that the intruder had broken in through the rear basement door. The two officers at the front of the building agreed to stay put in case the intruder tried to escape from the front entrance. A third car was dispatched and arrived within minutes. Two officers entered through the basement door whilst the two new arrivals stood by the back door to catch the intruder, should he manage to try to escape via the back of the building.

Sir George pulled up at the front of the building and got out of his car. He approached one of the officers and introduced himself. The officer advised him that two officers were in the building searching for the intruder. Sir George was told to wait in his car until either the intruder was apprehended or until it was established that there was no one in the building. Sir George did as he was advised and hoped that no damage had been done—and that nothing of consequence had been stolen.

Mike was frantically wriggling in the chair, desperate to break free of his restraints. In Jack's haste, he had not done a great job of restraining Mike, and within minutes Mike was free. He managed to slip the cord off of his hands, and then he untied his feet. He could only make out outlines in the darkness, so he found the light switches and turned on the lights. He knew that he had to get out of there fast.

The officers in the building had checked the basement and the first floor, and they were on their way up to the next level.

Mike looked at the remains of his clothes and wanted to cry. They were in shreds! He was going to have to make a break for it in just his socks. He assumed that the bastard Christian had discovered him ransacking his office and taken his revenge. He must have had help from his sidekick Tom to get him dragged all the way over to Lancaster Publishing. Those two buggers had really got their own back on Mike, and he was not happy.

The police made their way up to the second floor to discover that the corridor was in darkness, but they stopped in their tracks as they saw a door to an office being opened and light pouring out from the open doorway. They quickly ducked into an alcove. Seconds later Mike came running down the corridor. They saw his shape moving fast, and they jumped out to apprehend him. Mike saw the shapes of the men in the corridor too late, and he collided with them. *Fucking bastards!* he thought. *It must be Tom and Christian!* Mike lashed out with his fists and feet at the shapes and yelled, 'You wankers! I am going to fucking kill you for this!'

The officers were shocked by the frenzy of this strange, naked man. He was like a wild animal as they tried to restrain him. Eventually one of the officers managed to aim a hammer punch to the temple of the naked maniac's head, knocking him unconscious for the fourth time that night. They put Mike's hands behind his back and slipped on a pair of handcuffs. They cuffed him to a radiator pipe while he laid on his side. One of the officers then used his radio to tell his colleagues that they had caught one intruder and were now going to check the other levels.

A few minutes later they contacted their colleagues again to say that the rest of the building was clear, and that they believed that there was just the one intruder. They told the other police officers to meet them on the second floor. Sir George was advised that it was safe for him to enter the building, and they asked him to make his way to the second floor to see if he could help to identify the intruder.

Sir George took the lift to level two with the police officers, and when the lift door opened, he was horrified to see Mike Tyler handcuffed to a radiator wearing nothing but his socks.

A police officer was bending over Mike and trying to revive him. Mike was starting to come round. As he regained consciousness, he could see Sir George standing over him, and all he could say was, 'Oh fuck. I'm fucked.'

Sir George was confused and furious. He glared at Mike and said, 'Yes, I think you are right, you bloody cretin.'

'I presume you know this gentleman, then, sir?' one of the officers asked Sir George.

'Yes, I am afraid I do. Up until thirty seconds ago, he worked for me.'

Mike knew his career was finished, but he just wanted his night of hell to come to an end. However, it was not over yet. Sir George agreed for them to take Mike into his office, where Sir George very grudgingly allowed Mike to put on a spare suit that he kept in his office closet. There they discovered the vandalism to the computer along with Mike's shredded clothes, some tape, and some rope. Mike was asked to explain what had happened and he amazed himself by coming up with a fantastic story. He said that he had been working late in the building when he heard a noise from upstairs. He claimed that he had gone up to investigate and noticed that Sir George's office door was open. He decided to be brave and challenge the intruders. Upon entering the room, he said that he was overwhelmed by two men, who knocked him unconscious. He presumed that they must have ripped off his clothes and bound him to a chair after putting tape across his eyes and face. When he regained consciousness, he found himself tied up, naked, and unable to see or shout for help.

Mike went on to claim that with superhuman effort, he had broken free from his bonds and had removed the tape from his face. He turned the lights on in Sir George's office to discover his shredded clothes. With no thought for his own safety or how vulnerable he was in his naked state, he tried to head off in pursuit of the intruders. As he ran down the corridor, he had mistaken the police officers for the intruders, and that was the last he could remember.

Sir George felt terrible. He had misjudged Tyler, who had clearly suffered a lot in his heroic efforts to protect the office. 'I am so sorry, Mike. What an awful experience. But when you saw me, why did you say, "Oh fuck, I'm fucked"?'

Mike had forgotten about that and quickly tried to recover. 'Well, I was sure that you would be very upset that I had not managed to stop the intruders, and that you would fire me.'

Sir George told Mike that he was being foolish and that he was very proud of him. The police asked Mike if he had managed to see the faces of the intruders, and he said it had been too dark. They asked him if he had heard their voices, and he said that they never spoke.

Eventually the police left after trying to get some fingerprints from the office. Sir George called a twenty-four-hour number for someone to board up the window on the back door entrance to the basement. While he was waiting for them to come, he went to his drinks cabinet, poured two large brandies, and handed one to Mike. 'You look like you need this, my boy. Sounds as if you have had a pretty terrible experience.'

Mike agreed and sipped his brandy. Sir George praised Mike's bravery and said that he was also impressed that he had been working late. Eventually Mike left with the praise still ringing in his ears and the promise of imminent promotion. His head felt like it had been used as a baseball, but it had all been worth it even if Christian and Tom had got the better of him.

When Mike got back to his apartment, he took pleasure from knowing that although Christian and Tom had tried to shaft him, they had ended up getting him promoted. Nevertheless, he was still going to screw them for beating him up and trying to humiliate him with their warped idea of leaving him bound and naked in Sir George's office.

* * *

Christian had always mocked people who said that curry was an aphrodisiac. He loved the stuff, but all it usually did was give him bad breath and a dose of the shits the next day. But now, sitting in his favourite curry restaurant in Ealing, he was feeling very attracted to Julia.

He had suggested that they have a curry after the pub, and he had asked if she minded taking the tube to his favourite place in Ealing. Christian had said that he would buy the curry and pay for a mini cab for Julia to get home afterwards. She had secretly hoped that he might invite her back to his flat for a drink after the meal, and she gladly agreed to his proposal.

Christian was not sure what to do. He had only just split up with Lizzie, and so getting involved with someone else so quickly seemed wrong. Besides, Julia worked for him, and sleeping with one's staff was definitely unprofessional. Jinxie had also just passed away, and he had been one of Christian's best friends—it would be disrespectful to shag his daughter so soon after the funeral. So many concerns came into his head that he knew he had to suppress his attraction to Julia. In any case, he felt that she probably did not fancy him.

Julia was happy to be sitting with Christian. She would have preferred not to travel all the way to Ealing, and she would rather not be eating a curry, but she really hoped that he would ask her back for a drink and that he would finally fall for her.

Christian couldn't help it—he was getting more and more attracted to Julia. She really was very pretty, and he loved her soft Irish accent. He made up his mind: he would invite her back for a drink, and if she said yes, he would try to get friendly with her. If she was receptive, he would try to kiss her, but he would be decent and leave it at that.

In the restaurant he decided to lighten the mood and put her at her ease. 'I have been putting my writing skills to work, and I have been freelancing for a fortune cookie company,' he told her.

Julia was not sure to make of this; she actually thought it sounded quite lame. But she replied by saying that she thought that must be very interesting.

'Yes. I have come up with some very interesting predictions for some of the cookie messages for restaurant goers.'

'Sounds fascinating,' she said, but she certainly did not think so.

'My best one is, "Someone near you will be eating rice."' Julia laughed. Christian had succeeded in lightening the mood. He went on to say that he was developing a new concept for curry restaurants with the fortune naan. Based on most late-night clientele, he said he felt his best prediction message would likely be, 'You will have drunk too much beer, and will be deeply offensive to the waiters. They will probably shit in your curry.' Julia was relaxing, and Christian enjoyed entertaining her.

Two hours later, Christian rolled over in bed, exhausted. It had been fantastic. Julia really was beautiful, and having sex with her had been better than anything he had ever experienced before. She nestled into the crook of his arm, and they both drifted off to sleep knowing that at this moment, nobody could be as happy as they were.

* * *

But they were wrong. Billy and Wendy were in love, and they had finally had the guts to admit it to each other. While sleeping in the spare room of Billy's brothers flat in a single bed, they both wondered why it had taken them so long to get it together.

*   *   *

Tom was sleeping with Lizzie in his arms. Lizzie was still awake and was wondering why she had agreed to go home with him again. She had now guessed that Tom was in love with her, but she was still confused. Although she liked him a lot, she was not yet ready to fall in love again. But it was just a matter of time, and although she did not know it yet, she and Tom would soon be together.

*   *   *

Sadly not all the rats had been returned to their boxes on the night of the fateful Party of Plagues. A few of them had managed to scamper into an electrical cupboard and hide from the maniacs that had been chasing them. They had occasionally left the comfort of their new home to forage for food, but they had also become quite partial to chewing on the electrical wires.

Earlier that evening, the electrics in the upstairs bar of Moriarty's had finally gone terribly wrong. Bare wires came into contact with each other following days of being chewed by rats. Fire broke out, and Eddie acted heroically and cleared everyone out of the bar as quickly as he could. He tried desperately to attack the blaze upstairs, but as the fire engines arrived, he was forced to finally retreat to the street. Eddie was hospitalised after collapsing minutes later from having inhaled too much smoke.

Eddie was later told that the fire services had got the flames under control and that the pub had been saved. He was told that he was a hero and would probably get an award for bravery. Eddie did not care about the award—he was simply happy that his pub was safe because he loved Moriarty's more than any living thing.

*   *   *

Mike Tyler loved himself more than anything in the world, and although tonight he was battered and bruised, and his head felt like it was exploding, he knew that he was destined for greatness.

*　　*　　*

Lord Whitstop had loved the days when he was seen as a major public figure who stood up for social justice. Tonight he felt sure that his former glories would soon be restored, and he was filled with hope and anticipation as he drifted off to sleep.

Chapter 19

Talking about the weather in Britain had always been a national obsession—no surprise, really, when one could actually see four different seasons in the space of a week. A cold, icy wind whistled through the streets of London, and the sky was as almost as dark as night. Today an icy chill was going through the bones of a lot of people, but it was not going to have a lot to do with the freezing weather.

Mike Tyler was not feeling very well. His head was still hurting like crazy, and his forehead was now black with bruises. He went to the office early and was sure that today Sir George would reward him for his bravery and company loyalty.

*   *   *

Christian and Julia also woke early. Without the benefit of being inebriated, they were both nervous in each other's company following their first night of passion. They did not speak very much, and Julia headed off early to her flat to take a shower and to get some clean clothes.

*   *   *

Lizzie had sneaked away very early from Tom's flat, before he was awake. He was disappointed to find her gone when he finally got out of bed, and he hoped that he would get to speak with her later.

*   *   *

Billy was glad that his brother was away on holiday and had left a well-stocked fridge. Wendy was glad that she did not have to get up for work, and she was even more pleased that she would never have to work at Cosmet Sensicare again. Billy made some, coffee, eggs, and toast, and he brought a tray to Wendy in bed. He told her that he had to go to the printer, and she was disappointed to see him leave early.

*   *   *

Later that morning Christian, Julia, Tom, and Billy all met at Brown and Son as planned, and Julia did the introductions. Tom liked the idea that the magazine was going to be printed by a man called Tommy. They were chatting away, happy and excited, when Christian pulled the newspaper off Tommy's desk and exclaimed, 'Oh fuck!' Christian suddenly felt that his world was falling apart as he read the article.

Whitstop or Wits Stopped? Looney Lord Loses the Plot

Lord Whitstop, recently put out to grass in the House of Lords, the final resting place for the politically insane, has finally gone barking bonkers. Living in his own fantasy world, he has dreamed up a story that during the Falklands crisis, the Argentinean regime used chemical and biological weapons. During our interview at his private office, he delivered a very moving tale of ex-soldiers suffering from strange and unidentified illnesses in military hospitals that he believed were not post-conflict stress-related disorders, as previously suggested.

We checked out his story to find that whilst some post-Falklands veterans were in fact hospitalised due to suffering from post-conflict stress, all had made full recoveries many years back and were now leading normal lives.

Whitstop regularly referred to a Captain McIntyre during his emotional ramblings, so we tracked him down to get his side of the story. Captain McIntyre, a much-decorated and highly regarded veteran of the Falklands War, at first resisted our attempts to interview him, stating that Whitstop's crazy allegations were totally groundless and the result of an attention-seeking, senile mind.

McIntyre finally agreed to speak with us late last night and told us that Whitstop had been making his life a misery for months. Whitstop had been constantly writing to McIntyre, telephoning him, and even turning up at his office. McIntyre, now a director of a major insurance company, stated that he was seeking legal advice to stop Whitstop from bothering him.

Apparently in his communications to McIntyre, Whitstop repeatedly stated that he was on his side and was now committed to revealing the truth in order to help the brave boys who were still suffering.

Christian stopped reading and put his head in his hands as everyone sat in stunned silence.

'Oh my god. Why didn't I check out the story properly? I cannot believe I acted so naively! Jinxie said I should have contacted McIntyre. I thought of myself as a professional journalist, and I did not even do the most basic of checks. I was lost in my own little world, trying to get our magazine out first, and I even failed to do that.'

Julia and Tom, who were sitting next to Christian, tried to put their arms around his shoulder, but he flinched and stood up. 'I have let you down. I let my own ego and my feud with Tyler cloud my judgement, and I have let you all down.' Christian walked out of the office.

Tom got up to follow, but Julia insisted that he should stay. She would go out after Christian.

Tommy, the printer, was lost and did not have a clue what was going on. The only thing he did manage to work out was that Julia was clearly in love with Christian. Tommy felt a little sad. He had always known that one day she would find someone special, but he had hoped against all hope that one day she might fall for him.

* * *

Mike Tyler did not love anyone except himself. He was happy to make do with climbing the corporate ladder as quickly as possible and earning loads of money. He had been at work for a few hours now, and he was getting a little impatient. Sir George really should have summoned him by now to reward him with a salary increase and a promotion.

Meanwhile, Sir George was sitting at his desk looking bemused. He read the note that had come mysteriously glued to Mike Tyler's briefcase. Reception had taken delivery of the briefcase earlier in the morning in a huge envelope addressed to Sir George.

Initially Sir George had been suspicious of the package, and for one awful moment he wondered if someone had sent him a bomb. But on reflection, he saw no reason why someone should do such a thing to him, and he opened the envelope to read the note.

Now for the fifth time this morning he read the note again.

> Last night was just a warning. If Mike Tyler or any of your other cronies breaks into my office again and tries to fuck up my computers, you will wish that you had never messed with me.
>
> I hope when you found your boy Tyler in your office, you realised that I know who you are.
>
> Tell Tyler to eat the contents of his briefcase.

Sir George finally decided to open the briefcase and was greeted by the sight of what he could only assume was human excrement. He closed it quickly again and tried to work out what this all meant. Clearly the composer of the note suggested that Mike Tyler had broken into an office last night and damaged some computers. It also seemed clear that Mike Tyler had been lying and had been deposited in Sir George's office by the mysterious note writer. Sir George finally told his secretary to call Mike Tyler's extension and to tell him to come up to his office.

Mike was overjoyed and almost skipped up to the second floor. This was it—this was going to be another glorious step in his climb to the top.

He was ushered into Sir George's office and took a seat in front of the huge, polished desk. Mike could not wait to be praised, pay-raised, and promoted.

Instead Sir George said, 'Recognise this, do you, Tyler? You lying, conniving specimen of weasel shit.'

It was Mike's turn to look confused and also a little wounded. But more than anything, he was now very nervous as Sir George pushed his briefcase across his desk at him.

'Read the note and then open your case. Then I would like an honest explanation from you for once in your life, before I have you thrown out of this building.'

Mike did as he was told. He read the note and then opened his case to discover that some bastard had crapped inside it. He thought that Christian and Tom had really gone too far this time as he shut the case quickly and tried not to vomit from the smell. Mike tried to think of an explanation as quickly as possible and then opted for a blend of the truth and fiction. He admitted that his story about the intruders was pure fabrication, and he went on to admit that he had broken into the offices of ChrisTom Media last night. He claimed that he had good information to suggest that Christian had produced a good magazine that would draw attention away from *Alpha Male*. In order to protect the interests of Lancaster Publishing, he stated that he had taken enormous risks to try to sabotage the competition.

Mike then claimed that he had been surprised by someone returning to ChrisTom Media's offices, and that person had got the better of him in the darkness and knocked him unconscious. He said that his attacker had taped his mouth and eyes and had tied up his hands and feet. Mike said he was convinced that his attacker must have enlisted the help of a colleague to manhandle Mike into the boot of a car.

They must have taken him to Sir George's office and stripped him naked before being tying him to a chair. He claimed that he had struggled heroically with his bonds and eventually had broken free. Mike then described how he had rushed in to the darkened corridor bruised and naked, with no thought for his safety. He had in his confusion attacked the police officers, thinking they were the intruders.

Mike said that it had to be Christian and Tom who had attacked him last night and sent his briefcase to Sir George. He went on to say that he had every confidence that Sir George would not allow himself to be challenged by these upstarts and that he expected he would exact a swift and forceful revenge.

Mike had amazed himself at his ability to think on his feet under extreme pressure and with a throbbing head. Now he waited expectantly for Sir George to cover him with words of praise.

Sir George rose slowly to his feet, stared at Mike with veins pulsating on the side of his head, pointed to his door, and bellowed, 'What total and utter bollocks! You really must think I am some doddery old buffoon with the intelligence of an amoeba. I have never heard such an enormous pack of lies in all my years in business. You, Tyler, are without doubt the most unbelievable purveyor of untruths in the whole of this city. You are fired! Get out of my office, get out of this building, and never let me see your hideous face around here again!' Mike tried to protest, but Sir George grew even angrier and screamed, 'Get out of my office this instant, you arse wipe, or I for one will force you to digest the contents of your briefcase!'

Mike knew it was useless to argue anymore. His career prospects had crashed and died, and Sir George was in no mood to be reasoned with. Mike walked out of the office, took the lift to the ground level, exited in to the street, and threw his briefcase into a builder's skip.

*   *   *

Julia walked with Christian for hours round the streets as he castigated himself for destroying all their dreams. Today should have been one of the finest in his entire career. Today should have seen the first ever issues of *Style Inc* coming off the press, but now they were ruined thanks to his failure to do his job properly.

Julia told him that she was at fault as well, because she had also believed Whitstop. She said that no one could have known that Whitstop had lost his faculties and drifted off into a world of fantasies, but Christian insisted that he had not checked things out properly. If he had not been in such a hurry, he would have tracked down McIntyre, and they would never have ended up at the printer with a lead story that was a complete fiction.

Julia tried to get him to look on the bright side: at least they had found out *before* printing the magazine. Christian said that had they printed, he could not bear to think of the consequences. They agreed to return to the printers, and Christian would assure Tom and Billy that he would get working on another lead story as soon as possible. He agreed with Julia that the team looked to him for direction, and he owed it to them to make them feel that it was just a temporary setback.

When they reached the printers, Tom was very excited. The machines were running, and some of the magazine pages were already coming off the press. Christian could not understand what Tom was up to. 'Tom, are you crazy? We cannot print! We will be a laughing stock. Whitstop's story is total rubbish.'

'We are not going to run with Whitstop's story—we have a new, true, and even better story to run with.'

At first Christian thought Tom had gone totally mad, but then Tom told him all about Billy's story about Michael Freeman and Cosmet Sensicare. He explained that Billy had proof, with copies of confidential Cosmet Sensicare correspondence to Freeman and replies from Freeman. Plus, he said that Billy had pictures from the laboratory at the Cosmet Sensicare factory showing the cruel treatment of animals. 'And Christian, the icing on the cake is that Billy has a picture of Michael Freeman sitting in the boardroom of Cosmet Sensicare with the other directors! This is a really brilliant story—thank God you invited Billy to come and work with us.'

'Where is Billy now?' Christian asked.

'He has gone to Graphix D Sign, and he is putting in the text to the story directly on one of their computers. His girlfriend is going to meet him there with the pictures from the lab, copies of documents, and the picture of Freeman in the Cosmet Sensicare boardroom. The guys at Graphix D Sign have been brilliant. They say that they will have all the pages ready to come back here early this afternoon, ready for print. Tommy is getting on with printing the other pages, and I expect we shall have our first copies of *Style Inc* by late tonight. Graphix D Sign are also currently working on three new ideas for a front cover with the picture of Freeman on it. We should have those in a few hours, and then we can choose the one we like best.'

Christian was amazed. He had always seen himself as the guy who made things happen in the office, but now Tom was taking charge and was doing a good job of it.

Tommy walked back in to his office with some sheets off the press. 'Are you happy with the print quality?' he asked.

They all stared at the sheets and felt really proud to see *Style Inc* finally coming into the world. Yes, they were all happy with the print quality, but most of all they were relieved that the magazine was finally a reality and no longer just a dream.

Christian headed over to Graphix D Sign to help Billy craft his story, and he was very impressed with Billy's writing skills. Billy was very young, but Christian could feel the kid had what it took to be a great journalist. He knew that Billy had found his vocation.

Tom was still at the printers like an excited schoolboy, wandering around the machines and watching the sheets coming off the press. Julia was sitting in Tommy's office, chatting with him and drinking a coffee. All of the *Style Inc* team were occupied and were now confident that on Friday, Bookstall Solutions would be able to collect the magazines from the printers for distribution as planned.

Finally, after the ups and downs of recent weeks, everything was going to plan. But Christian could not help feeling that but for Billy, they would now be in serious trouble.

*   *   *

Eddie was desperate to leave the hospital, but the nurses told that he had to wait until the doctor had done his rounds and agreed that he was okay. While he was waiting, Nigel Winters from the brewery came to see how he was.

Nigel told Eddie that the brewery blamed themselves for not taking more care over the repairs, and he said that they were truly sorry for all he had gone through. He praised Eddie for his handling of the fire and said that the brewery was going to reward him for his efforts. He went on to tell Eddie that Moriarty's was going to be closed for nine months and was going to be given a total facelift.

Eddie was at first concerned that they would turn his bar in to some ultra-modern neon monstrosity, but Nigel assured him that this was not the plan. The brewery had decided to renovate all the original features and restore the bar to its original condition, when it was first opened in the 1950s. It was going to become an elegant, smart bar with dark, polished wood and brass fittings. Moriarty's would have a new kitchen to produce traditional English food, and the brewery was going to put new pumps in to serve real ales, as well as a range of temperature-controlled cabinets to house quality wines. Eddie was delighted, and it took a good ten minutes for Nigel Winters to finish having his hand shaken and being told what a good bloke he was before he could leave the hospital.

*   *   *

Mike Tyler had totally lost control of his senses and headed off to Christian's office.

Jack Beecham had not had a good meeting in Windsor and did not get the contract to provide bodyguards for a well-known boy band. He had not managed to eat last night because of the idiot who'd broken into his office, and his early start had caused him to skip breakfast this morning. He had parked his car at the back of the building and then gone up to his office to deposit his briefcase and papers.

The only joy he got this morning was playing back the message on his answering machine from one of his bodyguard employees, Tony, confirming that he had delivered Jack's package to Lancaster Publishing as promised.

Jack was bloody hungry, and it was making him irritable. He also badly needed a coffee, and there was none in his office. There was no chance of getting much work done this morning because his computer was totally fucked. Jack decided to head off round the corner to get some breakfast.

As Jack descended the stairs and reached the final level approaching the front door to the building, he was totally amazed to see Mike Tyler walking up the stairs. 'Are you some kind of fucking deranged lunatic?' he bawled at Mike.

Mike looked up, confused at this aggressive greeting from a total stranger, and as he did Jack punched him with all his might full on the nose. Mike flew backwards down the stairs and smashed against the door. His last thought before losing consciousness was that his nose was definitely broken. Later that day, as he left the hospital, he decided to leave Christian alone for a while, for the sake of his own health.

*   *   *

Billy finished his story, and Graphix D Sign put the pages together, ready for printing. Christian and Tom chose their preferred cover, a library picture of Michael Freeman giving a speech in Parliament. The text next to it read,

Freeman? But for how much longer?
Read the terrible truth about his animal cruelty lab.

Christian, Julia, Tom, Billy, and Tommy stayed through the night at Brown and Son printers to see the first copies of the magazine being bound. At 11.00 a.m. a van branded with the logo of Bookstall Solutions arrived. They all helped the driver load the van, and not one of them felt tired—they felt very proud and excited. By lunchtime they all agreed that they should call it a day and get some sleep. It was going to be a long weekend, waiting for the magazine to appear in the newsagents on the Monday morning.

Some days back, Christian had found the contact details of a lawyer amongst Jinxie's papers in his flat, and the lawyer had said that they did in fact have a copy of Jinxie's will. Julia had asked Christian to go with her to read it, and he had agreed. Now he rather wished he had not, because he felt totally exhausted. Although he was pleased that the magazine had finally been printed, he personally felt he had failed. Christian knew that Billy's story had saved the day. Christian had nearly doomed the magazine with his foolish Whitstop fable. He felt awkward in Julia's company, because he was sure that he would no longer be her hero. He was just an inexperienced, pathetic journalist incapable of telling fact from fiction.

They both returned to their own flats, freshened up, and changed their clothes. At 3.00 p.m. they both sat in the reception area of the lawyer's office reading ancient copies of *Country Life* that had been strewn around a coffee table. Some minutes later they were shown into the office of Jinxie's solicitor, Roger Blakes, and provided with very welcome cups of tea. Christian had delivered a copy of Julia's birth certificate to the lawyer's office to prove that Julia was Jinxie's daughter. They sat quietly and waited to find out the contents of Jinxie's last will and testament.

Roger said, 'I am glad that you are both here, because you are the two sole beneficiaries of the will of Mr James Jinks.'

Christian was surprised. He was sure that Jinxie would have made arrangements for Julia, but not for him. He now expected that perhaps Jinxie had left him some small tokens to remember him by, and the thought pleased him.

Roger Blake started to read the will, and it went pretty much as Christian had expected. He had left his flat and all its contents to Julia, as well as some bonds and some equity funds, and the sum of fifty thousand pounds. Julia was surprised and looked a little tearful.

Then Christian was told that he had been left Jinxie's collection of books of famous poets, as well as scrapbooks containing copies of Jinxie's articles from when he had been a war correspondent. He had also left Christian a collection of old, valuable pens that Jinxie had collected throughout his life. Christian was deeply touched.

Then came the final bequest. 'I hereby leave the sum of 120,000 pounds to Christian Davidson, on the condition that he takes a minimum of one year away from working and that, during this period, he either works on producing a collection of poems or writes a novel. If he accepts this condition, then the money shall be administered by my solicitor, and Christian Davidson shall be advanced twenty thousand pounds of the total. If he completes within one year a set of at least thirty poems or a book, then he shall receive the remaining hundred thousand pounds. If he fails to complete the aforementioned task, then the remaining sum shall go to my daughter, Julia Daley.

'It is by far the greatest of my last wishes that Christian Davidson shall accept my proposal. I very much hope that he shall not decline and live his life unfulfilled as I sadly did. I urge him to accept my proposal because I truly believe he has the gift.'

For Christian it was a double surprise. He had never really imagined Jinxie having very much money—the only new clothes he had seen the old man wearing was when he died. But the biggest surprise of all was that Jinxie really had believed that Christian could write, and that he was prepared to bequeath him a major sum of money to try to persuade him to become a writer.

Perhaps Jinxie was right. Perhaps he should try to write something decent before it was too late. Although his magazine was soon to appear in the shops, he knew that he had failed; only Billy's article had saved the publication. Christian now thought of gifting his interest in ChrisTom Media to Tom. But could he really become a writer?

Christian sat silently thinking, and no one said a word. Then out of his affection for Julia, he said, 'I hate to go against Jinxie's last and generous wish, but I cannot do it. He was my friend, and his friendship clouded his judgement as to my abilities. I am not a writer and never can be. Jinxie was in many ways like a father to me, but Julia was his daughter, and she should rightfully have the money.'

Julia tried to argue with Christian, but he refused to change his mind. Twenty minutes later they both left the lawyer's office.

That night Christian, Julia, Billy, Wendy, and Tom went out to celebrate the successful completion of the first issue of *Style Inc*. Christian still felt that he personally had failed, but he decided to keep quiet and let everyone have a nice evening. They were all happy that night and promised they would have a proper celebration in a year from that day, when *Style Inc* had completed its first successful year.

CHAPTER 20

EDDIE STOOD IN the newly renovated Moriarty's. It had taken longer than nine months for the refit—in fact it had taken almost exactly a year. He was pleased that the brewery had agreed that he could reopen the pub with a private party, and he was delighted with the final outcome of the renovations.

Tonight was going to be a double celebration: the reopening of the bar, and the first birthday of the highly successful magazine *Style Inc.* Lizzie was sitting with Eddie discussing the final preparations for their joint celebration. Following her successful recommendation to Westside Publishing to acquire the magazine some ten months ago, they had made her the publisher of the title.

Tom walked in, and Lizzie gave him a big hug and a peck on the cheek.

Eddie said, 'I can see you two have only been married a couple of months. That won't last long.'

For the first few months after *Style Inc* appeared, Lizzie and Tom still had a nervous and furtive relationship. But as time passed and it became clear that Christian and Julia were in love, they no longer felt that they had to hide their relationship.

By the time they made it public, Christian said he had already guessed and had no problem with Tom and Lizzie being together. At first Lizzie was just fond of Tom, and his love for her seemed unlikely to be returned. But in time she came to really love him, and when he proposed, she accepted straight away. They were married shortly after.

Style Inc had been an enormous success and sold out all the initial copies of the first issue within one week. The publication went twice into reprint during the course of the first month, and everyone said that it was a much better and more original publishing idea than *Alpha Male*.

Westside Publishing had agreed, with Lizzie's recommendation, that it was better to buy *Style Inc* than to attempt to launch another publication in to the same market sector. She became the publisher, and Tom joined Westside Publishing as business development director to create new publishing concepts.

Christian was invited to join Westside Publishing, but he declined.

Billy was offered a job with the *Guardian* newspaper, which he happily accepted. Billy had won widespread acclaim for his investigative story on Michael Freeman. The story had created a major stir, and Michael Freeman was forced to resign from Parliament and from his party. Cosmet Sensicare was investigated and found to have inflicted unnecessarily cruel treatment on animals. Criminal proceedings were brought against all the directors, including Michael Freeman. Billy was a hero to animal rights groups, but, most of all he was a hero to Wendy, to whom he had finally proposed four weeks ago. Wendy now worked as a veterinary nurse. She loved the job more than anything—except of course being engaged to Billy.

Mike Tyler had nearly thrown up when he saw that the sales of *Style Inc* were going through the roof. One month after being fired from Lancaster Publishing, Mike Tyler accepted a magazine publisher's job in Hong Kong. He needed to get away.

Mike had hated seeing Christian's magazine in every newsagent—it was a constant reminder of the success of his lifelong enemy. Going to Hong Kong seemed the best option available. He had found it hard to find another job in London, and it put good distance between him and what he felt was Christian's ill-deserved success.

Julia had not been offered a job by Westside Publishing following their acquisition of the magazine. They liked her but felt she lacked real publishing experience. She was not upset because Julia had wanted to take time to try to spend a year finding out as much as she could about her father's life. Over the last year, she had also healed the breach with her mother, and Siobhan was overjoyed to have her daughter back in her life. During her year researching her father's life and rummaging through his possessions, Julia understood why her father had been so keen to encourage Christian to become a writer. She found reams of hand-written poems signed by Jinxie. She realised that her father had never been able to fulfil his own potential and did not want this to happen to Christian.

No one had known much about what Christian had been up to in the past ten months, and no one had seen very much of him. Both Christian and Julia had kept away from the group for most of the year.

Tommy had worked hard on his printing business and had recently managed to order the latest printing equipment for Brown and Son. He met Jackie through Lizzie, and the relationship had blossomed. Tommy was hopeful that one day there would be another son named Tommy, to see Brown and Son continue printing long into the twenty-first century.

By 8.00 p.m. all of the old friends were at the party and were happy to be sharing in each other's news and successes. Only Christian and Julia were missing, and the group hoped that they would come, but feared that they might not. Tom knew that Christian would be pleased that they had all done so well, but that Christian's own sense of failure may make him too embarrassed to show his face. *Style Inc* had been a success, but Christian always insisted that he had failed to play any part in it.

Then at 8.15 p.m., just as they were becoming convinced that Christian and Julia would not show up, the two came through the door. Everyone stood in silence at first, and then Eddie spoke.

'Well, you two kept that very quiet,' he said, pointing to the pram.

Julia had found out she was pregnant only three and a half months after Jinxie's death. At first she was afraid and she did not tell Christian for over a week. When she finally plucked up the courage to tell him, he was delighted. During her pregnancy, he was the perfect attentive partner. It was incredible, but it seemed that she had conceived on the first night she'd slept with Christian, just as her mother had done when she had first slept with Jinxie.

'Does the little one have a name?' asked Eddie.

Christian beamed with pride and said, 'I would like you all to meet my son, James.' Christian had suggested naming the boy after Jinxie, and Julia had no hesitation in agreeing.

Everyone looked surprised to see Christian and Julia arrive with the baby, but now it was Christian's turn to look surprised because Julia opened her bag, took out some books, and gave a copy to all their friends.

Tom looked at the book and read the cover out loud.

Jinxie's Wish

A Poet's Heart

By Christian Davidson

He then turned to the inside page and read aloud the dedication.

> This book tells the story of the life of my friend and mentor, James Jinks, whom I came to know and love as Jinxie. I wrote this book because it was Jinxie's wish, and I dedicate it to his memory.

They all now understood what Christian had been doing with himself over the past ten months. He had worked with Julia to piece together Jinxie's life, and he had finally written a book, which had just been published.

Julia smiled with pride as everyone came up to Christian, shook his hand, and congratulated him on his achievement. He had not expected Julia to bring copies of the book with her, but he was pleased she had. Over a year ago, all their dreams had seemed impossible. Now they were living their dreams, and this time no one was going to spoil their party.

EPILOGUE

ONE MONTH LATER, all the friends were exactly where they wanted to be.

Billy was working on a major story at the *Guardian* newspaper.

Wendy was tending to a litter of puppies at the vet.

Tommy was supervising the installation of his new print machinery.

Tom and Lizzie were at a restaurant holding hands.

Julia was pushing James in his pram in Hyde Park.

Christian was at a book signing for his novel, *Jinxie's Wish*.

Only Mike Tyler was in the wrong place at the wrong time. He stood in a bookshop in Hong Kong. He stared wide-eyed and angry at a display of books. He read the book cover out loud in shock and horror. '*Jinxie's Wish: A Poet's Heart,* by Christian Davidson.' He stepped back, burning with rage. 'Thousands of miles from home, and I still cannot escape that fucking Toss Pot!'

Jack Beecham was on holiday. He was deeply shocked and stunned to see the maniac Tyler standing in front of him. But even worse than that, the madman Tyler was insulting him in front of his new girlfriend, Debbie. 'Call me a fucking Toss Post, eh? You bastard!'

Jack pulled back his arm, clenched his fist, and punched Mike with all his might full on the nose. Mike flew backwards, crashing into the display rack of *Jinxie's Wish*. He collapsed on the floor, surrounded by numerous copies of the book.

Incredibly, though thousands of miles apart, Christian and Mike found themselves surrounded by copies of *Jinxie's Wish*.

Christian was feeling very blessed.

Mike Tyler was sure he had been cursed.

So it was that both of them had been touched by *Jinxie's Wish*.

THE END

ABOUT THE AUTHOR

Having graduated from University in the early 1980's I started working for a publishing company in London. It was a tremendously exciting time and quite possibly the heyday of magazine publishing.

It was a very competitive sector, and a major recruiter of ambitious young graduates who loved the idea of being involved in the media industry.

Jinxie's wish is a work of fiction. It is, however, based on some of my experience of working in publishing in that era. Set in London, during the 1980's it reflects the hard working, hard drinking hedonistic culture of the time.

It is a slightly romantic nostalgic comedy that chronicles the dream of Christian a young journalist to launch the first UK lifestyle magazine for men. His struggle is made more extreme by his rivalry with the devious Mike Tyler who tries everything in his power to sabotage the launch of Christian's magazine. Their rivalry has the potential to destroy both of their lives.

This is my first novel, and I hope you will enjoy the bitter, but, often comic feud between Christian and Mike.

I dedicate this book to my wife Ruth and my children David & Mirna.